In Search of a Quiet Place

In Search of a Quiet Place

PHYLLIS C. GOBBELL

BROADMAN PRESS
Nashville, Tennessee

4273-23
ISBN: 0-8054-7323-8

Dewey Decimal Classification: F
Subject Heading: CHRISTIAN LIFE—FICTION
Library of Congress Catalog Card Number: 86-2692
Printed in the United States of America

Library of Congress Cataloging-in-Publication Data

Gobbell, Phyllis C.
In search of a quiet place.

I. Title.
PS3557.017I5 1986 813'.54 86-2692
ISBN 0-8054-7323-8

One

First the soil is cool to Rosemary's knees. Then the shade narrows, creeping toward the azaleas and star jasmine, toward the twining wisteria with its heady perfume. The heat begins to gather on Rosemary's back, low down, at the curve of her spine where she bends. It moves up to her shoulders and finally to the crown of her head. When she finishes weeding, the sun has slid well above the Grays' roofline. By Rosemary's calculations, it should be close to ten o'clock. The mailman is late, if she's right about the time, and she has spent enough mornings working around the picture window to make a good guess.

Friday—from April through September except when it rains—is Yard Day. Rosemary has been at work since John left at seven-thirty, mowing, trimming around the base of the two maple trees—almost grown now, like the two maple trees in every yard on the street—tidying up around the shrubs, the clusters of annuals, the alyssum that edges the driveway. She's fussier about her yard than her living room, but not many people see her living room. She clips the last holly bush and wipes her forehead with the back of her wrist, indulging a smile as her eyes sweep over a job well done, which is the only way Rosemary will have it.

The front yard is a three-hour project, which means the mailman is definitely late, but now at last Rosemary spots his vehicle up the street, the little white Jeep with red and blue stripes. She leaves her clippers on the steps with her spade and gloves and waits at the mailbox.

The familiar round-faced man grins as he hands her a parcel, the size of a shirt box, wrapped in brown paper and twine. "Here's what you've been waiting for, I believe."

"My daughter wrote that she'd send a package," Rosemary explains. She starts to tell him that today is her birthday, her fiftieth, but only the very young and the very old make such announcements. She doesn't even know the mailman's name. She should, for he's had her route since she came to Nashville fourteen years ago, but she doesn't.

He thrusts a handful of mail toward her. "Here's the other stuff, the fliers and all those envelopes addressed to Occupant."

"Maybe I'll get lucky and find a bill."

"You might, at that. I've been delivering water bills all this week." He raises an eyebrow toward the Grays' yard, as lush as a golf green. "Bet that's a bill you dread."

"August is the worst." It seems appropriate to nod earnestly, and Rosemary does, but the water bill is of little concern to her. Her yard is her one extravagance, and everybody deserves *one*.

"You do have a fine yard, though. You've put in quite a morning already, I see."

"Oh, well, the gardener didn't show."

"The gardener! Now that's a good one!" The grinning mailman presses the accelerator and the vehicle eases forward with barely a hum. He hears a "Thank you," which hardly anyone bothers to say anymore, and he glances back, returning a broad wave. But he sees Rosemary Gray shuffling through the mail, tucking one envelope behind the other sharply, as if she expected a letter that didn't come. As if he didn't *tell* her it was all junk.

And all the time, the brown package is mashed in the crook of her arm like so much trash, as if it didn't matter at all.

Rosemary didn't *expect* a card from Judith, but it annoys her that her firstborn forgot—or ignored—her birthday. It annoys her, too, that she lets it bother her.

The gift from Melissa is, not too surprisingly, an owl done in macramé. In her letters, which arrive once or twice a month, Melissa tells that already—just since winter when she took up macramé—she's selling as many plant hangers and wall hangings in the community as she can make. Rosemary pictures her at a rough-sawn table, dressed in faded flour-sack prints, her cornsilk hair hanging across the ropes she twists into an owl; she will sell the finished product for a handful of change, enough to buy milk for her babies.

It's not that way, of course—not exactly. Melissa's letters are cheerful, full of assurances that the crops are flourishing, that the children (who are no longer babies) are energetic and apple-cheeked, that she and Simon are thriving on hard work and clean air. Still, Rosemary cannot let go of the thought that Melissa's chatty letters are attempts to *seem* happy, to say in so many words, *I did not make a mistake.*

No letter accompanies the owl, but Rosemary would've been surprised at two in one week. She knows, too, having visited the log cabin once, that out there in the wilderness you don't just dash to the drugstore for a birthday card. She pulls out a crayon scribbling from Jason, no doubt; a backwards J is the only decipherable shape. At four, he ought to be printing his name or drawing stick people or *something* that you could make out, shouldn't he? Rosemary wonders if the kindergarten he'll attend in the fall is adequate, or, for that matter, if the county school system in which he and Bradley will grow up is any good. Will they ride the bus? Many such questions surface when Rosemary thinks of her grandchildren. What do they like to eat? Women who are allowed to have a hand in raising their grandchildren take such knowledge for granted. Rosemary has to depend on comments tossed to her like crumbs by way of the U.S. Postal Service:

"It's much easier to go camping this year, since Bradley is out of diapers." Now when did that happen? "Bradley is cutting two teeth at once." So, how many teeth does that make? The most basic facts about her grandchildren Rosemary cannot recite.

Abruptly, she drops the owl in John's recliner. She hurries herself along, for another three-hour job in the backyard awaits her. She layers mayonnaise, turkey, and lettuce on whole-wheat bread for a quick sandwich. Her taste buds yearn for a cool, tangy salad, but who has time to concoct one, to peel vegetables, to boil eggs, to section oranges or grapefruit? Certainly not on Friday.

Biting into her sandwich, she leans on the edge of the kitchen sink, where she often devours her lunch without tasting it. She can picture exactly the tilt of the umbrella, exactly where she would be sitting at the table, having her salad and her tall glass of mint tea, if John would give in to building the concrete patio. She still has the magazine from four years back with the patio and the planters, the rows and rows of bright perennials—which she could manage without a hitch—the contoured lawn furniture in subdued shades of green and blue. In the magazine, everyone looks so *content;* you know the neighbors are over for a visit, saying, *What a restful patio!*

Rosemary and her neighbors do most of their visiting over the hedge. From time to time Rosemary does invite Bonnie Truxler or Jean Hollingsworth to share a cool drink with her, but the dirty old redwood picnic table is only shaded in the late afternoon and the gnats are always bad out in the yard like that; so if the neighbors do visit, it just makes more sense to go to the kitchen. If John would give in to the patio, it would be a different story. Why, she wouldn't hesitate to invite *anybody* over for lunch, or for a cookout on summer evenings (if she could get John away from his recliner and the television). Robbie might not be so hesitant to bring his girlfriends by to meet his parents if his parents had a decent place to entertain.

Rosemary washes down her last bite with milk from a mug, since the mug tree is handy. She heads for the backyard and works through her routine at a steady pace, just short of hurrying. The chores are not disagreeable; it's just her nature to *press on,* like a runner who thrives on running, but always toward that *end,* the finish. When Rosemary puts away her tools and checks the clock in the kitchen, she finds that she has accomplished her task in two hours and fifty minutes. That adds immensely to her satisfaction.

She is headed toward the shower when the phone rings. Turning on her heels, she marches back to the kitchen. The Grays are no doubt the only one-telephone family left on the block. It's that nuisance that colors her rather snappish "Hello!"

"Am I speaking to Mrs. Rosemary Gray?"

Unaccountably, the answer is soft, tentative. "Yes, I'm Rosemary Gray." She stands perfectly still, her eyes fixed on the letters S-A-G-E in the spice rack. "Yes. . . . Oh. . . . Yes, I understand. . . . All right, thank you." Then something catches and Rosemary calls, "Wait!" She clears her throat. "What I mean is, are you *sure* it's my husband? I mean, John Gray is a very common name."

"Mrs. Gray, he gave us your name and number."

"Yes, well, I suppose there's no mistake then."

"I'm sure there's no mistake."

"All right. I'll be there soon. Tell him—tell him I'm on my way."

Rosemary showers, dresses, seeks out her most comfortable pair of shoes, also locates the health insurance policy among the neatly filed papers in John's old rolltop desk beside his recliner. It is getting on toward rush hour, and Rosemary contemplates the best route to the hospital as she locks the garage. The particulars of grooming and getting away have glazed over the more weighty details, but on the highway, Rosemary begins to piece together what has happened. All she knows for sure is that John has been in an accident. Car accident? The woman who called—a nurse?—didn't actually say. All she said, when you cut away the formalities, was that John had been in an accident and he was at the hospital. And, yes—Rosemary almost forgot—that he was able to tell her name and phone number, which has to mean he's conscious. Probably skinned up, getting stitches, maybe. A little blood would be all it would take to convince John that he's dying.

Which, of course, he is not. Not John, with his high potency multivitamins and extra mineral supplements, with his blood pressure apparatus that he uses every evening more or less to gauge how he handled the day's stress. Rosemary keeps telling him that he'll live to be a hundred. *But an accident,* something anxious in her insists. All right, suppose he did have a fender-bender. John not only obeys the speed limit; he stays well under it just to be safe. *Safe* is John's middle name, or would be if he had one. Why, he paid to have seat belts installed in his car way back before most people ever heard of seat belts. He must've called a dozen car places before he could talk to anyone who wouldn't laugh. *How could you drive, strapped in like that, Mister?* If John was in the car, he was buckled up. Rosemary draws a long breath. She was never one to borrow trouble; she doesn't intend to start now.

Some blocks short of the hospital, the tall building rises into view. All at once traffic, as if controlled by some distant lever, goes into slow motion. Rosemary taps on the steering wheel while she waits for an interminable red light to change. A flashy car cuts in front of her; she hits her brakes. "You've got the nerve!" she shouts, for no one's benefit but her own. The young man who could've been Robbie—

though Robbie has certainly been taught better driving manners—sails on without so much as a glance back. There is plenty of time to scrutinize the faces that appear in the other lanes, the bored man heading home from work, the rushed woman who is already late to pick up her children at the sitter's. The automobile dehumanizes nice, ordinary people who would say "Excuse me" if they so much as touched your sleeve in an elevator. They close themselves within the steel and glass frame, touch the steering wheel, and become part of the machine, darting from lane to lane, speeding under yellow lights. No one cares what the other's destination may be or how urgent; each is caught up in his own air-conditioned armor, nursing his own thoughts. One of these drivers may be on his way to rob a bank; another has just been told he has cancer; someone is about to jilt her boyfriend, and another is heading for the hospital to have a baby. . . . Rosemary blinks, overcome by a peculiar sensation: She has been here before, with the same notions whirling in her mind; the slant and coloring of the sunlight were exactly the same.

The sense of déjà vu grows more profound as she turns into the parking lot at the emergency room. A security guard stops her. He's even younger than Robbie; his croaky voice seems to still be changing. "This lot's full, ma'am," he says. "You'll have to go around the block and park in the main lot."

Rosemary points to a corner space. "I can fit in there."

"But that's not really a space, ma'am."

"My car will fit, I'm sure."

"The thing is, you can't park there. It's not really a space."

"Yes, you said that. But surely you can see that I wouldn't be blocking anybody."

"Well, no—"

"Then why shouldn't I park there?"

"Because—that's just a corner. They didn't mark off a space."

"You're wasting my time, young man."

"I have a job to do, ma'am," he says with a helpless little smile.

"Now look." She finds the voice that she has used a thousand times with her children. "My husband has been in an accident of some kind. I should've been here hours ago. But I was in the yard and couldn't hear the phone, then I *had* to clean up, I had no choice, and the traffic—well, you know how it is at rush hour, some of those drivers think the they're in a demolition derby—" She hears the chirp that has edged into her voice, and with a deep breath she carefully modulates her next words. "As long as one corner is available, you have no threats that can send me back out into that madness on the streets."

The guard's jaw goes slack, and then suddenly, like a kid spotting a merry-go-round, he points behind Rosemary's car. "There's one! See that space? Right behind you. See that Camero backing out?"

Rosemary twists to look over her shoulder. "That's convenient."

"Wait a minute. Now, come on back." He moves aside, motioning.

"Thank you." Rosemary shifts into reverse, and, as an afterthought, she says, "I didn't mean to cause trouble. I can handle it now."

But he's not about to dismiss her yet. She can read the message on his transparent face: *Get this crazy woman out from behind the wheel.* "Come on back. Take it easy."

"You, too," she quips, but if he hears, he doesn't show it. "Easy, now, take it easy . . ."

Two

Take it easy, now, she told herself. *Plenty of time. Easy, easy.*

Rosemary kept one steady hand on the steering wheel, using the other to press on the bulge that was her abdomen, and eased up on the accelerator until the contraction had subsided. It wasn't too bad yet, but no doubt the pain would get worse as the contractions came closer together. Best to get to the hospital while she could drive herself, considering that she was alone.

Rosemary was twenty years old, having her first baby, and John was out of town. He was *always* out of town those first years, but when Judith was born, being alone had not yet become a way of life for Rosemary. Married only fourteen months, she still marked off squares on the calendar when he was gone. She still slept with the lights on. Not that she wasn't busy. She spent the days dashing from one piano student's house to another. She spent the evenings sewing her own clothes, and, during her pregnancy, crocheting more booties than triplets would need. Still, John's absences kept her in a kind of limbo. She saw herself as just passing the time till he returned. You couldn't say that she was *used* to being alone; she was just learning to endure it.

And John had promised, more or less, that he would be there for the big event. That was what they called it, "the big event." They also referred to her condition as "expecting."

"Promise me you won't miss the big event," Rosemary had pressed, over and over.

"I certainly don't intend to," he always answered.

"Promise me."

"I've told you. It's all arranged."

When John laid out the plans in that level, unhurried way of his, it did seem to be all arranged. No one cared much about seeing salesmen from Christmas through New Year's anyway, he said, so he planned to stay off the road from December 22 through January 2. Rosemary's due date was December 27—"give or take a few days," the doctor said, and John had done just that in his figuring. Rosemary always felt reassured when he went through the dates. Still, he never out and out *promised* he'd be in town for the big event. And that very morning, leaving for his East Georgia territory, he'd said as an afterthought, "You do have Aunt Millie's Studebaker, just in case."

Rosemary had wanted to cry. He sounded so *detached* about the big event, when really it was supposed to be a highlight of their lives, for both of them—even though she was doing all the work.

She managed to swallow back the tears, as tears were a sign of immaturity, and she was trying hard to grow up before she became a mother. But she said, in a somewhat quivery voice, "I've been feeling funny, John," which was the truth.

"Funny? How do you mean?"

"Peculiar."

"Do you hurt?"

"Not exactly."

"Maybe you're just a little nervous."

"I'm a lot nervous, to tell the truth, but what if it's *time?*"

"But it's only the twentieth," said John, so reasonably that Rosemary could not argue. "After Wednesday, I'll be in town for twelve days." After Wednesday, he was saying, it would be all right to have the baby.

But the baby didn't consider anyone else's convenience. Judith never did, even from the beginning.

It was Rosemary's first experience driving through Greenville, South Carolina, first and last, for John was transferred to another territory in the spring. The chances were slim, however, that she would've ever driven in the heart of Greenville again if they'd stayed. That one traumatic afternoon—bucking the rush-hour traffic, timing contractions, all while studying the city map and looking out for street signs—was so charged with emotion that for a long time after, she wouldn't drive at all. The cars closed in on her from every side. They darted across in front of her to make a left turn when *she* had the green. Horns blasted when she stopped at a yellow light instead of rushing through. And then, when it was time for her to make a left turn, there was no break in the traffic moving toward her. She sat through two lights, with a line of honking cars behind her, until it seemed that her options had dwindled to one. She seized the brief moment between the time the oncoming traffic stopped and the cross traffic started, and floorboarded the Studebaker. She was in sight of the hospital anyway, if someone should ram her. The Studebaker, accustomed to Aunt Millie's delicate foot, strained and sputtered, embarrassingly so, but the noise alerted the traffic; the cars with the green light held back for her to make the turn. She was safely past the intersection before the next contraction hit.

Half a block from the hospital, Rosemary fixed her eyes upon the big red Emergency Room sign, and that was where she headed. She passed a sea of parked cars, turned into the Emergency Room entrance, and saw two empty spaces right before her. Maybe her luck was changing, she decided, passing up the first, pulling into the space nearest the door.

She reached over, with a groan, for her overnight bag in the floorboard of the passenger's side. When she raised up, a security guard was at her window. She *assumed* he was a security guard. He was in uniform, though by his lazy-lidded eyes and pox-scarred face one could mistake him for a leftover from a gangster movie. Rosemary cracked her window.

"You gonna be here long?" the guard asked in a whiny nasal twang.

"As long as it takes to have a baby."

"You can't leave your car here," he said. "This has a two-hour maximum. You have to be going to the emergency room."

"Oh, I'll go there first. This is somewhat of an emergency."

"But you won't be out in two hours."

"I wouldn't think so. Where do you suggest I park?"

"There's a twenty-four-hour lot over there," he indicated with a tilt of his head, without taking his hands out of his pockets. He stood stiffly, and Rosemary noticed that his breath crystallized in the air. She had no idea it was so cold. She was sweating, wearing nothing but a sweater, without having bothered to turn on the heat.

"I don't think I'll be out in twenty-four hours, either."

"Maybe your husband could move it before tomorrow."

Now he was getting personal. Rosemary said indignantly, "I'm afraid not."

The guard scratched in front of his ear. "I've never come up on this before," he said, showing his first sign of sincere interest in her situation. "People that are real sick come by ambulance, or somebody brings them. How long you think you'll be here?"

"A week, maybe."

"Nobody ever wanted to park here for a week."

Rosemary's thinning patience sounded in her voice. "Just where do they park?"

"Maybe they go through admitting. That's on the other

side of the building, all the way around. You'll see some spaces on the stree—Lady! Are you all right, lady?"

Rosemary might've exaggerated a little, but truly a contraction doubled her over at that moment. The guard sprang into action. "Hang on! I'll get help!" Before the wave had completely subsided, two men were there with a stretcher. Rosemary barely glimpsed the uniform as she was hauled into the emergency room. "Thank the guard for me, will you?" she told the attendant at the foot of her stretcher. She put the car out of her mind.

Inside the hospital, women in Rosemary's condition were neither a novelty nor a cause for alarm. No one gasped when she caught her middle and grimaced. There were procedures, and no one seemed the least bit anxious about what to do next. They went through their motions, but for the most part, Rosemary felt like an object on the assembly line, not any different in their eyes from the patient before or the one who would be next.

The nurse who met her just inside the emergency room patted her arm and said, "Don't worry about a thing," but then that one was gone. The one who took over and asked her a lot of questions seemed thoroughly bored. Name? Age? Doctor? Allergic to any medications? She changed expressions only when the questions came down to Rosemary's husband.

"John Gray," Rosemary told her.

"Middle initial?"

"He doesn't have a middle name."

"Just John Gray?"

"That's right."

"Is he here?"

"Not yet."

"He'll have to sign some insurance forms over in admitting when he gets here."

"I'm not sure when that will be. He's out of town," Rosemary heard herself fumbling. "I don't know when I'll be able to reach him." Then she added, "I'm telling the truth."

She might as well have called him John Doe. The nurse gave a disbelieving nod. "You can sign. I'll send the papers up to labor and delivery."

The nurse who had been first to meet her—the kind one—flitted by, pausing long enough to say, "Relax. You won't be alone."

She was right. Within the next hour, Rosemary had been questioned or examined by at least a half-dozen strangers, stripped of any shred of modesty. Once, in Dr. Bridgeman's waiting room, she'd overheard a young mother say that having a baby was an exhilarating, almost spiritual experience. Well, so far it had been downright humiliating, not to mention that it hurt something awful and was getting worse all the time. Maybe she'd misunderstood the woman. Maybe the woman had adopted.

At last she asked a nurse, "Where's Doctor Bridgeman?"

"He'll be along in a while."

"But when?"

"In plenty of time."

"Are you sure?"

"As far as I know, he's never missed a delivery. You shouldn't worry."

But I have good reason to, Rosemary wanted to say. *John told me not to worry, too.*

Her nurse, whom she now knew as Mrs. Pfaff, gave her a shot to take the edge off the pain, and the next hours were somewhat hazy. But at some point during that time, the insurance lady caught up with her, and she was called upon to answer another battery of questions—first, about her insurance, and next, about John.

"Husband's last name?"

"Gray."

"First?"

"John."

"Middle."

"He doesn't have a middle name."

"No middle name?"

"No, but he used to have."

The rotund lady shifted in the chair, which was completely hidden from view.

"Really. It was his father's name, Eustace. But his father ran off when he was just a boy, so when John turned eighteen, he went through some legal procedure and had Eustace dropped."

"Eustace," the woman repeated, dryly, glaring out of the corners of her narrowed eyes.

Rosemary fidgeted. "I looked it up in a book of names. It means 'healthy,' which John is, for a fact, but I wouldn't name a baby Eustace." How could anyone stare that long without blinking? Rosemary wondered. She went on, "I guess whoever named John's father had a sense of humor."

"I don't," the woman said.

"I'm telling the truth. I do have a husband. He just can't make the big event."

"We get girls from time to time who have to be responsible for their own bills. It's simpler if you just say so."

"My husband is responsible," said Rosemary. "His name is John Gray. No middle initial."

The woman took hold of the bed frame to raise herself out of the chair. "Well, at least you have insurance," she said.

Judith was born sometime after eleven that night. Rosemary's last coherent moments were around eleven, when all at once, there was a flurry of activity, a heightened noise level, and she was wheeled down a cold hall by yet another stranger. Once after that she heard unfamiliar voices, and she barely opened her eyes to see three mysterious masked faces peering over her. If she was dying, she was too weary to care. Later she learned that Judith's delivery coincided perfectly with the change of shift. They *said* Dr. Bridgeman was there. Mrs. Pfaff, of course, had gone home. And when she asked for John, naturally, she was told, "There's no one here named John."

Rosemary didn't completely wake up until morning, after which she was taken to her room. Soon she was allowed to hold the baby, who slept soundly through their first meeting. At first Rosemary had a roommate, but the other new mother was going home that day. "Do you think I'll get someone else in here?" Rosemary asked her.

"Probably, but I was lucky. I was alone for two days."

Rosemary couldn't imagine why that was lucky.

The roommate was named Sherry Lovelace. Sherry was twenty-six, but this was her first baby. She was the picture of a new mother, radiant, soft-spoken, *sweet.* The nurse who brought her baby drew the curtain between beds, but Rosemary could hear Sherry's soothing voice, cooing, crooning lullabyes, speaking in gentle, hushed tones. What she could be saying to a baby, Rosemary had not a clue; but then, Sherry had been a mother for almost a week, so she was somewhat experienced.

The morning passed quickly, and soon Sherry was packed, waiting for her husband to arrive. "Jerry was set on having a boy," she said. "I think he would've been awfully disappointed if we'd had a girl. I was secretly hoping for a girl, but of course I wouldn't take the world for Stevie."

"I think John wanted a boy, too," said Rosemary.

"Oh, but he's thrilled with your girl, isn't he?"

"He doesn't know about her yet."

"He doesn't *know?*" Sherry held her hairbrush in midair for a minute, and then she came to Rosemary's bedside. "You mean he hasn't been here?" she asked. John would never believe how much interest was generated over his absence. Sherry's questions were not like the others', however; hers brimmed with genuine concern. When Rosemary had laid out the situation—trying hard to be matter-of-fact about it—Sherry said, "Do you have a number where you can reach him? I'll go downstairs and call him for you right this minute."

"He's already out on the road by now," said Rosemary. "He won't be back at the motel till tonight."

Sherry gave a sympathetic smile. "You're a brave girl. But promise me that you'll get someone to reach him for you tonight."

"Oh, yes."

"Is there someone else I could call for you?"

"Well, my mother doesn't know. She lives outside of Atlanta."

"Write her number down." Sherry got her purse and pulled out a little pad and ballpoint pen. "I'll go downstairs and call her for you right now. Won't it be nice when hospitals have phones in every room? Well, in a few days, you'll be up and around, and you can use the pay phone yourself."

Rosemary felt a flood of affection for this woman she had known for three hours, this woman she'd never see again. It occurred to her that *all* the people who had attended her during this big event had been strangers, people she'd never see again. Somehow she couldn't believe that the woman in Dr. Bridgeman's office, who had lauded the experience of childbirth, had gone through it with strangers.

"If you'll hand me my purse, I'll get some change for the phone," said Rosemary.

"I wouldn't think of it! It's my treat."

"But I can't let you *pay*."

"Yes, you can. I can afford it."

She laid her long white fingers on Rosemary's arm. Her diamond was the size of a plum. No doubt she could afford a call to Atlanta; still, Rosemary was not used to such generosity. She started to protest, but before she could speak, the door swung open, and a man straight off the pages of a Sears and Roebuck catalogue flashed an adoring smile at Sherry. He brought a bouquet of daisies, tied with blue ribbons, and a football. Sherry laughed and cried at the same time. They hugged and kissed. Then she turned to Rosemary. "This is Jerry."

Rosemary had an inkling that was who he was.

"I'll call your mother the minute I get home," said Sherry as they left. "I'll tell her what a brave girl you are."

Rosemary didn't feel a bit brave, especially after Sherry, Jerry, and Stevie were gone. This was a peculiar ordeal, a *lonely* ordeal. Certain pleasant people had popped in and out, but the bottom line was, she *was* alone. No one had *seen her through* it. Where were those shoulders to lean on? Her husband didn't even know he was a father, and she wouldn't be the one to tell him. He would hear the news from the first person who didn't mind going down to the pay phone. The same with her mother, who would probably go on and on to Sherry, but Rosemary wouldn't hear it or even hear *about* it. She was sure this despondency wasn't what a new mother ought to be feeling, and she was annoyed that she couldn't get past it. Why, *why* couldn't things be the way they were *supposed* to be?

The baby slept through her second visit. When the nurse came to get her, she asked, "Have you named her?"

Rosemary was fairly certain that John had agreed to the name Judith; she was already calling the baby Judith. But she said, "I'll talk it over with my husband first."

"We'll need a name on the birth certificate by tomorrow."

"That's fine," said Rosemary. "He'll be here tomorrow."

Never in all her life had tomorrow seemed so far away.

The new shift came on at three o'clock, new faces, more questions. As luck would have it, Tuesday was Dr. Bridgeman's day off. A young doctor, perhaps an intern, was taking over his rounds. "How are you feeling?" he asked, to which Rosemary answered, Fine. "Any problems?" No. "How's the baby?" Just fine. "Dr. Bridgeman will see you tomorrow." *It doesn't matter now,* she wanted to say. When it *had* mattered, he hadn't been there.

When Judith was brought to her in the late afternoon, asleep, Rosemary began to worry. "Is something wrong with her?" she asked. "Babies do open their eyes, don't they? I mean, they're not like kittens."

The nurse howled. This one was a dyed blonde, stout, pushing fifty, by the name of Miss Prentice. There was something about her that reminded Rosemary of a teddy bear.

"Sure they open their eyes," she said, through her laughter. "You can wake her up, you know. Just give her a jiggle."

"Oh, no, I don't—"

But Miss Prentice was bending over the bed, squeezing Judith's plump foot, calling, "Wake up, lazy bones! Your mamma wants to see those pretty eyes."

Judith's eyes opened right up. Miss Prentice kept on babbling, "You lazy girl, you had your mamma worried. See, Mamma, there's nothing wrong. Babies just like to sleep, that's all."

But Judith didn't pay any attention to all that chatter. She was looking at Rosemary. Rosemary learned later that according to medical theory, babies can't focus at first, but Judith most definitely did. Rosemary still didn't know what to say to a baby. But she had the distinct impression that Judith knew who she was, that this newborn baby was sizing her up already, forming an opinion. "Well, well," said Rosemary. For years after, she wished she'd tried to come up with something more intelligent. It was as if that first communication told Judith everything she needed to know. Her opinion was formed from that moment. What did she think of her mother? She yawned and closed her eyes.

By that night, Rosemary was glad she had no roommate, for she had begun to leak tears. That was what it was, really, not crying; the tears just kept forming behind her eyes, and when she couldn't store them anymore, they leaked out. She knew that by now, John would be in his motel room. Thinking of him made her eyes leak more, but not because of the same old *missing* him. Missing him was just an emptiness that she knew well, always remedied by his presence. Something else, odd and troubling, had entered that void, and she was not sure that John's return now could make it all right. Not having a phone in her room was actually a relief.

When Miss Prentice first found her leaking tears, she attributed the trouble to postpartum blues. She explained all about how new mothers often felt scared and just generally "blue" and how it was important for her husband to understand that this was just natural, and to pamper her a little through it all. Then she asked, "Is he coming by tonight?"

Rosemary explained one more time; she had told her story enough now so that she didn't think about it too hard as she recited. Remarkably, Miss Prentice believed her. "You want me to call him for you?" she offered.

"Would you mind? I have the number of the motel and a whole bunch of dimes."

"Sure, if it'll make you feel better. I'll have to say, though, I'm not sure the jerk deserves our trouble."

"Oh, John is really a very, very good husband!" No one had ever spoken a word against John before, and Rosemary was not only shocked, but defensive as well. "After all, it's not as if he went off on a *vacation.* He has to work. And the baby did come early. Why, he'll be as disappointed as I am that he missed it."

"Whatever you say, honey. Far be it from me to cause friction. Now where's that change?"

Miss Prentice was back shortly. "Well, I got him. Delivered the news."

"Oh. Good. Well, I really do appreciate it."

"You need anything before I go?"

Rosemary shook her head absently. "Was he all right—my husband?"

"Sounded fine to me. He asked about you."

"He did?"

"I told him you were just dandy. I figured you wouldn't want me to say anything about the blues."

"I'm glad you didn't."

"I'll check on you later."

"Oh, Miss Prentice? Did he seem happy about the baby?"

"I'm sure he was." She wrinkled her chin. "I've never been a married woman, so I don't read men too well—especially talking on the phone to some man I've never laid eyes on."

"I just thought he might've said something."

"Well, let me think now. He wanted to know if the baby was OK. I told him she was a little doll. I don't know what it is about some babies. I see babies every day, hear those newborn yells in my sleep; why, no telling how many thousands of babies I've diapered. But once in a while, one sorta wraps me around its little finger. I don't know why. Of course I didn't say anything like that to him. I just said she was a little doll."

Rosemary plucked at the sheet. "Did he say anything else?"

Miss Prentice frowned, touched her chin, seemed to *know* that there should be something else. "Well, he did say to tell you he'd see you tomorrow. Best I can remember, there wasn't anything else. I'm sorry."

"It's okay," said Rosemary. "I didn't think so."

Judith was brought to her once more that night. "Well, at least she's awake this time," Rosemary commented. She couldn't have known, of course, that Judith was already on schedule, sleeping through the day, staying awake at night.

"She's just been lying in the nursery, looking around," said the nurse. "Best little thing you ever saw." And she laid Judith in the crook of Rosemary's arm. Judith promptly began to yeowl. "Why, I can't believe this," said the nurse. "First time I've heard a peep out of her."

On Wednesday, John arrived just as Rosemary was about to dig into her meat loaf and lima beans. She was raising the first bite to her mouth when she saw him standing in her doorway, turning his hat in his hand, looking as if he wasn't sure he was welcome. "Come on in, John," she said. She laid down her fork and tried to push a few waves in her hair. It occurred to her how washed out she must look, after almost two days of wallowing in the bed. She had put on lipstick earlier, but now she couldn't taste it. Who ever said new mothers were supposed to have a certain radiance about them?

John would notice, too, for he put great stock in appearance. There he was, suited and starched, without so much as the knot of his tie loosened, and his face so scrubbed that you could use his forehead for a mirror. Rosemary had time to observe these details as he came toward her, for he moved with a strange caution, as if he might have been approaching a skittish horse. Rosemary couldn't believe she looked *that* bad. "Is something wrong, John?" she asked.

"No, no," he answered too quickly. Then he bent over and kissed her on the top of her head. "How about you? Everything all right?"

"Yes, fine."

"The baby?"

"She's fine, too."

"Good. That's fine."

He laid his hat on the bedside table and then looked for

a chair to pull up beside her, though not too closely. Rosemary figured he'd given her no reason so far to let her meat loaf get cold. "Do you mind if I have my lunch?"

"Not at all. You've got to keep your strength up."

Rosemary pulled her tray closer. She hadn't considered while her waistline was expanding that it might not immediately shrink back to normal size, so she was somewhat ashamed of her thick middle. But it was well covered. Surely that wasn't why John kept watching her.

Finally he said, "It was exactly a week early, wasn't it? A week to the day."

Rosemary was chewing. It? The big event. She nodded.

"I meant to be here. How was I to know it would happen a week early?"

Rosemary swallowed. "You couldn't."

"You're not mad, are you?"

"Of course not."

"Good. I was disappointed, too, you know. How do you think I felt when I found out it was over and I'd missed it?"

"I'm sorry. I know it was a disappointment."

"I was afraid you might hold it against me."

That, she understood, was the reason for the scrutinizing looks. He was trying to figure out how much trouble he was in. He wasn't *sorry;* he was just *sheepish.* Did he think she'd keep him after school, or what?

"Let's just forget it, John. I managed all right."

"I never doubted for a minute that you'd manage. But still, I meant to be here. Even if I couldn't do anything but pace in the waiting room, I meant to be here."

"I know. I'm sorry."

He seemed to feel better, for he took a deep breath and said, "I wonder if I could get a look at that baby."

"I don't know when the curtains are open, but you could check."

"I think I will."

Rosemary cleaned her plate. She even took her spoon and scooped up the juice from the canned peaches. At that particular moment, her waistline didn't seem to matter so much.

John was gone maybe ten minutes; he came back saying the curtains weren't open.

"Where were you then?" asked Rosemary.

"Oh, just looking around." Evidently, he'd seen flowers in someone's room or perhaps a florist wheeling a cart of flowerpots through the hall, for he said, "I would've brought you some flowers, but I guess I was in too big a hurry to get here. I got up at four o'clock. It's better than a six-hour drive, you know."

He didn't sit down this time. After they'd settled on the name for the birth certificate, they seemed not to have a lot to say. It reminded Rosemary of their first date. Then she remembered about her car and, without going into the whole story, told him how she'd parked in the emergency room lot, without the guard's blessing.

"I'll go move it," said John, who seemed almost relieved. "In fact, I'd better try to get it home. I need to check in with the office, too. Oh, what time do you think I can see the baby?"

"I get her at two o'clock. I think they'll let you dress up in hospital greens and hold her."

"You think so? Well, then! I'll certainly try to make it back by two."

Rosemary wasn't surprised, though, that he didn't. She knew he'd be there shortly, explaining how much trouble he'd had getting the Studebaker home or how he'd dropped by the office and the boss detained him. And she would be apologizing that the nurses didn't let Judith stay in the room longer.

She wasn't surprised, and she was only a little disappointed.

Judith slept, of course. Rosemary examined her—fingers, toes, ears, hairline, the shape of her mouth—which was what she was used to doing while Judith slept. Then she noticed that it was time for the nurse to be back, and she said, "Just you and me, one more time." Her own voice startled her, but once she'd broken the ice, it seemed quite natural to talk to the sleeping infant. "John is a *good* person, the best, really. I think he's just a little *afraid* of you. Don't take it personally, though. For some odd reason, he seems to be afraid of me, too."

Then something dawned on her. *One* tiny person had seen her through the last two days, maybe not as someone to lean on, but she had *been there,* through it all, which was more than anyone else could say. When you came right down to it, the thing between a mother and baby was something that no one else *could* be part of. She'd never dreamed it would be that way, but now, as she brushed her cheek against the fuzz of Judith's head, she was beginning to believe that was how it was supposed to be.

When John came back, he brought a little heart-shaped box of chocolates. If he'd noticed her waistline, Rosemary decided, he wasn't worrying about it. Sitting at her bedside, he kept asking, "Can I get you anything? Do you feel all right? Is it warm enough in here for you?" He did all the things an attentive husband should do, trying so very hard to make things *right* again. Rosemary saw all this, understood it, appreciated it. She tried, too. She never spoke a word about how scared or lonely or humiliated she had been, the day Judith was born; she stuffed that all away, like old clothes, boxed up and pushed to the back of the closet. And after a while, she insisted that John go on home and get some rest, since he'd made such an early start that morning. After all, wasn't she in good hands here? She'd be just fine. At last he gave a long sigh and said, "If that's what you want." It wasn't, but she was trying to let him know that she didn't blame him for missing the big event or for any difficulties she'd had or for *anything.* She didn't. She truly didn't blame him for anything.

She noticed how his shoulders drooped as he eased out the door. Maybe he realized, too, how delicately they handled each other now. Maybe he was wondering, as she was, just what had gone wrong, and whether anything could ever make it right again.

Three

Finding John is something of a scavenger hunt. Yes, they had a John Gray in emergency, Rosemary is told. He was sent to 4-East. She takes the stairs, rather than wait on the elevator, scolding herself the whole time for not asking the nature of his injuries, his condition, just exactly *what happened.* They probably wouldn't have told her, but it wouldn't have hurt to ask.

Through no one's fault but her own, she winds up on 4-West. At first she doesn't know this, and when the R.N. at the nurses' station says, "We don't have a John Gray," Rosemary is poised to huff. Then the nurse goes on, "Not *Grant?* We have a John Grant in 4011, but no John Gray."

"Did you just get him in—the man in 4011?"

"He was admitted this afternoon."

A clerical error, no doubt. Rosemary thanks the nurse and heads for 4011.

The door is slightly ajar. Rosemary pushes it gently and takes a few hesitant steps inside. "John?" The bed appears to be unrumpled. A high-backed vinyl chair is turned facing the window; as Rosemary moves closer, she sees an elbow. "John," she says again, but the words have barely left her lips when she stops. It's not *her* John's elbow. And the thought has barely made connection when old, piercing eyes peer around the high back of the chair, and a blue-veined hand goes up.

"Is that you, Agnes?"

"Oh, no, excuse me. I've made a mistake."

"What? Speak up, Agnes."

"I'm sorry, but I'm in the wrong room," Rosemary says, raising her voice.

The man, swallowed by a kelly green robe, waves his thin, almost transparent, hand. "Come around here so I can see you."

Rosemary quickly moves around the foot of the bed to the side of his chair, anxious to correct her mistake. She has wasted too much time as it is. "I came to the wrong room. I was looking for someone else. Please excuse me for disturbing you." She enunciates clearly, as if speaking to someone with a minimal understanding of English.

"I forgive you," he says.

"Thank you. Well, I'll be—"

"I forgive you for everything." He points a crooked finger. "Don't mistake what I say. You didn't fool me for a minute. You took my money out of coldhearted greed, not because you thought my screws were loose. But I forgive you anyway. It's nice of you to stop by."

"But I'm not Agnes."

"Speak up! My hearing's no better than it's been for twenty years and I don't expect it to improve now."

Rosemary's lips part, but nothing comes out. She can turn on her heels and exit, but she doesn't. The man's narrow eyes—a purer blue than the sky in April—hold her. Easing closer, more in front of him, she sees how dwarfed he is by the big chair. He'd do well to tip the scales at a hundred. His white hair is thin on top, tufted at the ears. His face, though remarkably unwrinkled, is long and gaunt. He regards her with a scowl; why does she get the impression that he could burst out laughing in an instant? If he had a hat to match his robe, and pointed little shoes, he'd make a wonderful leprechaun.

"How about a pear?" he asks.

"What?"

"A pear? Or a banana, orange, apple, take your pick." He gestures toward a fruit basket on the higher of two shelves, impossible for him to reach. "It's from Fanny Malone. At the home."

"The *nursing* home?" Rosemary ventures.

"What other home do I have, thanks to you? But I've already said I forgive you. Have a pear."

"No, thank you, but I'll be glad to get one for you."

"That's obliging of you."

Rosemary reaches for the basket, unties the cellophane, hands him a ripe pear. He shines it on his sleeve and takes a hearty bite. "It's a fine thing to have all your own teeth at my age," he says, chewing. "Take Fanny Malone with her dentures. She has to cut her fruit up, can't bite in like this—," and he takes another chunk out of the other side of the pear.

Rosemary says, "I came in here by mistake, Mr. Grant. My name is Rosemary Gray. I thought this was my husband's room. His name is John, too, John Gray."

"—but that's better than mashed bananas, which is about the only fruit you can eat when you're gumming it."

"I really do have to go. My husband has been in an accident, and I haven't been able to find him."

He chews more thoughtfully, and, swallowing, turns an intelligent gaze upon her. "Go if you have to," he says, in a quiet voice that seems considerably younger.

She touches the cold rail on the foot of the bed and takes a step backward. She starts to say good-bye; instead she says, "You've been putting me on, haven't you?"

He lets his eyelids slide down over the blue gaze, and turns his head. Rosemary does not see, but rather feels, that he is smiling.

"Good-bye, Mr. Grant," she says sternly, hiding her amusement.

Outside, she is no longer amused, realizing how much

time she has lost. She hails a cleaning woman, who directs her to 4-East. This time, when she inquires at the nurses' station, the answer comes quickly from a girl with a pony tail. "Yes, we have Mr. Gray. Are you his wife?"

As she says yes, an older nurse who is writing at the desk looks up, speaking to the other. "Dr. Nebbins wanted to see her first."

"I know, but he's gone now."

"What is it?" asks Rosemary. "What happened to my husband?"

"Dr. Nebbins wanted to talk to you before you went in." The girl's eyes widen as she spots a third nurse, a thin woman with an aristocratic profile and a tall starched cap. She motions for this one, explaining, "Mrs. Krantz is the head nurse."

"I want to see my husband."

"Mrs. Krantz, this is the wife of 4223. I thought you'd want to talk to her, since Dr. Nebbins had to leave."

"Hello. It's Mrs. Gray, isn't it?" Her lips are so thin, they're barely visible. Her salt-and-pepper hair is slicked back into a bun. "Your husband has been concerned about you."

"I was working in the yard. I couldn't hear the telephone." She frowns, her voice suddenly irritable. "Could you please tell me what happened to him?"

"Yes. Let's move right over here, out of the way. Now. Your husband had an accident around noon."

"Yes, I know that. But what kind? How *is* he?"

"He has some chemical burns. I believe it had to do with a car battery, but I'm not clear on it all."

"Burns?"

"On his arm, and in his eyes."

"Oh." Rosemary frowns. "Is he all right?"

"He's resting comfortably. His arm will be fine."

Rosemary nods impatiently. "Where is he? I want to see him."

"Mrs. Gray, you do understand—about his eyes?"

Half turned to leave, Rosemary stops. "He has burns," she says. "Chemical burns."

"Dr. Nebbins will tell you more tomorrow about what you can expect. Of course the bandages will have to be on for a while."

Rosemary nods.

"You can go on in to see him now. He's in 4223. Right down that hall on the left." She smiles stiffly; her lips disappear.

John's door is closed. Inside, the room is dim, the blinds drawn shut. Rosemary's gaze goes to the thick bandages that cover John's eyes. So white; are they luminous? She doesn't speak at first, moving quietly toward the bed, getting her bearings. But John stirs and calls out, "Rosemary?"

"I'm here, John."

She lays one hand on his cool arm and, with the other, straightens the hospital gown on his shoulder. "What have you gone and done to yourself?"

"I can't see."

"Well, yes. You'll have to keep the bandages for a while."

"No. I mean, I can't *see.*"

Rosemary's mouth is dry. She runs her tongue around her lips.

"Did they tell you what happened?"

"No one gave me a straight answer about *anything,*" she says, lightly.

"I was helping a girl with her car." He draws a long breath—from pain or weariness, Rosemary cannot tell. "A girl about like Melissa. Had a couple of kids. The battery was dead." His words slide together.

"You can tell me when you feel better—"

"I never knew a battery would explode. I was using the

jumper cables, and there was a spark." He flicks his fingers. "That's the last thing I saw."

"All right, now." She rubs his arm, the one without bandages.

A moment later, he asks, "What did the doctor say?"

"I missed him."

"He wouldn't say how bad it is."

"We'll talk to him tomorrow."

"He doesn't have to tell me I can't see."

"You rest now. I'll be right here."

For a moment, he lies still. Then his lips move. His words are slurred, spoken with effort. "I think I'm blind."

"Sh-h-h! When the bandages come off, it'll be different. We'll talk to the doctor tomorrow. Rest now."

He is determined to keep talking. "Where were you?" he asks, drowsily.

"In the yard, John. I'm sorry I couldn't hear the phone."

"I forgot it was Friday."

"Please, John, be quiet. I'm sure they've given you something to make you rest. So rest."

She moves a chair to his bedside. A nurse comes in to check on him, telling Rosemary, "He was so *agitated* till you got here."

"Yes, well, I was delayed."

"He's had something for pain. Maybe he'll give in to it now."

Rosemary waits until the sheet on John's chest begins a slow rising and falling again. Then she goes to the window and opens the drapes. The gray room is too oppressive. John can't *see* the difference, but perhaps he'll *feel* it.

The sliding drapes make the faintest sound, but it's enough to rouse John. He first feels the edges of his bandages. Then he calls, "Rosemary?"

She answers, "I'm here, John."

There is a telephone in the room, but when Rosemary finds a chance to slip out for a minute, she goes to a pay phone. She tries Robbie at the center where he works, but he's already left. She dials her house, and Robbie answers.

"Did you forget I'm taking you out for your birthday? Where *are* you?"

She tells him. She tells what she knows, which doesn't seem like much.

"I'll be there in half an hour," he says.

Rosemary peeps around John's door to see that he's still asleep. She's not used to one chair or to one room; she needs the light of the corridor, the noise of the cart bearing the dinner trays, the chatter of the nurses, the *activity.* Every few minutes she looks back in on John, but she stays in the hall until Robbie arrives.

She sees him step off the elevator, but he doesn't see her, and he stops at the nurses' station. Oh, what a smile the girl with the ponytail gives him. *Don't waste it, honey,* Rosemary thinks. Robbie has never had any idea what a charmer he is. Not surprisingly, he flashes a quick, impersonal smile as he thanks the nurse, *but you don't know it's impersonal, do you?* Robbie is too nice to everybody. He says, *How are you?* with such warmth that whoever he asks believes he actually wants to know.

He tugs at his collar as he starts toward Rosemary, seeing her now. Rosemary knows he's itching to be rid of his sport coat, which he's wearing tonight only because he was taking his parents to a nice restaurant. Even in dress clothes, he looks incredibly boyish for twenty-one. Tall enough and broad-shouldered, he has not really changed in five years, with his light brown hair, always on the shaggy side, perfect teeth—without the aid of an orthodontist—and one giant dimple that shows itself even when he talks. His manner, however, betrays his appearance. No all-American boy is supposed to be so subdued, so philosophical, so serious.

"How's Dad?" he asks, still several feet away.

"He's sleeping. He talked a little when I first got here. I don't think he was in any pain."

"How are *you?*"

She tosses off his question. "Oh, I'm OK." But how many sons would bother to ask?

"Can we go inside?"

Clearly, Robbie wants to see that his father is all right, so Rosemary shows him in. Inside the door, she raises her finger to her lips, for at last John is sleeping peacefully, making a little whistle as he breathes out.

Robbie stands near his father's bed for several minutes, looking him over. When he turns back to Rosemary, she notices the ridge between his light brows. Someone else would call it a frown, but Rosemary knows it is the indication of deep thought or, in this case, worry.

"Does the doctor think he'll be all right?" Robbie whispers.

"I haven't talked with the doctor." Their whispers don't seem to bother John, so Rosemary continues in a comfortably low voice. "I don't know any more than I told you on the phone. The doctor is supposed to be back in tomorrow."

"Do you think there's any permanent damage?" Robbie asks, still whispering.

"I'm certainly not counting on it!"

Robbie glances at his father. "Before the bandages went on, could he see?"

"He was sketchy about the whole thing, Robbie. Just wait till we talk to the doctor. There's no point in jumping to conclusions."

She settles in the chair at John's bedside, and Robbie goes to the window, leaning on the ledge where flowers are often set. They continue to talk in low voices, but not about John. Robbie will graduate at the end of the summer. He has finally received approval on the job that has been in the works for a good while, counseling at a state juvenile detention center. Rosemary is relieved to hear that it's final. Not that working with criminals was *her* choice for Robbie, but it's a good sign that he's over his ridiculous whim to be a preacher.

"You'll be good at it," she says, and it's true. But he would've been a good doctor, too. He's only twenty-one, Rosemary reminds herself. She has not stopped hoping.

The nurse with a ponytail—H. Connelly—comes in twice to check on John. The last time, she says, "The cafeteria closes in thirty minutes. It's a good time to eat. They know they're not going to run out, so they give you extras. I'm going down myself." She looks from Rosemary to Robbie and back as she talks, but Rosemary is fairly sure her comments are for Robbie.

"Why don't you go and eat, Mother? I'll stay here." He truly doesn't catch on. Rosemary suspects that his simple, honest approach to life, taking everything at face value, is part of his attraction. "You go if you like," she tells him. "I'm not hungry at all."

"Neither am I."

The girl's face falls dramatically. "Well, I'll be back later," she says, making no effort to conceal her disappointment. "Someone will check on Mr. Gray while I'm gone."

"Don't feel that you have to stay, Robbie," Rosemary tells him. "There's not much you can do."

"I'll stay until you leave."

"Oh, no. I'm going to be here all night. I'm sure I can get a cot."

"But you just said that we can't do anything."

"I said *you* can't. John wouldn't like it a bit if I left."

"Then will you at least get something to eat?" He knows there's no point in arguing about the night, but he does persuade her to take a break.

She remembers a vending area on the first floor. "I'll get

a cold drink and a snack," she says. She isn't hungry, and besides that, Nurse Connelly will be sulking in the cafeteria.

John is awake when Rosemary returns, but quiet. Drowsy, perhaps, or just not talkative. Robbie doesn't have much to say, either. The worry ridge is back between his brows. He has no trouble getting a cot for Rosemary. He asks at the nurses' station, and within ten minutes, an orderly, accompanied by Nurse Connelly, brings it. From John's fourth-floor window, a wide field of lights glitters. With the settling of night, Rosemary feels a great heaviness settle. Whatever small talk they make, their unspoken fears weigh upon the air.

A few minutes before visiting hours end, Robbie decides to go. He sees that his father has dozed off to sleep again and motions for Rosemary to follow him into the hall.

"I thought I ought to tell you. He says he couldn't see at all after the accident."

"I know. He told me that, too."

"He did?" Earnestly, as if he doesn't think she comprehends the seriousness of the situation, he says, "Mother, he may be blind."

"It's natural for him to be scared, Robbie. Don't you think so? He probably *couldn't* see, but no one has said the damage is permanent. Let's hear what the doctor tells us before we panic."

Her tone, so often used successfully with Robbie, doesn't appear to reassure him this time. But he nods, lets it go, and promises to call in the morning.

Then, turning back, he says, "I'm sorry about your birthday, Mother."

She dismisses it with a wave. Birthday parties are for children and old people anyway.

That is what she tells John later, when he mentions what

day it is—or was, for it's well after midnight and Rosemary is just drifting off to sleep when he remembers.

"That's why I was at the mall. I stopped to get you a present. But this girl had the hood of her car up. And two children, hanging out the windows, crying."

"Try not to think about it, John."

"I never got into a store."

"It doesn't matter, about a present, I mean."

"She said one of the kids must've turned her lights on when they went into the mall. Must've been a defective battery."

Rosemary is too tired to reply. She waits, and after a minute, he says, "Well, happy birthday, anyway."

She hopes John can't hear her laugh into her pillow.

Four

Rosemary had a birthday party when she was ten years old. She'd never asked for a birthday party, not being one to call attention to herself, but her mother contended that she was due one. "We've certainly bought *our* share of presents!" Virginia Lowell declared, though presents were beside the point, the point being that Rosemary had never known the thrill of being the birthday girl herself. Virginia had also realized that her daughter was outgrowing noisemakers and pin-the-tail-on-the-donkey. Actually, Rosemary and her friends hadn't played pin-the-tail-on-the-donkey since they were six; perhaps it had been just long enough to seem like a new game. When Virginia tacked the donkey outline upon the wall, the girls squealed and cried, "Me first! Me first!" They slipped on their party hats with giggles and asked if they could take home balloons, which, of course, they were allowed to do, since the dining room was decorated with at least seventy-five. If the party was too childish—and that thought had occurred to Rosemary—not one of the twenty-five guests seemed to mind.

Though Rosemary's *real* birthday fell on Thursday, the party was held after school on Wednesday because that was her father's afternoon off. Jarvis Lowell was the only doctor in Darlington, which meant that he *could* be summoned any hour of any day or night, but he never scheduled appointments on Wednesday afternoons. He'd been telling his patients about this party for weeks, so no one even called the house for a word of reassurance on this particular Wednesday.

His presence was a treat, not just for Rosemary, but for her guests as well. Fathers generally didn't attend little girls' parties, and those who did usually hung to the outside edges, looking thoroughly bewildered by the tinkling voices and unharnessed energy. Not so with Rosemary's father, who had brought into the world practically every one of her guests, who still treated them and their parents, too. He scurried about, clicking his camera, urging Betty Chandler to show off "those swell braces." A chorus of laughter rose when he told Mary Margaret Wade that the last time he saw her, she had three hundred chicken pox bumps on one arm. He listened politely to a few complaints from mothers and inquired about family members. "How's your pa's rheumatiz?" he asked Mrs. Kirk. "Did Jimbo's rash go away?" he asked Mrs. Patton. "I'm pretty sure chocolate caused it, but if it comes back, be sure to let me know." And to Mrs. Davis, whose fourth baby was due anytime, he even dared to ask the loaded question, "How are you feeling?"

Dr. Jarvis Lowell was "Doc" to everyone in Darlington, including Virginia. She had been his nurse for six years—two years before they were married, and after, until she was expecting Rosemary. By that time Virginia was twenty-nine, Doc thirty-nine. The way they doted over their little girl was a source of humor in Darlington. Doc Lowell, who had delivered hundreds of babies, must've said fifty times, "This delivery was more awesome than my first, and I was twice as jittery." When Doc Lowell's baby turned over, cut a tooth, or sat alone, it was public knowledge in Darlington.

And then there was Virginia, who called Doc more than a few times with complaints like, "The baby's running a slight fever. What do you think?" or "She hasn't wanted her bottle all day. Do you think she has a sore throat?"

Miss Dexter, who had replaced Virginia in the office,

delighted in sharing these little anecdotes with the patients (behind Doc's back, naturally). Certainly no malice was intended by Miss Dexter or by any who tittered over the Lowells. The rather naive behavior of two people with Doc and Virginia's background, and at their age, simply struck a chord of amusement among people who were genuinely happy for them.

It occurred to Rosemary when she was quite young that her parents shared something exceptional because they had worked together. Her father often remarked to her mother about an article he'd read in one of his journals, and her mother used medical words right along with him. Serious ailments of patients were rarely discussed in front of Rosemary, nothing more than *Mrs. Tipton jerked her back out of place again today.* But Rosemary often eavesdropped as her parents discussed cases, locked in a private world where voices and expressions changed. Such occasions made Rosemary wonder if her mother missed doing what she'd been trained to do, working side by side with the man who still respected her as a nurse. Rosemary would ask, or hint at asking, just to receive the answer that always contented her. "Oh, no, my days as a nurse are over! Not that I didn't enjoy them *then,* but *now*—well, my life right here in this little house is exactly what I want!"

Virginia made the dress that Rosemary wore at her birthday party, a white organdy pinafore over blue cotton, edged in lace and ribbon, worn over layers of stiff petticoats. Though Rosemary itched all through the party, the discomfort was a small price to pay for all the compliments she received. She knew she was not pretty, in spite of her parents' continual assurances that she was beautiful. She was quite plain, really, taller than her friends, pale-skinned, with feet that too often got in the way. But the dresses that her mother made always drew compliments. The pride that she felt was not just in her appearance, though she certainly *felt* prettier, dolled up in organdy and lace. But she felt *important,* too, when other mothers clucked over the intricate handwork, and other girls exclaimed, "Your mother sewed that herself? Gee-e-e!" *Yes, she loves me that much,* Rosemary thought. It was the same with the birthday cake, which Virginia made from scratch, a cake in the shape of a gingerbread house, decorated with jelly beans, cinnamon drops, and candy corns. Rosemary knew of no one else whose mother put that much time and trouble into a birthday cake. It all meant to Rosemary that she was an adored child, a *special* one to the only two people who really mattered.

At the end of the party, each guest received a unique favor, two hair barrettes on which was painted the girl's name. This craft was another that Virginia had picked up since hanging her white uniforms in the back of the closet. "You've gone *all out* for this party!" Mrs. Chandler told Virginia, and, turning to Rosemary, added, "What a lucky little girl you are!"

Rosemary smiled, not knowing exactly what she was expected to say. Her mother dismissed the comment, laughing, "It was pure delight for me!" Then she winked at Rosemary as if imparting a secret, but it was no secret at all. Virginia drew her happiness from making her family happy; Mrs. Chandler knew it; the whole town knew it. What Rosemary knew was very simply that she was her mother's prize, her father's, too. That impression had always been with her, but never did its sweetness etch so deeply as on the day of her tenth birthday party.

When the guests were gone, Rosemary slipped out of her party clothes, into the cotton dress and brown shoes she had worn to school. She picked up the diary that someone had given her for her birthday and grabbed a sweater, calling to her mother that she was going out. Virginia didn't ask where, but she called back, "Don't be long." The sun was dipping behind the trees and already the shadows were chilly. Something joyful and buoyant made Rosemary want to fly, but she settled for running, all the way to the bridge and down the hill to Parson's Creek.

Only at this time of year, after spring rains, was there any water at all in the creek bed, and even now, hardly enough to get feet wet. When Rosemary's father had first brought her here, the water tumbled over the rocks with a fierceness that sent her scrambling into his big, safe arms. But she was hardly more than a *baby* then; that was before the dam was built upriver and Parson's Creek dried up. Now the only sound was a drone of insects, which was not at all unpleasant. The only danger was that a snake might slither from the brush, or so her mother had warned her. But since Rosemary had never seen a live snake, this possibility seemed remote. In fact, she couldn't imagine that *any* threatening creature would invade what she considered her private territory. This was not a place to share even with friends.

The bank that led down from the street was rutted and rocky, but gently sloping, so that Rosemary felt sure-footed as she ran. At the bottom she caught her breath in great gulps of air so damp and earthy-smelling that it made her dizzy. Here the ground was level, with weeds growing up through the gravel; this was the creekbank. It fanned out to a surface of smooth pebbles, showing that the creek had once been as wide as a street. Rosemary walked out to the ribbon of water that wound silently through the creek bed, hopped across it and back, across and back. The rocks made a crunch beneath the soles of her sturdy brogans, sending a blue dragonfly flitting away. Now straddling the narrow stream, she hopped on one foot and then the other, following the water back under the bridge. This was the best place of all, where Rosemary did her best thinking, a hiding place of sorts, though she never hid from anyone in particular. At first, she'd had to ask permission to "go under the bridge," naturally, so it was no secret from her parents, but they wouldn't bother her. Her father never took walks anymore, and her mother never had.

She propped against one of the wooden pillars, the one she'd spent hours scraping clean, and stretched her legs out on the round rocks. There was a rumble overhead, a car crossing the bridge, which always made a thrill ripple through Rosemary's arms—*I know you're there, but you don't know I'm here.* When the noise of the car had died away, a strange silence fell, an almost-perfect absence of any sound at all, except for a soft hum that could be a monotonous song of crickets, or, as easily, a ringing in Rosemary's own ears. Such a *stillness,* she thought, as if this was a world apart from the one at street level, and in this world there was no movement of time. Such *quiet:* It seeped *into* you.

Rosemary opened her diary, taking out the pen that was fastened to its binding, and wrote on the first page: *Today Mamma and Daddy gave me a wonderful party for my tenth birthday and all my friends brought wonderful gifts and I felt just like a princess. . . .*

That same year, Rosemary learned to play the piano.

On a sweltering August morning, a secondhand upright was delivered to the Lowells' house. One of Doc's patients, it seemed, owed him for many months of treatment. Though Doc never pressed for payment, the old gentleman was a proud man who insisted on "making an arrangement," and he assured Doc that the piano was merely gathering cobwebs since his wife was gone. Virginia was forever scolding Doc about such arrangements in lieu of cash, but a cash payment seemed unlikely and the piano did have some value, so she made the best of the situation. She called the only piano tuner in town and the only piano teacher in town. By the end of the next week, Rosemary was taking her first lesson.

Old Miss Clarice Markham, who smelled of mothballs,

whose heavy makeup would've cracked her face if she'd ever smiled, had a reputation for whacking fingers with a pencil whenever they struck a wrong note. Rosemary never knew whether that was true, for she was a model student who demonstrated technical correctness and a keen ear as well. Miss Markham often came close to smiling when sitting on the bench with Rosemary, who at recital time performed not one but *three* solos. Though Miss Markham's idea of praise was a slow sideways nod, her gesture of giving a student three recital pieces communicated something more powerful than words. The printed program itself was good evidence that Rosemary was favored, and her performance left no doubt among the audience that she was Miss Markham's star pupil. When Rosemary gave her timid curtsey, the ringing applause indicated how remarkable it was for a first-year piano student to play "Libeistraum" with such flow, such balance. It was not until then that Rosemary actually grasped the depth of her talent; mirrored by others, she could finally *see* herself. If some of her girlfriends rolled their eyes at each other, if a few mothers clapped stiffly, Rosemary didn't notice, nor did Doc or Virginia, who had always known their daughter was precocious.

Like being the birthday girl, being the star of a recital was short-lived. Rosemary's musical ability was soon taken quite for granted, even by *her,* so natural it was for her fingers to dance up and down the keyboard. She practiced her hour a day (Miss Markham required thirty minutes' practice of her other students, but for Rosemary, an hour) and spent countless other hours picking out her own tunes. She played songs from her mother's old music books. Virginia, who had once dabbled at piano, had kept a stack of yellowed music, "Cruising Down the River," "Let Me Call You Sweetheart," and such. Sometimes both Doc and Virginia would join in on a familiar chorus. Neither could carry a tune, which only made their attempts more entertaining.

It often occurred to Rosemary, as the three of them warbled "Mockingbird Hill," that her parents were more fun than any of her friends.

Rosemary didn't have a best friend. She usually walked to and from school with Pauline Grady, but Pauline's interests were quite different from Rosemary's. Pauline stayed on the go, flitting from one girl's house to the other in the afternoons (while Rosemary practiced piano) and attending movie matinees so she could giggle at boys. She followed boys, in fact, to the vacant lot where they played ball, and she seemed to delight in being told, "Get lost!" Once she invited Rosemary to stay overnight, but Rosemary promptly invented an excuse. Why, Pauline herself told that she sleepwalked, which seemed too bizarre for Rosemary's liking. It seemed sensible to spend her first night away from home with someone more stable.

But no one else asked. Rosemary's friends, or the girls that she had for years considered friends, were beginning to behave a lot like Pauline. They had become more giddy, more daring, and—she screwed up her face when she thought about it—more *boy crazy.* Rosemary didn't mind, however, the lack of companions, pulling at her, squealing in her ear. She liked school, enjoyed her music, loved her family. All in all she led a happy and pleasantly full life.

The summer after she had turned thirteen, her father decided that the trim on the house needed painting. Rosemary went with her mother to the hardware store and they brought back three gallons of paint. That afternoon, which was Wednesday, her father removed the shutters from across the front of the house and opened the yellow paint.

Rosemary watched with curiosity while the perspiration rolled down his cheeks and off the tip of his nose. It was a rather balmy June day, and the shutters he painted were laid out in the shade, but he very soon drenched a handkerchief. Then he shed his undershirt, baring the pasty flesh of his stomach, which jiggled as he worked. He drained a pitcher of water, and finally, after painting one shutter and half of another, he handed Rosemary his brush. "Whew! I've gotta cool off," he said. Rubbing his face and neck with an already-soaked handkerchief, he plodded toward the house while Rosemary considered whether she should try her hand at finishing the shutter. She made a few feeble strokes and saw how easy it would be to mess up her father's job, so she wiped the brush on an oily rag and laid it on a newspaper. Naturally she'd managed to get her hands splotched with paint. It took a minute to dab them with turpentine and a few minutes more to dawdle at the outdoor faucet. Altogether some ten or fifteen minutes passed before she heard her mother's cry.

Doc Lowell had stretched out on the sofa in the living room, closed his eyes, and died.

Someone, during the blur of days that followed, droned to Virginia and Rosemary in deepest sympathy, "You *will* get over it." Of all the condolences that were offered them, Rosemary remembered only that one, for her mother had answered with a sweet but distant smile, "Rosemary will, but *I* won't." And when the consoler urged, "Yes, dear, you *will*," Virginia snapped, "No, I will *not*, I promise," which seemed to Rosemary an odd, if not eerie, thing to say. Later, from the far stretch of dreary months and years, Rosemary understood that her mother had meant exactly what she said. Virginia made a promise, and she kept it.

Rosemary was not included in any of the business that wound up her father's affairs. The banker called on her mother, and so did Mr. Bascomb, a friend of the family who was also an insurance agent. Then one day Miss Dexter, Doc's nurse, came by and brought a cardboard box that she could barely reach around. Though Virginia promptly whisked Rosemary into the kitchen, Miss Dexter's resonant voice penetrated the thin walls, and Rosemary heard her say, "I thought you might need these accounts receivable, but to tell the truth I wouldn't expect much."

Rosemary's curiosity was reasonably aroused, and frankly the secrecy insulted her. When Miss Dexter was gone, she asked, "Is anything wrong, Mamma?"

"Nothing for you to worry about," her mother said sharply. "I'm taking care of everything."

Rebuffed as she was by the reply, Rosemary didn't doubt at that point that her mother *was* taking care of everything, or, in any case, that she *would.* For parents always did. True, the shutters were still lying in the yard, one painted, one half painted, and the others untouched. (Rosemary had cleaned the paintbrush and carried the paint to the back porch, all on the afternoon that her father died.) The clothes hamper was full of smelly clothes, and grocery shopping consisted of Rosemary's hurried trips for milk, bread, and cereal. But Rosemary still assumed her mother was in charge. She didn't worry until Miss Markham gave her a reason.

It was on a sultry morning at summer's end when no breeze stirred through the tall windows of Miss Markham's Victorian living room. At the close of the lesson, the stiff-backed teacher laid a blue-veined hand on Rosemary's arm, which was very out of character, and said, "Answer me a question, child. Tell me truthfully, What does your mother intend to do about paying for your lessons?"

Then, while Rosemary fidgeted, Miss Markham explained that she had not been paid in three months, that as much as she enjoyed a gifted student, her livelihood came solely from teaching piano and she could not give lessons to *anyone* free of charge. "It pains me to discuss this with a child," she said, "but I've sent three notices in the mail and your mother hasn't responded."

"Oh!" Rosemary chirped. "I'm sure they must be in the stack of mail that she hasn't opened."

"For *three months?*" Miss Markham glared from under her penciled brows.

Rosemary gave a sheepish nod.

"That's very peculiar, don't you think?"

"I hadn't thought."

By the time Miss Markham dismissed her, Rosemary was nursing a big case of humiliation and a worse case of worry. If her mother wasn't paying Miss Markham and wasn't opening mail, was she paying *any* bills? Wasn't *she* the one who always fussed when patients failed to pay? Did this mean they had no money, or that her mother wasn't really *taking charge?* Either way, it was Rosemary's business now.

Virginia was in the kitchen, nibbling from a box of corn flakes, which was her lunch, when Rosemary said, "Mamma, you haven't paid Miss Markham in three months."

Virginia closed the box top and wiped her mouth daintily with a napkin, as if she'd finished a proper meal. "Your father always took care of that," she said. "He paid bills on the first and fifteenth."

"Yes, but—" Need she say such an obvious thing, that her father couldn't pay the bills now? The words caught in her throat, and when at last she spoke, her voice had lost the ring of a child's unquestioning trust. "*You* have to take care of it now."

Virginia propped her elbows on the table and rested her head in her palms. "There's so much to do, so much to know. Doc never even let me write a check. Then he left me with *everything* to handle."

"I'll help you," said Rosemary. She eyed a basket on the counter that overflowed with sealed envelopes. Gathering it up, she set it before them. "Let's open some of the mail."

"I'm not up to it."

Rosemary pretended she hadn't heard. "Some of these

look like plain letters, maybe people writing to say they're sorry about Daddy."

Virginia rubbed her temples. "It's so over*whelming*."

"Once we get started—"

"It's not that *simple*." Virginia drew a weary breath and let it out so slowly, it wouldn't have made a candle flicker. "Doc left a small insurance policy. That's what we have to live on."

Rosemary nodded.

"You don't understand. I shouldn't expect a child to understand."

"I'm thirteen, Mamma."

Virginia patted Rosemary's hand absently. "So you are." And then she shared the secret of Doc's business affairs, which was very simply that he'd treated too many patients for free. Some had moved away; others right there in Darlington were billed regularly but never paid; and a great many were never sent bills. "I had no idea it was this bad," Virginia wailed. "A few times, when I was his nurse, he'd say, 'Don't bother billing so-and-so. He can't read. He'll come in and pay when he can.' Just a *few* times. But later on, why he must've handled the whole town that way! I never *dreamed* it was so serious!" Beyond that, whenever Doc failed to take in enough to meet *his* obligations—which he never shirked—he drew from savings, so that the savings account was virtually wiped out. Virginia's lips quivered. "We had a position in the community. Now you and I are practically paupers. You see where his kindness left *us!*"

Rosemary had heard more than she'd bargained for, but none of it would change the way she remembered her father. Maybe he hadn't managed their money well, but he had always *taken care of them.* Who would take care of them now?

She made a stack of cards and letters, a stack of bills, a stack of junk mail. After a while, Virginia blew her nose and said, "I'm glad I told you, honey. It takes a great burden off my shoulders." And, calling for the checkbook, she tackled the stack of bills.

Virginia wrote checks; Rosemary addressed envelopes. Some bills had to wait, but all that were overdue were paid, with twenty-three dollars left over. "And we're due some insurance money soon," Virginia added. "We'll manage, won't we, honey." Then dropping her pen, she covered her face and moaned, "Why did you go away, Doc?"

Rosemary paid no attention to her mother's latest tears. She said, "We need groceries. If you'll make a list, I'll go to the store."

"Better get it on credit," said Virginia, sniffling. "It's going to be like this from now on. Bare necessities."

"I'm going to take Miss Markham's check by her house on my way to the grocery. Can you make a list?"

Virginia dabbed at her eyes. "We can't afford music lessons anymore, Rosemary. You tell Miss Markham."

Rosemary offered not a word, except to ask, "Can you make the list now?"

A few patients who owed five or ten dollars for recent treatment did make their payments, but those with long-standing accounts made no effort to pay. Virginia scooted the box of bills under her bed and, as far as Rosemary knew, never pulled it back out.

But Doc's patients were not entirely insensitive. To his wife and daughter they brought berries and vegetables in summertime, apples in autumn. For weeks after Doc's death, had it not been for the corn, squash, okra, and tomatoes from country gardens, Virginia and Rosemary would've eaten poorly indeed. That was during the time when Virginia was neither grocery shopping nor cooking, when meals were raggedly observed by opening a can of tunafish or pork and beans. Understandably, Rosemary was delighted to find a farmer at the door. It meant her mother would prepare a legitimate meal.

A ham at hog-killing time, a gallon of sorghum molasses —the offerings from people grateful to Doc Lowell continued not just for a few months, but for years after. It was one of Doc's former patients who finally hung the shutters that had laid on the ground all summer, and another eventually (two summers later) painted the yellow trim.

In these ways, they *were* paying, Rosemary thought, at least some were. She couldn't help believing, like her father, that people were basically good, or that they *wanted* to be. But Virginia was not so willing to cancel their debts. She resented the situation that forced her to accept their generosity. "Why do they do it anyway?" she muttered, slicing Mr. Baird's ham. "I'll tell you why. For themselves! To soothe *their* guilt! Barney Baird knows he never gave Doc a cent for delivering their last baby, and that child's at least four now." Then she went into her familiar chorus. She was *Doc Lowell's wife.* She shouldn't have to live hand-to-mouth, to make over last year's clothes for Rosemary. Life was, oh, so hard without a husband!

Virginia imagined, too, that none of her old friends cared about her now, for they had stopped calling. "It was Doc they all loved," she said. "What do I care? If anybody did invite me anywhere, I have no decent clothes to wear and no money to buy any." It was, of course, that self-pitying drone which put the kindest friends off, even loyal Miss Dexter, who at first had made a point of calling every week. *Is there anything I can do for you, Virginia? No one can do anything for me, Betsy.*

By the time Rosemary was sixteen, she considered her mother an old woman. Virginia's brown hair was turning gray, but not in shiny streaks, which might have lent an air of dignity. The gray had crept in like an evil intruder, changing the color to something dull and mousy. The

French twists that she fashioned as her hair grew long somehow always came out a bit shaggy. The dresses that she chose to wear were faded and mended many times over; they were the ones with pockets for her dainty handkerchief, as tears were apt to come almost any time. The tall and stately, large-boned woman that she had been came to look quite fragile and hollow-chested as she shuffled about in house slippers, her shoulders drooping.

Rosemary worried about Virginia's rapid deterioration, but any efforts to revitalize her mother only turned on her. "No, I will not go to the beauty shop and spend good money trying to look young again! My youth is spent! You don't cheat Time, and it's vanity to try to!" Or, "Are you ashamed of how I look, Rosemary? I gave my best years raising you, and now you're ashamed of me." Virginia inflicted guilt with the skill of a champion archer, consistently sending her arrows to the bull's-eye. On one level, Rosemary understood her game, but on another, where logic had no place, she was convinced that somehow she was indeed responsible for her mother's misery.

And so, except for the time she was in school, Rosemary was at home trying to do what she could to make life easier for her mother. The world of parties, ball games, and movies was essentially unknown to her, except for the rather exaggerated view that came from Pauline. Pauline still walked to school with Rosemary, but she generally had pressing business in the afternoons, like watching the football team practice.

It was just as well, Rosemary told herself, that no one visited the once-bright cottage, now badly in need of repair. The back porch was stacked with two examining tables, an old solid wood desk, boxes of tongue depressers, and countless other items from her father's office. The screen door had come off in front. And inside, the house had come to reek of a curious odor, a heavy, sour smell that no amount of airing on breezy days could take away. Better for the girls that she loosely called friends to remember the day of her birthday party—the gaiety, the energy, the affection—than to sniff the foul air that had settled upon the house, upon Rosemary's life.

One evening, however, Pauline rattled the door with a vigorous rapping. "It's just *me,*" she called, when Rosemary peered cautiously through a crack between the curtains. Pauline had no concept, naturally, of how rare it was for the Lowells to hear knocking at their door. Nor could she imagine how relieved Rosemary was when she showed no inclination to come inside.

"I need a favor," said Pauline, popping her gum. "If I don't make a B on my mid-term, I'll flunk algebra for sure. So could you come over to my house and help me study?"

"When?"

"Tonight! Now! Mid-term's *tomorrow,* silly. When did you *think* we'd study?"

Maybe this whole last week, Rosemary could've said. Maybe this afternoon. Of course Pauline had been busy with her *real* friends. Rosemary was a convenience, a straight-A student who happened to live down the street. As far as she was concerned, Pauline *deserved* to flunk.

"Well, what about it? Will you?"

What could she say? Certainly not that her mother never wanted her to leave the house, which was the truth. "All right, I'll be there in a few minutes," she said.

Virginia's response was not entirely unexpected. "You were just out *last* night, Rosemary. You're becoming a regular gadabout."

"It was two nights ago, Mamma, and anyway I was at the library working on my term paper."

"Pauline is a gadabout."

"We're just going to be at her house studying."

"Isn't this just another excuse to leave me alone?" Virginia brought out a limp handkerchief and held it to her nose as her eyes turned glassy bright.

Rosemary looked down at her feet. She could not answer no in complete truth, and knowing it made her oh so ashamed. "I suppose I don't have to go," she said.

Then Virginia took a peculiar approach. At once dry of tears, she said softly, "Never mind me. Why, I used to be pretty and lively myself, with friends and interests. I just forget sometimes, now that my only interest is you." And with a feathery wave, "Go on to Pauline's. Enjoy yourself. And tell her mother hello for me. We used to stroll our babies together."

It was dusk, and the wintry air, warmed earlier by a bright sun, had turned frosty. Rosemary could see her breath crystallize as her long legs carried her away, though not really *away*. Her mother's dependency was as real as a rope that kept tugging at her, reminding her of her obligations. The irony was, she had slipped into the noose herself, willingly, by gradually taking over responsibilities that should've been her mother's, by humoring her, by giving her a shoulder to lean on. Perhaps if she'd kept acting like a child after her father died, her mother would've eventually taken charge. She would've *had* to. But how could a thirteen-year-old girl, even a bright one, have figured that out?

Rosemary's brisk hike took her not to Pauline's, but to the bridge, overlooking the ravine where she used to go back in simpler days to tune out the rest of the world, her quiet place. It was possibly still quiet, but not a place she'd care to go anymore, for it had become someone's dumping ground. Besides the bottles and cans, there were tires, the rusty remains of a stove, a hat, a lady's slipper. A mangey dog sniffed at a heap of old garbage. The sight was revolting, and Rosemary could not get away fast enough.

But it *had been* clean once; it had been safe and attractive and very quiet. And she had spent thirteen years in a family that was exactly what a family was supposed to be. Those things, she promised herself, were what she would remember, and she dug her hands deep into her pockets, heading for Pauline's.

Miss Clarice Markham was seized by a stroke one afternoon as she whacked little Marcella Wade's fingers, and Darlington's only piano teacher was, after a spell in the hospital, confined to a convalescent home, her right side paralyzed.

The day that Rosemary quit her lessons, Miss Markham had loaded her arms with old music books. After that, whenever Rosemary returned one, Miss Markham would say, "Let me hear you play, Rosemary. *Staccato! Staccato!* This is a happy tune, child, not a funeral dirge!" The old lady actually became quite amicable after Rosemary ceased to take formal lessons, even to the point of confiding, "You'll soon go beyond anything I could teach you. Not one of my pupils has your natural ability or your persistence." No doubt Rosemary grieved over her illness more deeply than did any of her students. Miss Markham had *meant* something to Rosemary, and now she was lost to her forever.

"Wonder what will happen to all her pupils," Virginia remarked.

Rosemary hadn't thought past her own sorrow.

"Why, *you* could teach them, Rosemary. If you let it be known that you'd give lessons, why, you'd have Miss Markham's entire class signed up before the day's end."

"I'm not a teacher, Mamma."

"But you *could* be. You've taught yourself. You just follow what's in the book, don't you? Besides, who else in Darlington could teach piano now?"

As it turned out, Virginia made good sense. Within a week, Rosemary had lined up all the pupils she could handle after school and on Saturdays. She taught them at their own homes, which Virginia hadn't considered, but Rosemary held fast to that condition. At first Rosemary's piano was too desperately in need of work to be used for lessons, and later, after the students and their parents were used to the arrangements, it seemed unreasonable to change. When summer came, schedules were reworked, but by then Virginia was quite pleased not to have children traipsing in and out, for she had at last found an interest besides Rosemary.

Virginia was painting what she called "Personalized Trinkets," using a kit she'd ordered from the back pages of a magazine. The kit came with bracelets, key holders, Christmas tree ornaments, and barrettes, which Virginia painted like the ones she'd once given as favors at Rosemary's birthday party. "I should've started a business like this," Virginia muttered, leaning close to the tiny paintbrush. "I had the idea first. But my family took up all my time. Not that I regret what I sacrificed. Those were the happiest days of my life."

Rosemary had assumed that her mother would sell her creations, but who did she ever see that might order from her? And who would buy a bracelet with the name Zennia already painted on it? Virginia's interest quite obviously was in painting, not in selling. She frequently ordered refills, which became rather costly, but the expense wasn't what Rosemary minded. It was the "displays," the rows of jewelry that filled the coffee table and later the dining room table, the ornaments across the mantle, the key holders strung on a piece of clothesline at the window. Crowded with "personalized" objects and all the other trinkets that Virginia had accumulated over the years, the Lowell house was taking on the character of a bazaar, it seemed to Rosemary. Little wonder that in her recurring dream she shrank while her mother's collections swelled, and she awoke, smothering, terrified that she was *losing* herself.

Graduation came, but without bells and whistles for

Rosemary. A handful of her classmates went to college or to business school. Some, including Pauline, got jobs in Atlanta. A few got married or busied themselves with plans to marry, and those remaining generally found jobs there in Darlington. Rosemary ran an ad in the paper that she was now offering piano instruction for adults, and she added fourteen students. "What a bright future you have!" her mother declared as she made ready for a round of lessons. She left Virginia humming a bright tune. Now that she was really and truly locked into Darlington, her mother had every reason to believe that she'd be there, taking care of things, forever.

One of Rosemary's pupils was the wife of the young Reverend Hogan, a new minister in Darlington. Mrs. Hogan had the notion that a pastor's wife ought to play the piano, which was a pity, for her sense of rhythm was nonexistent, but she was diligent in her efforts. The Reverend repeatedly praised Rosemary's God-given talent, adding that she ought to use it in church, to which Rosemary feebly replied that she guessed she should and maybe one day she would. The Hogans were, in a way that Rosemary couldn't quite put her finger on, *different* from other families who employed her services. Nevertheless, she grew quite fond of them, and trusting, too. That was why the stranger at their house didn't alarm her. The Reverend had left a note vouching for him, and any friend of the Hogans had to be all right.

"They were cleaning fish for supper," said the man, "and Janice sliced her hand. So they had to rush to the doctor, and *I* stayed to baby-sit with little Jimmie Lee." He laughed at himself, and then, noting that Rosemary was fidgeting, he said, "I'm afraid you made the trip for nothing. Let me get the baby and I'll take you home."

"Oh, I'll just walk," said Rosemary.

"Mark asked me to drive you, and I'll be glad to."

The Reverend had scribbled, "John is an old friend of mine. He'll explain why we had to leave. Let him take you home, and please accept our apologies." Rosemary had walked just four blocks from the Dudleys, but her house was well over a mile away, and the Reverend always gave her a ride. She figured that if Jimmie Lee was safe with the "old friend," she surely would be, too.

The backseat of the man's car was full of suitcases. He explained that he was a salesman for a line of men's clothes, on his way back to Atlanta after a week on the road. "Mark and I were in high school together," he said. "I heard that he'd moved here, so I just looked him up. I got directions from Joe Downey."

The mention of Joe Downey at "Downey's Best Peach Cobbler in Georgia" was as good as a proper introduction.

It crossed Rosemary's mind that her mother would most certainly view this as being reckless, riding with a stranger, a salesman from Atlanta, a man who was at least twenty-five and maybe older, but he was nice, and Rosemary was nice back. As she bounced Jimmie Lee on her lap, she paid careful attention to her new acquaintance, to each expression and gesture, and by the end of the short drive, she had formed an impression of John Gray that was quite favorable. He was rather dashing in a conservative sort of way, but beyond that, Rosemary construed that he was gentle, mature, solid, a man of deep convictions. "I was wondering—" he said.

Rosemary smoothed the folds of her skirt that hung to her sock tops.

"I come this way from time to time, and I was wondering if maybe I could call on you."

"That would be nice."

"I'll be through next month for sure," he said.

And very boldly she said, "I'll be counting on it."

Five

The next afternoon while Robbie sits with John, Rosemary gets home for a few hours.

"You shouldn't be driving back and forth every day," John says, sulking. "You're not used to traffic."

"You haven't been to the grocery with me lately," she tells him. "Don't worry. I want a bath in my own tub and I need to pick up a few things."

What she doesn't say is that she wants to call Judith and Melissa and talk with them privately.

To reach Melissa, Rosemary has to telephone her nearest neighbor who isn't near at all and leave word for Melissa to call. She tells the neighbor about John's accident, for she can't conscientiously send the woman driving a mile and three-quarters without giving her a good reason. She is, however, reassured when the neighbor says, "I won't let on to Melissa, though. I don't like to be the bearer of bad news."

No one does, Rosemary says to herself as she waits for the call and lets her thoughts roll back to the doctor's visit that morning. How cool and detached he seemed, telling John that the chances for having his sight were minimal. How *technical* he was, describing the damage. How quickly he exited, meeting another doctor outside John's door and making some joke that caused the other to chuckle.

There must be a course in med school on bearing bad news, Rosemary decides. *Never show your feelings; make it brief;*

get out and promptly forget it. John's so-called specialist is no Doc Lowell, nothing like the sort of doctor Robbie could be.

Melissa is a little breathless when she calls. "Mother, is everybody all right?"

Rosemary can count on one hand the times she's telephoned Melissa since she retreated to the wilderness; once was to tell her about the death of her grandmother.

"Yes—well, there's a little problem with your father."

When Rosemary has given an account of John's situation, Melissa says, "That doesn't sound like a *little* thing."

"I guess not, but we're not going to let it *overwhelm* us." It annoys her that she has to explain herself continually to her daughters, and the irritation creeps into her voice. "When the bandages come off, the doctor can tell us more. We'll take one step at a time."

"You're right; that's the only way."

Melissa at least doesn't mind admitting that her mother is right, which is more than can be said of Judith. But Rosemary shakes Judith out of her mind, John also, and says, "Tell me about my grandchildren."

And for a minute, she smiles, listening to Melissa's stories. The boys have caught a turtle that draws into its shell whenever anyone comes around. Bradley bawls and Jason questions why the turtle doesn't like him. There are other anecdotes, and once Rosemary laughs out loud. Then quite suddenly Melissa says, "Mother, I'm pregnant."

"Oh!"

"About eight weeks now. I didn't say anything in my letters because I was planning to call you."

And when was that going to happen? Rosemary wants to ask, but she doesn't. "So how are you feeling?"

"Fine, except for the nausea, which is apt to come on at any time. I never appreciated morning sickness that happened just in the mornings."

"And what do you do with the babies when you're too ill to take care of them?"

"Simon's usually around, and, Mother, they're not babies. They'll be three and five soon, and they're thrilled about the prospect of a baby brother or sister. Simon and I are thrilled, too."

"I'm sure you are." Rosemary wonders how they will afford another child, but that isn't something a mother asks. She's fairly certain they haven't considered it anyway. "Take good care of yourself, and tell Simon and the children hello for us. I should be going now."

"Mother, is Dad really all right?"

"I've explained the best I can, Melissa."

"There's nothing you're not telling me?"

"Of course not."

"I'd like to see him. If I weren't so sick all the time, I'd try to get there somehow."

"Don't mention it, Melissa. Your children need you, and you couldn't do anything for John."

"You're sure his feelings won't be hurt?"

His feelings, somehow, have always mattered to the children. "I'm sure of it. I'm sure your father doesn't expect you to rush to his bedside, and I'm sure that having you get sick in his room would only upset him."

"You *will* explain to him, won't you?"

"That's what I'm saying, that there's nothing to explain."

"Well, if you say so." Cheerfully now she says, "Be sure to tell him our good news! Tell him I'm thinking about him and that I'll be checking on him—oh, you know what to say!"

And Rosemary, who has spoken for her children a thousand times, says, "I'll take care of it."

When Rosemary glances at John's recliner in the den, the crumpled owl reproaches her in some strange, tender way. At first, yes, she did wonder where she could use it, being the practical type and not a person to collect *things.* On the smooth uncluttered surfaces of her house are found only objects with a purpose—lamps, coasters, a few family pictures on the wall. No glass figurines, as in her mother's house, where Rosemary dusted enough to last her a lifetime. And after the funeral, oh, the boxloads of *things* they carted away to the junkyard! Dozens of musty, fraying pillows, trinkets no one else would have—chipped ceramic knick-knacks, a miniature Statue of Liberty with the gold paint flaking off, gaudy floral-painted vases, on and on. Not to mention the collection that her mother had painted over a period of three or four years and had continued to display. If the barrettes and bracelets hadn't been "personalized," or if the names had been Jane and Sue—but where would one find a girl named Desirée? It was heartbreaking to discard all that dime-store junk that were her mother's treasures. But what other end could her mother have expected for such a useless menagerie?

The owl hanging is, of course, different. Handmade by Rosemary's own daughter—and without some unfamiliar name attached—it *is* special. Though it's obviously more compatible with wind chimes forever clinking in a dorm room than with a brown Naugahyde recliner, or, say, the solid cherry poster bed, Rosemary will certainly find a place for it. It's just that—she raises the owl in front of her, eye to beaded eye—Melissa wouldn't give an apron to someone who doesn't cook, would she? She wouldn't send John, in his present condition, a book. Mothers, on the other hand, are supposed to cherish anything, every scrap of paper on which a child has slid a crayon across the page, every popsicle-stick recipe-holder from Vacation Bible School, every owl a grown daughter knots together out of ropes and beads. Why does it irritate her so? At least Melissa remembered. Even if she wrapped the first item she could reach when she did remember, she did make an effort. More than Judith did.

She holds the owl at arm's length, giving one last close appraisal, and slowly she begins to nod. All he needs is a brass ring tacked on at his feet, and he'll make a dandy holder for hand towels. As a matter of fact, the bathroom has needed one for a long time. She folds up the owl, altogether content with her gift, now that she's found a use for it.

Normally, Rosemary is not a procrastinator, but she continues to put off the call to Judith. Melissa, with her odd notions, can be aggravating, but Rosemary cannot say that she's ever dreaded a conversation with her younger daughter. With Judith, there is *something,* something that Rosemary has never been able to name, something that has led to one clash after another. It has been two years since Judith was home (and she would surely resent the reference to *home,* for her home is a high-rise in Chicago that Rosemary has never seen). It has been several months since she called, telling her plans for skiing in Colorado at Christmastime. A part of Rosemary wants to hear Judith's voice and to know she's all right, but another part fears the inevitable conflict. Has Judith ever agreed with her on any issue? It doesn't seem so. She tries to dredge up a memory of some pleasant conversation with Judith, but the exchanges she remembers are either loud and angry or low and tense. And so Rosemary bathes, dresses, gathers into an overnight bag the items she needs at the hospital, waters her houseplants, and even then, when she dials, she's half-hoping Judith's phone is busy. But it's not.

Judith answers in the professional, impersonal tone that she has acquired as an attorney, and Rosemary says, "Hello, Judith, it's your mother."

"Mother?" There is a pause. "Yes, hello, Mother."

What is it about us? Rosemary wonders. Already she hears it in Judith's voice, in the hesitancy, the pulling back. Then it sounds in her own voice as she asks, "How are things with you?" This is destined to be one of the low and tense conversations.

"Just fine. How about you?"

"That's why I'm calling. Your father has been in an accident. He's in the hospital with eye injuries."

"How bad are the injuries?"

"The doctor explained that there's extensive damage to the cornea in both eyes. That's the outer covering of—"

"I know that, but what does it mean, Mother? Can he see?"

"We have to wait until the bandages are off for the final word."

"He may be blind. You're saying he may be blind."

"It's very possible."

"This is incredible! He's been so health-conscious all these years, and now—You said it was an accident. How did it happen?"

Rosemary explains to the best of her knowledge. The business of a battery explosion still doesn't make sense to her, but the point is—and Rosemary emphasizes it with Judith—his eyes sustained chemical burns. No need to play down the facts with Judith.

"Does he have a specialist?"

"Of course, Judith. He's receiving good care."

"The *best* care, I would hope! We're talking *eyes,* Mother. What does the specialist intend to do?"

"He hasn't been very specific. It just happened yesterday."

"Somehow the idea of just waiting around until the bandages come off isn't reassuring. Is there just one specialist on the case?"

"He did say something about calling in a surgeon."

"A surgeon? So maybe this is something that can be corrected by surgery."

"Sounds reasonable, but he didn't say it in so many words."

"Sometimes you have to *ask.* You have to show that you're concerned about the details."

"Of course I'm concerned!"

"Anyway, maybe it's not as hopeless as you made it sound at first."

"Hopeless? That wasn't the impression I intended to give, Judith. I simply tried to be straightforward. But after all, this is not a *little* thing."

"No, it's just that you've always been the one to look for the silver lining, and frankly I couldn't detect much of a silver lining when you said Dad was in the hospital, probably blind. But we're getting off track, Mother."

"So it seems."

"Maybe I should fly down there."

"That's not necessary."

"Then why don't you give me the name of the doctor, and I'll call him."

"That's absolutely not necessary! I'll see that John gets proper attention, and I'll let you know of any developments."

"I could get a better feel for how serious the situation is if I could speak with the specialist."

"The situation is under control. Trust me."

Judith's sigh is not at all subtle. "All *right,* Mother. Whatever you say."

And the conversation ends rather quickly, another disaster in communication, Rosemary is convinced. She wishes she knew how to operate John's blood pressure apparatus.

When Rosemary arrives back at the hospital, Robbie is reading in one of his textbooks while John naps. "No problems," he says. "You're back sooner than I expected."

She pulls her chair close to his and speaks softly, so as not to wake John.

"What do you think of Dr. Nebbins?" she asks.

"I haven't met him."

"That's right."

"Why? What do *you* think of him?"

"My mailbox has more personality than he has, but it's hard to say how he rates as a doctor." She glances at John, at the white layers that cover his eyes. "If there was something that should be done that's *not* being done, if there's a hot-shot specialist somewhere that could give John his sight and I didn't find him—what I'm saying is, John is depending on me."

"Do you have some reason to believe this Dr. Nebbins doesn't know what he's doing?"

Rosemary thinks about it. "No. As a matter of fact, he gave the impression that John's situation was nothing out of the ordinary for him. Maybe that's what I didn't like about him."

"Maybe what you didn't like was that he couldn't give you the news you wanted to hear."

She looks again at John. "He's not in a position to take care of himself. It's up to me."

"That's how it's always been. You've taken care of all of us. You're good at it. So don't worry."

That is what separates Robbie from the sons of Rosemary's friends. That is what separates him from his sisters. Not just that he's *nice* to his mother, but that he can make her believe for a little while that she's appreciated.

"All right. I won't worry," she says, knowing very well that it is a promise impossible to keep.

Six

"I want to take care of you," John said by way of proposing marriage. He was twenty-seven. Rosemary was nineteen. It was an autumn night, and they stood at the Lowells' gate, under the glittering stars and an orange-gold moon. Rosemary, in a thin sweater, was shivering, and John took off his coat and draped it around her shoulders. Oh, he was gallant in those days! Then he made that romantic declaration, that he wanted to take care of her, *take care* of her! No love poem could have charmed her more.

They were married by the Reverend Hogan in his living room, with Mrs. Hogan, little Jimmie Lee, and Rosemary's mother in attendance. Mrs. Hogan baked a wedding cake, three tiers, topped with bride and groom until just before the wedding when Jimmie Lee climbed upon the dining room table and took possession of the couple. Resourceful Mrs. Hogan whipped up a new batch of frosting and smoothed over the spot where the decoration had stood, so that no one would've been the wiser had not little Jimmie Lee toddled up to Rosemary after the ceremony and handed her the figurines. It was certainly no fault of poor Mrs. Hogan that the bride's head was broken off, and, after all, Jimmie Lee was not even two. It was just one of those things, Rosemary told them. Her mother was aghast when she said, "Let me keep it as a reminder not to lose my head," but really, far too much was made of the incident in Rosemary's opinion. All in all, she remembered her wedding day as just about perfect.

Rosemary had expected her mother to object to the marriage, and Virginia hadn't disappointed her. The arguments had been predictable as well. "You're only nineteen, and what do you know about men? What about your career? It will take you *years* to establish yourself as a piano teacher in Atlanta—if you *ever* do. John Gray seems like a nice enough man, but you haven't even known him a year, and that's just a few hours here and there. Besides which, he's a *salesman.* Salesmen spend their lives on the road. There you'll be, in a strange city, without husband or mother, either. Not to mention that you've never in your whole life spent one night away from your mother!"

Rosemary smiled complacently. "You forgot to say that he's eight years older than me."

Virginia recognized the trap. "Doc was ten years my senior," she said indignantly, "but I happened to be twenty-five years old when we married. I knew what I was doing."

"So do I," said Rosemary.

She was very sure of John, and in that light, very sure of herself. The number of hours that they'd spent together—or *hadn't* spent together—seemed unimportant, when couples like Gloria Brown and Ted Travis could grow up on the same street, sit in class together for twelve years, go steady all during high school, and break up because Gloria cut her ponytail off without asking Ted. Rosemary was too level-headed to call it love at first sight, but it hadn't taken her all those months to figure out that John Gray would make a fine husband. What he was, he had been all along, from that first evening. Unlike the Ted Travises who still had to grow up, John was already the man he was going to be. He wasn't apt to change; he would just become more of what he already was.

That was what Rosemary believed, anyway.

One point which Virginia might've belabored was the obvious effect of Rosemary's marriage upon *her.* Along that line, however, Virginia actually had little to say. Rosemary was grateful that her responsibility to her mother didn't become an issue; she was also somewhat shocked that it didn't. But it seemed that John must've forestalled that argument when he promised to have a telephone put in for Virginia, "so you can call Rosemary whenever you like, if you run into any problems, or if you just get lonesome."

The time came for Rosemary to leave with her new husband, to leave her mother and Darlington. "Atlanta is only an hour away," she said. Virginia nodded. "The telephone man comes this Tuesday. I want you to call collect as soon as he gets it put in." Virginia nodded.

Then, slipping her hand into Virginia's, Rosemary said quietly, "Mamma, you've been swell about all this. I know how you must hate being left by yourself."

"I do have my trinkets to keep me busy," said Virginia.

And so Rosemary left Darlington with a great lump in her throat, thinking about the disparity in her own promising future and the lonely existence to which she was sentencing her mother. But John told her that good-byes were always hard, that no mothers *really* enjoyed seeing their daughters leave the nest. Rosemary didn't ask how he knew so much about mothers and daughters; he seemed to know a lot about everything, just as her father had. He said that Virginia had depended on her too much, that now she'd probably be forced to make her own friends. He said exactly what she needed to hear. Already he was taking care of her.

A honeymoon, a *real* honeymoon, was not possible because John was in his busy season of selling, but he promised that they would go to the coast in the spring. They went directly to John's rooms in Atlanta. When he stopped the car in the driveway between two large old houses, Rosemary looked out on her side and saw a lovely second-story veranda extending all the way across the front of the white-shingled house. A rose trellis screened the side of the lower porch; a United States flag was displayed. Rosemary was on the edge of her seat, wide-eyed. "Is the whole upstairs yours?"

"Oh, hey, it's *this* one, Rosie!" John said, laughing. "That one belongs to the American Legion Auxiliary. Those ladies really take care of it. Right up there, Rosie, that's home." And he pointed to the steps leading up the side of a very plain brick house.

John lived in half of the upstairs. The other half had been rented by another salesman but was, at present, vacant. The downstairs was occupied by the landlady. John's rooms were large, furnished simply, and uncluttered, less depressing than the outside. Actually, it was in fairly good condition if you didn't compare it to the showplace next door, and Rosemary wasn't going to brood over that. "Everything's nice and clean," she said.

"I'm not here much to mess it up," said John, "but it's true, I don't like dirt."

"My father was like that. After he died, I guess Mother and I sort of let the house go—well, *you* know how awful it is. I'll never let your house get in that shape."

"*Our* house, Rosie."

"Yes."

"The wallpaper's old and dingy, but the landlady has talked about replacing it."

"I'm used to dreary wallpaper."

"If you want to buy new curtains, we can probably afford them."

"They're not too bad." Rosemary looked around. "I haven't seen the bathroom or kitchen."

"Didn't I mention that? The bathroom and kitchen are downstairs. Everyone in the house shares them. Of course, it's just us and the landlady right now. It's not bad, really." He unlocked a door that Rosemary had thought was a closet. "You go down these stairs. Kitchen's left, bathroom's right."

When John had locked the door again, he noticed that Rosemary was frowning. "I hope everything's all right," he said. "If it's not, Rosie, tell me."

There was one thing, not the wallpaper or curtains, not even the kitchen and bathroom that had to be shared with strangers. "The place has a peculiar smell, that's all."

John sniffed. "Yes, maybe. I guess I'm used to it. I hope it's not offensive."

"Maybe all old houses smell the same," said Rosemary, but she knew better. It seemed very odd that the air in her first residence of married life was no different from what she had left in Darlington.

On Monday morning, after not quite two whole days of marriage, John left for the week. Rosemary had made coffee in the kitchen and was pouring herself a cup when a short, squatty woman with coppery hair came in. "You're Rosemary, aren't you? John showed me your high school picture."

"I beg your pardon."

"I'm your landlady, Amelia Banks."

"Nice to meet you, Mrs. Banks."

"No Mrs. to it. I'm just Amelia."

"All right, Amelia," said Rosemary. She was unaccustomed to calling women as old as her mother by their first names, but she figured that being a married woman changed some of the rules.

"Is that my cup?" asked Amelia.

"Oh, *is* it? I'm sorry! I thought John said it was all right to use any of the dishes, but if you'll tell me—"

Amelia cackled. "Don't be so nervous, sweetie. I'm just a harmless old bag of wind that wants a cup of coffee." She wobbled over to the table and sat in a chair that squeaked beneath her weight, which Rosemary placed at about two-seventy-five. "A coupla lumps of sugar, if you please, no cream."

"Could I fix you some breakfast?"

"Oh, no, I had mine. But there's a package of sweet rolls in the bread box you might hand me."

Amelia shared one with Rosemary and ate the remaining three herself, while she talked a blue streak. "John Gray's like a son to me, a peach of a man. You've made yourself a fine catch. And looks like he did pretty well, too," she said, winking. "I'm gonna enjoy having you around, Rosemary. It gets awfully lonesome for me, and I can't get out much anymore. Tires me just walking to the bus stop. The grocery store delivers, but from time to time I have to call on John to run errands for me."

"I'll be glad to help you out," said Rosemary.

"You wouldn't mind?"

"Certainly not."

"Young lady, you're a gem! This partial's about to drive me crazy." She jerked a section of bridgework from her mouth. "The dentist is on Curry Avenue, right on the bus line. Tell him to file off this rough edge, right here."

Amelia needed dye for her hair and a card for someone who was having a birthday. The leaky bathroom faucets needed new washers. There was a mix-up about Amelia's taxes and she was required to bring certain papers to the courthouse, which, Rosemary explained to John, probably would've killed her, as she could barely make her way to and from the clothesline. In time, Rosemary started hanging out her clothes, too. Rosemary took over scrubbing the bathroom and kitchen; bending was such a hardship for Amelia. And somehow—Rosemary was never quite sure how it came about—the two of them began to take their meals together, with Rosemary cooking, naturally. She never learned to say no to Amelia.

But Amelia returned kindness as she could, by making her piano available to Rosemary. It was an old upright that needed tuning, but Rosemary gratefully accepted the chance to play. And when she mentioned that she'd taught piano, Amelia wouldn't rest until she located two children who wanted lessons. Actually they were granddaughters of the grocer and were already taking piano lessons, but Amelia was such a good customer that her food supplier would not refuse her. He spread the word, too, and others came to Rosemary. Soon she was teaching six children and two adults on Amelia's piano. The only hitch to the arrangement —after Rosemary paid to have the piano tuned—was that Amelia remained in the living room during lessons, her arms folded on her stomach as if it were a table, her eyes closed, her head rocking to the plinkety-plink of the keys. It was the most joyous sound Amelia had heard in many years.

She did, for the most part, allow the young couple their privacy on weekends. However, she couldn't resist wandering into the kitchen whenever she smelled something cooking, and what could one say except "Won't you join us?"

John was never unpleasant to Amelia. As a matter of habit, he continued to ask if she needed anything when he was going out (though she never did anymore) or if he could fix anything in the house (though Rosemary had proven to be a capable handyman). And once, before he taught Rosemary to drive, he took Amelia to the doctor on a Saturday morning. He was polite, like an obedient son. But privately he said to Rosemary, "I can't afford to feed Amelia. Don't invite her to have every meal with us."

"I can't be rude to her," said Rosemary.

"It's rude on her part to barge in on us every time we're in the kitchen."

"She doesn't mean any harm."

"Do you know how much our groceries are costing these days?"

"I buy them, John, but what can I do?"

"Just don't say, 'Come on, Amelia, pull up a chair.' "

Rosemary didn't disagree with what John was saying, but she couldn't bear to hurt Amelia's feelings. "Look at it this way," she said. "I make a little money giving music lessons because Amelia lets me use her piano. Maybe we do spend what I make on extra groceries, but couldn't we just call it even?"

John looked at her in a very peculiar way. He didn't answer, but he didn't say any more about it, either.

Then Bertie MacArthur moved into the vacant upper half of the house, and Bertie, a dried-up prune of a woman who could actually out-eat Amelia, became a regular at mealtime, too.

"Every week she gives me five dollars for groceries," Rosemary said to John. "That's fair enough."

"You're the cook," he said. And Rosemary let it go at that, because she couldn't tell whether he was joking or being catty, and it was better not to know.

John didn't mention the belated honeymoon that was supposed to take place in spring, but it was just as well with Rosemary, for when spring came, she had something besides honeymooning on her mind. She was sick. One who had never spent a day in the sickbed, she could barely drag herself to her feet. The smell of food made her queasy. She lived on crackers. One morning, racked by a wave of nausea in the middle of bacon-frying, she had to lie down right there in the kitchen, across two chairs.

"She's kind of green," said Amelia.

Bertie, who had spent thirty years as a licensed practical nurse, washed Rosemary's face and laid the cool cloth on her forehead. Knowingly, she said, "That's how it is with morning sickness."

"Morning sickness?" gasped Amelia. "You mean—"

"Isn't that right, Rosemary?"

By that weekend, Rosemary had seen a doctor and could tell John, "The doctor says I'm going to have a baby," omitting the fact that it was Bertie who had enlightened her. Later, however, she wondered if it wouldn't have been better for him to think her naive than for him to believe that she'd deliberately cheated him out of being the first to know.

Actually, the older women were making an effort to be considerate that next morning, for they fixed breakfast and Bertie brought a tray upstairs to John. She pointed to the crackers and tea and said, "That's for Rosemary. Good for her ailment." And Amelia, standing at the foot of the stairs, called, "Can you picture how it's gonna be around here with a *baby?* You a daddy, and Bertie and me, well, as close to grandmas as we'll ever get!"

Handing Rosemary her crackers, John said, "They already know."

"There wasn't much way to keep it from them," said Rosemary, meaning that they were naturally aware of her morning sickness.

But John said, "We don't have a speck of privacy."

"Now that's not true, John. This is a very nice place to live."

"Yes, for you and Amelia and Bertie," he said, and he walked out and got in the car.

He stayed gone until five o'clock that evening. When he came back, he behaved as if he'd been around the corner for a loaf of bread, asked how Rosemary was feeling and if she wanted to go the Dairy Queen for a hamburger.

"If you want to," she said, stiffly, knowing all along that what she *ought* to say was, "I'm sorry that Amelia and Bertie knew something that you probably should've known first, but the fact is, Bertie told *me;* I didn't tell her."

But in the first place, she was not anxious to admit that she hadn't recognized morning sickness for what it was. In the second place, while John's interest in this business was touching, it was also a little silly for him to get his feelings hurt over such a trivial matter as *who knew first.* And in the third place, he hadn't said a word about where he'd been all day while she'd wrung her hands.

So their first tiff just died, more or less. They didn't fight it out, and they didn't kiss and make up. They just pretended it didn't happen, and that was the way they generally handled disagreements from then on.

Not more than a month later, John announced that he had been transferred to a new territory, and they would have to move to Greenville, South Carolina.

Maybe it was all for the best, Rosemary told herself, but Amelia and Bertie just boo-hooed.

They were all in the kitchen, naturally. It was supper, this time. Amelia couldn't even eat her second tunafish sandwich, she was so heartbroken. "We won't ever get to be grandmas now," she said, burying her face in her plump little hands.

"It won't be the same without your music," Bertie said, trying to maintain her dignity as she wiped her eyes.

"Oh, what will we do?" cried Amelia. "What will we ever do without you, Rosemary?"

John stood by with his arms folded, saying nothing.

Seven

"I wondered if you'd still be here," says Rosemary to the little man who looks so very much like a leprechaun.

John Grant, sitting up in bed this time, is once again bundled in his roomy green robe. "Come in, Rosemary!" he calls.

"I'm glad you're not going to pull that line about Agnes again."

He shrugs. "You're back, I see. What made you come back?"

"Curiosity, I guess."

"So there."

Rosemary wags her finger at him. "It wasn't very nice. I was in a hurry."

"Sure, sure. Everybody is. Just think about it. You come in, you say, 'Pardon me, I've got the wrong room,' and I say, 'OK, fine, so long.' Are you ever gonna give me a second thought? Now come on and be sociable. I can get fussed at by the nurses. Sit down."

She has been sitting all morning, glued to John's bedside, but now, taking a chair in Mr. Grant's room, she settles comfortably. It's not at all the same here, knowing she can leave when she pleases, here where no threads of responsibility tie her.

"What are you in for, Mr. Grant?"

"My friends call me Buddy."

Rosemary raises her eyebrows. "Buddy. All right, if you say so."

"It's the truth. Sure, I had to give my *real* name to the hospital. That's what's on my Medicare papers. But I've been Buddy since my first day in the primer class. We had four boys named John in school. One was J. R. 'cause his name was John Robert, see, and the other was just plain John. The teacher pointed to another new boy and said, 'You're Johnny.' Then she turned to me and said, 'Well, Buddy, what about you?' That's how it got started." He scowled. "You still don't believe me."

"I happen to know that you like to concoct stories. But if you want me to call you Buddy, that's what it'll be."

"Ask Fanny Malone. Or anybody at the home. Just call up the Eastside Nursing Home and ask."

Rosemary lets a grin break through.

"Why would I lie about my name?"

"I *believe* you! I believe you, Buddy."

No pears are left in his fruit basket, but Rosemary peels and sections an orange for him and takes an apple for herself. "He's not on a special diet, is he?" she asks a nurse who checks in briefly.

"Oh, no," the nurse answers. "He can have whatever he wants. We've had a problem getting him to eat *anything*."

"You could've asked *me* if I was on a special diet," Buddy says with a pout.

"You wouldn't have told me if you were."

"I might've."

"And you certainly wouldn't have told me that you aren't eating. What's that all about, anyway?"

Buddy bites into an orange section. "No seeds."

"Why aren't you eating?"

"I am." He makes a show of plopping the other half into his mouth, chewing, swallowing. "See me? I'm eating."

Rosemary wets a brown paper towel and hands it to him. "Do you need anything else?"

"Nothing. Just sit down. You make me jittery, flitting

around. Sit." She does, smiling at his audacity, which for some reason doesn't offend her.

"You never did tell me why you're in the hospital."

"Bunions."

"All right, it's really none of my business."

"I just told you."

"You're in the hospital because you have bunions?"

"I am. Bunions are a bigger problem than you might think. They hurt so I can't walk, and the women at the home have started treating me like an old man. I've got to get back on my feet."

"Well, yes, that would be a problem."

"It most certainly is. But the operation ought to take care of it."

"You're having an operation?"

"In the morning, they tell me."

He seems to be on the level. He names his doctor and knows that the doctor is an orthopedic surgeon. Rosemary doesn't doubt his story this time, but for her benefit he says to another nurse who drops by, "You say my operation's at eight o'clock tomorrow?"

"I think that's right," says the nurse.

Buddy folds his arms and looks smug.

Rosemary stays another few minutes. Before she leaves, she tells him, "Sometime after your surgery, maybe I can wheel you down to my husband's room. He'd enjoy a visitor."

"What happened to him?"

Yet again, Rosemary tells of the bizarre accident and John's eye injuries. It has become like reciting for school; she speaks the words without letting their meaning sink in too deeply. But Buddy turns quite solemn. "That's a terrible thing."

Something about the remark touches her. She has been away from John's room too long. His lunch will soon be served, and he cannot manage eating without help. "I've got to get back," she says, "but I'll check on you after your surgery."

"Would you?"

"Of course."

"If I don't come out of it, would you please tell Agnes I forgive her?"

"Now, Buddy, I thought we dispensed with Agnes."

He squares his frail shoulders. "Your skepticism is boring, Rosemary! Agnes is my daughter, my scheming daughter. Have you ever heard of Nathan Periwinkle?"

"The judge?"

"He's my son-in-law. It's the truth. Everything I said that day about Agnes is the truth except—well, I've already told you that I didn't actually think *you* were Agnes."

"How long since you've seen her?"

"Oh, I couldn't say. She's been to the home a couple of times. Nathan drops in whenever anything needs signing. He was here yesterday about my operation. But you won't catch me giving *him* any messages for Agnes. He'd turn 'em around. He turned around everything I ever said in court and made me out to be a fruitcake. Agnes went along with him, but she didn't enjoy it as much."

"If she knows about your surgery, maybe she'll come by."

"Nope. Nathan said they were leaving for Ha-wa-ya this morning." He raises his forefinger to make a point. "Nathan talks to me. I don't talk to him. Anyway, if I don't come out of it tomorrow—"

"You will, Buddy. I'll check on you after the surgery."

He extends a bony hand for a very formal handshake. "Remember what to tell her."

"If I get a chance," says Rosemary, "I will tell her plenty."

The lunch trays are being delivered, but Rosemary reaches John's room ahead of the cart.

"You just about didn't make it," he says.

She knows what he means; after thirty years, she can read between the lines. She knows how anxious he is over the thought of managing his tray alone. As meticulous as John is, he can't abide the thought of making a mess with his food. "I said I'd be back before your lunch came, and I am." She wants to be reassuring, but somehow it isn't coming across. She squeezes his hand. "You mustn't worry, John. I've been here for every meal, haven't I?"

"I hear the cart. You just barely made it back this time. Where have you been anyway?"

"I went to visit another patient. I told you all about him. Don't you remember?" Again, she sounds more annoyed than she intends.

"John-Somebody, you said."

"John Grant, who goes by Buddy, incidentally, who happens to be about ninety years old and is about to have surgery on his bunions. You've heard of Nathan Periwinkle, haven't you?"

"Somebody else you've made friends with in the hospital, I suppose."

She lets it pass. "I know you've heard of him, John. He's a judge, always being quoted in the newspapers. Well, he's Buddy's son-in-law. Buddy's daughter, Agnes—Nathan Periwinkle's wife—evidently had her father declared incompetent, or whatever the legal term is—"

"You've lost me," says John, without interest.

"Buddy's daughter got his money and put him in a nursing home."

"Is that what the old man told you? Old people get confused about things, you know."

"Buddy is a sharp old codger. You'd like him, John. You would."

"You don't know anything about the man, Rosemary."

"I know that when he goes into surgery tomorrow, there won't be anyone in the waiting room who cares whether he comes out of it or not. His daughter left for Hawaii today."

"Maybe she didn't think bunions were life-threatening."

"Maybe she didn't care whether they were or not."

"You get too involved with other people, Rosemary, too involved with *strangers.* There's a lot of trouble in the world, sure, but you don't have to go looking for it. Why is it that you want to shoulder everybody's problems? Isn't a blind husband trouble enough?"

The clattering cart stops in front of John's door, and it's a good thing, Rosemary thinks, for it nips in the bud a discussion that neither of them needs. "They're bringing your lunch," she says.

"I know. I can hear. When you lose one of your senses, the others get better and better, they say. Why, I can probably sniff my tray and tell you if I have carrots or corn. I can tell when the elevator stops on this floor. Maybe I could count the times it opens and closes. That might be—"

"John, *please,*" Rosemary says quietly, and the girl who has brought lunch pretends not to hear as she sets the tray before John. Rosemary thanks her, and she leaves in a hurry. "Let me prop these pillows behind you. No, not too—"

But John, in sitting up, has managed to knock over his iced tea, flooding his beef stroganoff and green peas, soaking his roll.

"It's all right, don't worry about it, nothing broke, and I can order you another lunch, it's not a big thing." Rosemary wipes quickly, keeping the spill confined to the tray except for one icy puddle in John's lap, at which he doesn't so much as flinch. He turns his bandaged eyes away from Rosemary and lies perfectly still, without a word, while she cleans up.

Buddy comes through his surgery without a hitch. Rosemary makes a point of dropping in to see him each day, usually in conjunction with her lunch, but she no longer mentions it to John. She doesn't say any more about wheeling Buddy over to John's room, either, with John so down-in-the-mouth. It's peculiar: Visiting Buddy provides, in the sluggish day, the only five or ten minutes that actually dance by. Rosemary wonders if subconsciously she enjoys being sneaky. There is something entertaining about Buddy's eccentricities, to be sure, and joking with the leprechaun man provides a brief escape from the weighty and *real* situation that awaits in John's room. Odd as it may be, she feels rested and renewed after a chat with Buddy; it's almost like slipping away to that quiet place under the bridge at Parson's Creek.

But John had a point, too: She *does* seek out troubles to shoulder, strangers to take under her wing. Strangers are somehow *easier* than family, though it shouldn't be that way. It has something to do with the matter of *choice,* Rosemary knows; with family you can never say, "Forget it!" With family, you are always grappling with guilt for not doing more.

At the end of the first week, Dr. Nebbins suggests that Rosemary start spending nights at home. Actually, he insists. "We don't want your husband to become helpless, do we, Mrs. Gray?" he remarks, with a wooden smile. Naturally she answers no, but the doctor isn't interested in her answer. "Let him eat by himself, as much as possible. As long as you do everything for him, he'll make no progress in coping with his situation. Give him the chance to develop some self-confidence." All of which is sound enough advice, Rosemary supposes, but she can't help resenting being reprimanded as if she's been a naughty child, as if it's *her* fault that John isn't doing more for himself. And of course the doctor doesn't happen to mention this to John. Rosemary is left with that little chore when the orderly comes to take her cot out of the room.

"No, John, I won't be needing it anymore. I'm going home at night from now on. The doctor thinks it's a good idea."

Since John's eyes are covered, Rosemary has learned to read his reactions by the various movements of his lips. When he's anxious, he opens them as if to speak, closes them, opens and closes, and when he is considering something, he licks his lower lip. Now he purses his lips, a sign that he is annoyed. Rosemary goes on to say, "You can always call on the nurses if you need anything. It's not as if you'll be *alone.* Maybe I haven't let you be independent enough."

"If that's what you think," John finally says.

"It's not what *I* think. It's what the doctor ordered."

He doesn't say anything for a moment. Then, rather shyly, he asks, "What about breakfast?"

"Yes, breakfast, well—if a nurse can help you get started, you know, tell you what's what, why, you'll do fine. The doctor said so."

"I guess you'd have to get up at four o'clock to get here before breakfast."

"But it's not that, John. It's not that at all."

"You'll be here by lunchtime, though."

"Yes, long before. But what I'm telling you is, Dr. Nebbins doesn't particularly *want* me here at mealtime. Do you see what I'm getting at?"

"I can't *see* anything, Rosemary, but I guess you're saying that I might as well get used to fumbling in the dark. And I guess you're probably right. Come to think of it, you're almost always right. So if you think you ought to go home at night, well, go on. Whatever you think."

At home in the evenings, the telephone won't stop ringing. Their minister Dr. Lyons calls to ask about John. Rosemary has to apologize for the time that he came by the hospital and John said he wasn't up to having visitors. Marjorie Dye, also from the church, phones to say that Rosemary needn't worry about the ladies' meeting which was supposed to be at her house this month; they've changed it to Elaine McDonald's house. But if she wants it in August . . . The piano tuner returns her call, made the day before John's accident. "I've tried a dozen times, lady. . . ." One of the men from John's office calls, saying he just got back from his vacation and just heard the bad news. Can John have visitors? No one in the office seems to think so. Rosemary has to tell him to wait. And it seems that the light-bulb and magazine salespeople have been waiting for her to get home so they can be told *No* once again. Then there is Jean Hollingsworth from next door who pops in every evening or so to ask about John, offering to help out if she can, but of course she can't. Rosemary has so many things to catch up on that there is really not much time to chat. Jean, fortunately, takes a hint, so her visits are brief.

It doesn't take Rosemary many days to decide that staying at the hospital, where the hours march by slowly, is a lot less taxing than driving back and forth, with evenings at home a far cry from relaxing, with nights a far cry from restful. She cannot sleep for wondering if—doctor's orders aside—she has abandoned John.

"Why, he's doing just fine," says Head Nurse Krantz when Rosemary corners her one afternoon.

"He hates messes," Rosemary tells her. "He worries about dribbling his sleeve in chocolate pudding, dropping a green bean in his lap, things like that."

Mrs. Krantz gives her a scolding look. "Mrs. Gray, such things are to be expected. And we do check on him, you know. If his sleeve needs wiping, we take care of it. Really, he's had no problems with his meals."

"You don't just leave him to fend for himself then?"

"Of *course* not, Mrs. Gray."

"And he doesn't complain to you?"
"Never. He's been very cooperative."
"He eats well?"
"Yes."
"Why, then, does he give me the impression—" Rosemary stops; she knows the answer.

So does Mrs. Krantz, but Rosemary would've been just as happy not to hear her say it: "Your husband manages *very well* when you're not here, Mrs. Gray."

Rosemary tells him that night, "I won't be back until tomorrow evening. It's Yard Day, and I missed it last week." If John does so well without her, it shouldn't be any problem.

The backyard has less grass to mow than the wide, level front lawn, but it requires more of what Rosemary thinks of as manicuring. Weeding in the thick sedum clusters that jut out from the base of the willow, trimming back the ivy that climbs on the brick, clipping the boxwood hedge, spraying for bugs on the white iris, with their regal heads held high. Rosemary's backyard is not merely a springtime showplace. She has carefully set out her plants so that from March till November, a new crop of diverse colors and textures is always in bloom, rising up to replace each dying one. And in winter the evergreens show up, the holly berries, the boxwoods and the white pine where the birdhouse seems to suddenly appear, though it's been there all along.

Rosemary does not rush today. She inspects each plant and gives special attention to one azalea at the corner of the house. It's a slow bloomer this spring, not dead, for there are sparse patches of new growth, but it hasn't taken off like the others. They are a vivid, glossy green, thick with buds ready to burst into white blossoms. Rosemary can't find a bud on this puny bush. *Puny,* she says to herself, calling up the image of her mother pouring a spoonful of Castor Oil for the pale, quiet girl who was a late bloomer herself. With that brief reflection, she decides not to replace the bush quite yet. She makes a mental note to buy fertilizer.

The yard was, of course, why Rosemary wanted the house in the first place. It has been a fourteen-year process to create an established, *rooted* look that the suburbs rarely give, but Rosemary saw that potential from the beginning. Was it the willow tree that sold her? The ivy, the hedge, all the flowering plants grew only in her imagination when she told John, "*This* one." It was the third house that they had been shown in Nashville. Two other houses in the neighborhood with the same floor plan were listed at the same price. Rosemary could tell that John was partial to the white brick. He kept saying that corner lots were nice. But since there was no dollar difference, he let her choose. That is more or less the way John is. He isn't likely to ever put his foot down unless there's a question of at least a couple of dollars.

By the time Rosemary gets to the hospital, it's late afternoon. Three shifts have changed during her absence, and she has a peculiar feeling that she's missed something. Which nurses were on duty? Did Robbie call? What did John have to eat? Did he listen to the radio? Did anyone come by?

John, grunting most of his answers, finally gets around to relaying two pieces of news. Buddy has been discharged. He sent word about ten o'clock that he was leaving. And Dr. Nebbins is planning to take off John's bandages tomorrow.

"Well! I'm a little surprised—so *soon.*" Rosemary tries to sound cheerful, but a false note rings in her voice.

"No more hoping or speculating," says John. "Tomorrow we'll know. If the news is bad, there's no more kidding ourselves."

"Don't talk that way, John." But he has hit the nail right

on the head. "Can I get you anything? Do anything to make you more comfortable?"

He shakes his head.

"Are you sure?"

"You might call Robbie. He wasn't planning to come by tonight. Oh, I don't know. You probably shouldn't bother him."

"Why shouldn't I?" It seems the natural thing to do. Rosemary is already dialing.

Eight

Robbie was a *different* sort of child. He just was. It was *all* different with Robbie, from the very beginning.

Rosemary didn't need a Bertie MacArthur to tell her she was pregnant the third time. She didn't really need a doctor to tell her, either, but she made an appointment early on. Maybe someone had improved pregnancy and delivery since she'd given birth to Melissa eight years before. She wanted to get off to a good start. She wanted everything to be *right* this go-around.

They were in Louisville, Kentucky, the farthest north that they'd lived, the fifth city in ten years. Every move meant new doctors, sometimes for Rosemary, though she hadn't bothered to find a doctor for herself in Mobile, and always new pediatricians for the girls. John had in the past couple of years become inordinately concerned about his health, which as far as Rosemary knew was perfect, so he'd found himself a doctor in Louisville that he highly recommended. "And he's from Georgia, too. Makes you homesick to hear him talk." But Rosemary declared that she was homesick enough as it was, and she was going to see an obstetrician this time. Not that she had anything against general practitioners, certainly not. Her father had been one, and Judith and Melissa had been delivered by G.P.s, but *this* time, she wanted the best and most up-to-date care. One of their neighbors recommended a Dr. Corning, and he became Rosemary's obstetrician.

"My obstetrician says to go light on salt."

"My obstetrician gave me this booklet about breast-feeding."

"My obstetrician said that exercise is fine. He recommends it."

More than a few times, she had to say to John, "Just *indulge* me, please. This will be our last baby. I want everything to be the way it's *supposed* to be, that's all."

Dr. Corning, fiftyish and gray-haired with a beakish nose and sincere eyes, was easy to talk to. In fact, at the end of every visit, he would ask, "Now, Rosemary, what's on your mind?" An expectant mother always had a question or a worry, and he never cut her off. "Anything else? Are you sure?"

Once Rosemary had the courage to say, "My husband doesn't seem very excited about this baby."

Dr. Corning propped against the wall and folded his arms. "Did he *want* another child, Rosemary?"

"Well, no, not really."

"You have daughters, right?"

"Yes."

"And they're how old?"

"Eight and nine."

"So you've been out of the baby business for a while."

"You could say that."

Dr. Corning scratched his chin. He gave Rosemary a rather scrutinizing look and then scratched his chin again. "Men aren't always as crazy about babies as women are, Rosemary. Babies take a lot of time. They take a lot of the wife's energy, and, yes, they divert her attention from her husband. Plus, a new baby is an extra financial burden. Your husband has a whole different viewpoint from yours."

"Yes, I guess so. Well, thank—"

"This baby was more or less unplanned, I take it."

Rosemary looked a little sheepish. "I guess you could say that."

"Your husband was surprised."

"Well, yes." *Shocked* was more like it, but the doctor needn't know everything.

"Maybe the two of you had even talked about how nice it was that your girls were getting so self-reliant, and that as sweet as your babies had been, you were glad that phase of your lives was over."

Rosemary fidgeted. "I see what you mean, Dr. Corning. Thanks for pointing it out to me." She began to gather her purse and coat.

"If he loves the other children, he'll love this one."

"Oh, he does. He's a good father." And Rosemary said a hasty good-bye.

Dr. Corning was a smart fellow, all right, figuring how John looked at the prospect of a third child. Not that John had actually *said* those things, but she could tell, and Dr. Corning had hit the bull's eye. Maybe if she'd stayed longer, he would've come around to *her* viewpoint, which might've been interesting. Would he have said she was terrible? Or would he have nodded patiently and told her that she wasn't the first woman to feel the way she'd felt, to do what she'd done? She'd never know, for she certainly wasn't going to discuss the subject with Dr. Corning again.

The day that Rosemary had started to want another baby—and she could narrow it down almost to the minute—that day, the girls ate breakfast, dressed, and left for school without one cross word. None of the usual "She's got *my* ribbon!" or "Didn't you wash my pink blouse?" or "I forgot that I'm supposed to bring paraffin for science today." And when Rosemary checked their room, the beds were made—sort of—and Melissa had written on her blackboard, "I love Mom." It was a rare morning.

The ladies at the church were hosting a luncheon, and Rosemary had just stuck her chicken casserole in Irene Pauley's car when another car drove up. It was her friendly neighborhood cosmetics saleslady, Charlene, and along with her samples she had a baby. "He belongs to my sister," explained Charlene. "She's laid up with mumps, of all things, so I've been keeping Wally. But I couldn't put off working any longer. I just had to bring him along."

"I don't mind," said Rosemary.

"Some people don't like it. I can tell. I suppose it's *not* very businesslike to lug a baby around."

"Don't you worry about it."

The four-month-old baby posed no problem for a while. He seemed content, sitting in Charlene's lap as she tried to show some new colors in lipstick, except that he was fascinated by Charlene's curls and she had to pry his plump little fist open again and again to retrieve her hair. Then somehow, as Charlene took the top off a bottle of cologne that she wanted Rosemary to sniff, Baby Wally bumped her hand just so. The bottle went onto the floor before Rosemary could dive for it and the rug was soaked with Morning Dew.

"This just isn't working!" cried Charlene, while Rosemary dabbed at the rug.

Then Rosemary heard herself offer to keep the baby.

"Do you mean it? Oh, I'd be *so* grateful! He won't be a bit of trouble."

And he wasn't. Of course, Rosemary had to make some adjustments. She called the Brownie troop leader and bowed out of selling cookies at the shopping center that afternoon, and the favors that she was making for Melissa's class party had to be put up. Irene Pauley called from the church in a panic, needing more help in the kitchen, but Rosemary had to decline and only felt a *little* guilty. She kept the baby until just before the girls arrived from school, and he was the most pleasant child you could ask for, gurgling, blowing bubbles, making those cute faces. And he felt so *good* in her arms.

John got home early in the afternoon, as he sometimes did on Fridays. Then he spent a while making out sales reports for the week. But that day, he left his paperwork a couple of times to fool with the baby, tickling Wally's double chin and talking in the foolish way that grown-ups talk to babies.

"Isn't he sweet?" said Rosemary.

"Cute as can be, as long as he belongs to somebody else!"

Rosemary had asked Charlene to pick up Wally before the girls got home, for the girls were going to a Girls' Auxiliary social, and she would need to drive them to the church. But Judith said, "Jill's mom offered to drive us," and Melissa chimed in, "Isn't that nice, Mamma? You don't have to bother." They were in remarkably good spirits that afternoon, especially Judith, who made a peanut butter sandwich for herself and one for her sister as well.

And when they were gone, Rosemary stood before the mirror, telling herself that thirty was too close for comfort, that her girls weren't going to *really* need her that much in the years to come. And if, just *if* she were to think about having another baby, well, her candle was burning lower all the time.

Robbie was born a year later, and he was a wonderful baby. John was finally present for the birth of his third child—present in the father's waiting room—and he was very proud. While John was holding Robbie for the first time, he looked at Rosemary and said, with a foolish grin, "I guess he's all right. We couldn't have done better if we'd planned him."

And Rosemary knew that she couldn't tell him—he wouldn't understand in a million years—that Robbie *was* planned by one of them.

Robbie wondered about things, and he worried about things. In the simplest questions, he saw shades of meaning that were never intended; even as a little boy he did. But if that was a sign of genius, it was missed by his teachers, who saw Robbie as "quiet, cooperative, and such a *pleasant* child!" His dimpled smile counted for more than any perceptive answer that he might feed back on paper (which might very well be marked wrong if it wasn't what the teacher had in mind). Robbie was not one to raise his hand and ask an enlightened question. No, his teacher might think he was showing off, and he would *never* want that.

So he generally kept his thoughts in his head, and Rosemary was the only one who believed he was brilliant; she *knew* it. At the same time, he was so loving, so good-natured, so unimpressed with himself that Rosemary wasn't anxious for anyone to put a tag like "gifted" on him. He'd discover his gifts soon enough.

Within the family, Robbie was the pet, no doubt about it. His sisters were eight and nine when he was born, and though Judith was by nature nothing like the little mother that Melissa was, even Judith had her moments.

"I'll let you use my pens," she offered when he wandered into her room one day. She scooted her work over—that was in Birmingham when the girls had a built-in desk—and for a half-hour, Robbie sat in her lap, making red and blue R's and O's.

Then Melissa came in to get a sweater. "Hey, Robbie," she said, "wanna go see Mr. Vickers' new puppies?"

"He's busy," said Judith.

"I wanna see the puppies," said Robbie.

Judith turned to the side and dropped him off her lap, right into the floor. "Well, *go,* then! You're bothering me, anyway, and look at the mess you've made!"

It was one of Robbie's earliest memories, and one in a long line of lessons on how Judith could change from honey to vinegar in a snap.

Then there was Robbie's father, who was almost as hard

to read as Judith, maybe because he just wasn't *there* a lot, but now and then he would say things like, "We *men* want to watch football, don't we?" and somehow those little implications were enough. Robbie didn't seem to need a show of affection or the kind of attention that other fathers gave their sons, the fathers who were on the sidelines at every Little League game. *His* dad was away doing something important (his mother said) and that was all right. What he never had, he never expected and never missed.

His mother taught him to play ball. Not that she really knew much about it, but she was the one who got out in the backyard in the afternoons and pitched to him. "You're going to be so good that those big boys will *beg* you to be on their team!" she told him. Then when he did learn to hit, she took him herself to the lot where the neighborhood boys played. There, as sides were being chosen, she handed Robbie a sackful of chocolate chip cookies and said, "You can share these cookies with your team." Robbie's was the next name called, as his mother marched off the field.

And she was the one who kept saying that he was going to do something special when he grew up—"like your grandfather, who was the only doctor in the town where we lived, and he took care of everyone."

"Was he famous?"

"Well, I wouldn't say that he was famous. But he was important. What he did *counted* for something. And what you do will count for something, too. Wait and see."

"How do you know, Mamma?"

"Because you're special."

Robbie had to believe it, so often did she tell him. When his Sunday School lesson was about David, shepherd boy anointed king of Israel, his mother pointed out that some people were *chosen* to do great things.

"But who chooses, Mamma?"

"Why, *God* does."

"How would I know if he chose me?"

"I think you'll know," she said with a smile that she saved for him alone.

Oh, there was no lack of warmth and tenderness toward *him,* but it seemed to Robbie that if his family could've spread a little of it around to each other, they would've all been better off.

From the time he was three weeks old attending his sisters' baptism, Robbie was a regular in church. His mother saw to it. Not just on Sunday mornings, either. Sunday nights and Wednesday nights at prayer meeting, he slept on the pew beside Rosemary, for she was sure he would cry if she left him in the nursery. He sat on a blanket and stacked cans while Rosemary worked in the food closet that the church provided, and he sat in a little chair beside her piano bench while she played for his sisters' choir.

In Birmingham for four years, the Grays lived close enough to the church to walk, Robbie clutching his mother's gloved hand, his father a step behind with the Bible, Judith and Melissa in front with their ponytails wagging merrily. Robbie didn't remember that it was ever winter in Birmingham. They always seemed to walk past lilac hedges in bloom, the warm breeze rose-scented.

Then there was the move to Nashville when Robbie was seven, and the character of Sundays changed. Every Sunday morning Melissa tied up the bathroom so that they were late. Every Sunday morning Judith, who was beginning her private rebellion against organized religion, announced that she wasn't going to church anymore, and Rosemary declared that oh yes she was. John went out and started the car twenty minutes before anyone was ready, and Robbie tugged at his bow tie with one hand and chewed his nails on the other.

But in church, in the vaulted sanctuary with stained glass

windows, where the organ swelled and the congregation lifted up great hymns of praise, Robbie was so attentive, so *absorbed,* that the difficulties in getting there seemed to fade out. The ringing anthems, the ardent prayers, the Scriptures interpreted by the velvet-tongued preacher—church was so *spiritual.* Robbie caught what he could and mulled over it. In church, he often felt very close to *getting at* that essential *something,* and he was sorry when the benediction was pronounced and his family would climb into the car, complaining about the long service and too-tight shoes.

There came a time when Robbie was impressed with a strong urge to *do* something, to *say* where he stood, more or less. He was twelve years old, and his profession of faith was exactly *that,* an affirmation that he did believe in the Lord Jesus Christ, an expression of faith in that he accepted something which was beyond understanding. But there was so much still that baffled him, the concept of eternity, of something that never ends, and the creation, that time when there was nothing, *nothing* but the spirit of God. Robbie wanted to *get hold* of such largeness, and he couldn't. Heaven, hell, the devil, the soul—oh, he could give the right answers well enough, but what did they *mean?* It wasn't so much a matter of wondering *How can it be?* as of wondering *What does it all mean?* The more he contemplated God and life and the universe, the more certain Robbie was that there was some connection that he was missing. There were ministers and wise teachers whom he could ask, but he couldn't even establish the right questions; how could he possibly expect the right answers?

The only sport that interested Robbie was baseball. He started out in Little League and played during high school, and he might've qualified for a baseball scholarship if he'd pursued it. At least his parents thought so. The one time he mentioned it to his coach, however, he came home saying,

"Coach Willis doesn't think I'd have much of a chance," which more or less put an end to the discussion. If the coach didn't encourage him, well, maybe he should forget it.

What the gravel-voiced coach had said, exactly, was this: "You're a good kid, Robbie, and you got a lot of natural ability, but it takes somethin' more to play college sports. Call it the old killer instinct or just plain *drive,* you don't have it and never will, and you know it!"

Robbie knew it. For four years, the coach had bellowed at him—at the rest of the team, too, but especially at him—to get tough. *Get tough!* Every coach he'd ever played for had said the same thing, just with different slogans. *Give it all you got! Bear down! You gotta put out a hundred and ten percent!* Nobody spouted that old cliché, that it's not whether you win or lose but how you play the game, except your mom. Any little guy who'd ever been fitted for a uniform could tell you, if you lost, it meant you should've played harder.

Robbie's problem or weakness or failing was in the fact that he played baseball for fun. That didn't mean that winning was nothing to him, but it wasn't everything. He liked the dull impact of a fly ball plopping into his glove; the *feel* of it was satisfying, whether his team was ten points behind or ten ahead. He relished the moment that his bat made contact with the ball, when he could tell by the *cr-rack* that it was headed over the fence; the thrill was the same, with or without the bases loaded. Knowing that he had performed well, making his coach and his teammates proud all figured into his enjoyment of the game. Winning was just a piece of all that.

Robbie was a good consistent player—one coach in Little League had called him the glue of the team—but he wasn't an outstanding athlete, not one who'd knock a homer at the bottom of the ninth with the score tied. The ones who did, the "stars," were out there to win, and they wouldn't settle for anything *but* winning, and that consuming passion was the *drive* that Robbie lacked.

"You've gotta want it!" Coach Willis had told them when Robbie's team went to the state play-offs his junior year. "We can do it, we can have this victory if you want it bad enough, but you've gotta want it so bad you can *taste* it!"

Well, the truth was, Robbie didn't. He *thought* he did, and he played hard, but when they lost, he could slough it off and be grateful they'd gone that far, which was just the difference between him and the teammate who'd pitched his heart out and said, "We've got nothin' to be proud of! Nobody remembers the team that comes in second!"

So Robbie was neither surprised nor disappointed when his coach told him he never had *it* and never would.

He said, "Yes, sir. Well, thanks just the same."

"Hey, Robbie," said the coach, motioning him back. "Listen, like I said, you're a nice kid. I wish you lotsa luck."

"Thank you, sir."

"What I said, well, don't take it the wrong way. I didn't mean that I wouldn't put in a good word for you if you were set on trying."

"Thanks, Coach, but I'm not."

Jabbing a thick finger into Robbie's chest, the coach grinned out of the side of his mouth. "That's exactly what I mean!"

Not being *set* on anything in particular, Robbie chose to go to college in Nashville; it just seemed sensible. He could save money by living at home. He'd been working with recreation at a boys' center part-time except in baseball season, and he was confident that he could keep the job in college. Most of his friends were eager for a change—a new place, new faces, greener pastures, freedom! Robbie, however, viewed change from a different angle: Why spoil a good deal? He was not unhappy. There was a fuzziness, yes—like looking through the lens of a camera while focusing, just before the image sharpened—but it wasn't dissatisfaction. It was just a gathering of clouds, a sense of impending *something,* not necessarily bad. When he moved to the boys' center after two semesters, it was, again, for practicality's sake. He'd more or less floated into the position of a live-in counselor-assistant working nights. It was a good job for a college student; it was a sensible move. Robbie had no illusions about change of scenery. He wasn't looking for some dramatic life-altering event around each bend. He was too levelheaded.

And that made it all the more remarkable when it happened.

Rosemary could brag to Jean Hollingsworth. It was an unspoken agreement between neighbors; Jean bragged about her Dobermans, Rosemary about Robbie. Rosemary smiled inwardly at Jean's silliness over six dogs, even though they did win blue ribbons; Jean, who had no children, found it just as amusing that Rosemary doted on a grown son. Jean knew full well that Rosemary didn't care a flip for her Dobermans, and Rosemary knew how foolish she appeared in Jean's eyes, but that was all part of their understanding. They indulged each other.

It was Rosemary's turn, because the pups had won their blue ribbons last week, which was old news, hashed and rehashed, and because Robbie was coming home. "He might as well be living across the country instead of across town," she said. "We haven't seen him since he moved out the first of June."

Jean didn't mention, of course, that it was just July. "So tell me about his job. He's a counselor or something?"

Rosemary enjoyed explaining what she understood about it; the job was apparently a highly responsible one. Robbie hadn't said it in so many words—he didn't have a boastful fiber in his body—but Rosemary had the impression that sophomores were rarely live-in counselor assistants. The other two who worked nights with Robbie were both seniors. Some twenty to twenty-five boys lived at the center, and Robbie and the two seniors had responsibility for them at night.

"Troubled boys," said Rosemary, dicing celery into the potato salad. "All of them. That's why they're there."

"Troubled?"

"Oh, you wouldn't believe! Most have had some kind of trouble with the law. A lot of them have been in juvenile detention centers. And drugs—that's a big thing with most of the boys. They're supposed to be rehabilitated when they come to the center—they've already been through a drug rehabilitation program—but I guess *staying* clean is the hard part. Robbie has seen boys as young as ten who've been addicted." She stopped to see that Jean was appropriately shocked, and she was. "But the reason they're living at the center," Rosemary went on, "is that they can't function at home. Sometimes the parents have such problems themselves that they can't provide what their troubled children need, but you'd be surprised how many of the boys come from what you'd call nice homes, where the parents have a good income and they aren't alcoholics and they don't beat their children or each other. I don't know how some kids make such messes of their lives." She stopped again, thinking how lucky she was to have a son like Robbie. And Judith and Melissa had done all right, too. They certainly hadn't ever been in *trouble.* Rosemary guessed she hadn't been grateful enough for that.

"It does seem that Robbie has a lot of responsibility." Jean said it with sincere admiration. She liked Robbie. He'd walked her dogs when he was younger, when she was raising Golden Retrievers instead of Dobermans.

"Yes, he does." Rosemary heard herself, wondered if she might've sounded a little *too* proud, and added that most of the counseling as such was done by psychologists and social workers. "Robbie has to be *available* at night. That's the main thing."

"But still, you know problems are bound to come up."

"Oh, yes."

"And that, with his classes and studying and his social life—"

"I wouldn't think he has much time for girls," Rosemary put in.

"—well, you can see why he hasn't been home much."

"I suppose so." *Is* there a girl? she wondered.

At that moment she heard a car pull into the driveway, and she brightened like a child who'd heard the ice-cream truck. "He's punctual. He said around five and it's five o'clock sharp." She washed and dried her hands without hurry. She was trying very hard to be casual.

"I've got to run," said Jean. "Unless I can help you finish up dinner."

"Oh, no thanks, it's just picnic stuff. Robbie isn't company."

Jean had counted eleven dishes prepared for this "ordinary" meal, but she supposed that Rosemary smiled, too, when she fed sirloin to her pups.

"You've outdone yourself," John said for the second time, and Rosemary smiled. Robbie could find something polite to say about cold beans from a can, but this was going overboard for John.

Rosemary didn't get a lot of practice accepting his compliments. After "thank you," what did one say? "It's nothing special, John, nothing that I don't fix for *us*." Then, fearing she sounded cross, she sliced him an extra thick slab of chocolate cake, which he did not bother to praise.

"None for me," said Robbie.

"Nonsense."

"I don't have room."

"Of *course* you do." Rosemary set a slice before him that was not quite as large as John's. There was a time when Robbie would've devoured that much in three gulps and asked for more, but tonight he toyed with a few bites and pushed his plate aside. There was something else, Rosemary noticed, in that he didn't eat it to please her or apologize for leaving it. Small things, but mothers paid attention to things like that.

"Are you keeping up your schoolwork all right?" asked John. Naturally he hadn't noticed anything peculiar; fathers didn't. They didn't notice "weak" eyes that meant a fever or the breathless answer, offered too quickly, when a child had something to hide.

Robbie answered yes, he was managing to keep up. John asked if his job was interfering too much with school, and Robbie said no. John asked a couple of other questions, which Robbie answered absently, clinking his fork against his plate. How many times had Rosemary scolded him for clinking the silver against the china? This time she reached over and took hold of the fork, but the gesture was lost, for he let go of it and flattened his palms on the table, leaning forward. "I've got some news," he said.

Well, that was it. That explained his distraction. *Surely* he wasn't getting married! But it had to be something on that order, for the light in his eyes told that he considered his news to be good.

"I've been meaning to talk to you, but it wasn't something I could just toss out over the phone."

John folded his arms, slightly squinting. Actually, he looked quite scholarly. Rosemary raised her eyebrows. She'd often wished for those meaningful discussions around the dinner table (where Mr. Cleaver says to Beaver, "Son, let's talk about this"), but the Grays never got the hang of the family pow-wow. Their discussions were conducted with one party in the living room calling to another in the kitchen, or on the way out the door ("By the way, we've got to move to Mobile").

"Well, what is it, Robbie?" Rosemary was impatient; she doubted that she would've been very good at a family conference.

"Let me tell you what happened last week," he said, and Rosemary could see that he was a long way from the point. "I was studying one night about midnight, and I just got a strange feeling that I ought to go check on my hall. So I did. And when I passed one of the rooms, there was this soft whimpering sound coming from inside—it turned out the boy was crying. I knocked, called out to him—his name is Sam—and finally he let me in after I told him I was going to use my key. He kept saying, 'I don't want to die,' and at first, of course, I thought he'd *done* something, taken pills maybe, but he hadn't. He said, 'I don't want to die because I know I'll go to hell.' Well, we talked for a while, and I said I'd get Richard, one of the counselors, to see him the next morning. But he said, 'It's my preacher I need to see.' Now Sam is fourteen and he's been in and out of juvenile hall since he was nine. But he comes from a religious family. Why and how he got off track, maybe no one will ever know. Anyway, he hadn't seen this minister in three or four years, but the next day, he got permission to call him, and the minister came that afternoon. That night, when I got to the center, Sam couldn't wait to tell me. He said, 'Everything's changed. I'm gonna be all right now.' What's changed is Sam. I can see it. Everyone there can see it."

"That's lovely," said Rosemary. She was sincerely touched by the story, but particularly by the fact that Robbie was so sensitive to a boy's spiritual needs. A mother couldn't help being proud. "Things like that don't happen often at the center, I suppose. I'm glad for you."

"No, wait, that's not all."

Rosemary stood up. "Go ahead. I'm just going to pour the coffee."

"I don't want any," said Robbie.

"I do," said John.

"Go on, Robbie. You said there was more."

"The rest has to do with me."

"Good. I'm listening."

"I've decided to go on to the seminary after college. I want to be a minister."

Rosemary poured hot coffee on her hand, but she barely flinched. She was numb. She heard John say, "Well! That's fine. I always knew you'd choose something worthy for your life's work." And when she looked, they were shaking hands. *Shaking hands,* a gesture of such finality! Rosemary forgot the coffee cups. She wasted no time getting back to the table, taking charge.

"Just hold everything," she said, and she perched on the edge of her seat, straightbacked, in her chairman-of-the-board posture, lacing her fingers, resting her hands on the table between her and Robbie. "This isn't something you jump into on a whim." Robbie tried to speak but his mother didn't stop. "It's all very moving about the boy and his experience. Obviously you were impressed by how the preacher helped him—oh, it's certainly understandable, Robbie. You've *always* taken things to heart, maybe too much so, and you've just been caught up in something. But that's not a good reason—it's a *bad* reason—for taking such a drastic course!"

"Drastic? I thought you'd be pleased, Mother!"

"Robbie, listen to me. I want you to be happy. You know I do. I just couldn't stand by and watch you make a dreadful mistake. This incident at the center has swept you away, muddled your thinking. It'll wear off, but I know how you are. If you commit to something, you won't turn back. So please, *please,* don't rush into this."

"I didn't finish telling you about it," said Robbie, disappointed and annoyed at once.

"All right, tell us," she said in her humoring tone.

"It wasn't a case of getting swept away. What happened to me was that everything finally came together. All that I'd tried to figure out about God and the great scheme of things and how I fit in—it suddenly made sense. I was back in my room that night after I left Sam, and I raised my window. The moon and stars were so bright that you could've read the newspaper outside. It was breezy and warm, calm, a beautiful night. Did you know that the nearest star is more than a hundred light years from earth, and a light year is six trillion miles? Beyond imagination!" He waited, as if something had to jell in his own mind.

"It seems to me," he said, earnestly now, "that everyone and everything in creation is connected somehow. Wherever the outer boundaries may be, it all belongs to a *whole,* and there has to be a great design behind it all. But if that's so—and this is what has always bewildered me—shouldn't life have some higher meaning besides day-to-day plodding, making a living, playing baseball? I've wondered about it for as long as I can remember. Why was I here? Surely God put me here for a reason, for I'm part of this perfectly ordained unit that He created. I guess I believed there was a spiritual plane to *live in,* that we had to attain it to touch God. Well, as I was looking at the skies that night, it came to me in a single simple thought. I can't touch God except through people. There's something spiritual in us, yes, and there *are* moments when we rise above the mundane, but we are flesh and blood and it's through our *humanness*—the way we live out each day, relating to our fellowman—that we act out the part that God intended for man. Do you see?" Expectantly, he looked from his mother to his father, back and forth again.

John, hanging on each word, nodded almost imperceptibly. Rosemary said, "That's very *deep,* Robbie. I'm not sure I can follow it all, but I do understand that you feel you've found a key that unlocks a mystery for you."

"Yes! Yes, that's it exactly. Everything fell into place. I knew what my life was all about."

"Helping people."

"That's part of it, yes—"

"But you can help people in all kinds of ways, by being a counselor or a teacher. Or a doctor."

"It's not the same. I saw Sam with all his problems, asking for a minister, and I realized that he was calling out from his *deepest need.* It's that need, Mother, that I want to minister to."

He kept his eyes fixed on her, waiting for her approval—yes, she knew it, but she said, "A *preacher,* Robbie!"

Her voice, the lament of blighted hope never before poured out upon her favored child, was a slap in the face. "I thought you'd be happy!" Robbie insisted.

"Happy that my son is giving himself to a life of sacrifice? Because that's what it is, you know."

"You used to talk about being *called* to do something special. Mother, you *said*—" But he didn't finish. He could not bear to hear her say it all meant nothing.

In the lull, John spoke up. "Remember the Hogans, Rosemary? Mark Hogan was one of the finest men I ever knew. I wouldn't have ever set foot inside a church house if it hadn't been for Mark."

"Yes, and after three years in Darlington he was booted out because he invited a black family to church."

"That's not exactly true. Some of his congregation *did* disagree with him, but you have to remember, that was in the fifties."

"They moved every two or three years for as long as we kept up with them. Janice Hogan is still probably hauling that piano from parsonage to parsonage, hoping to put down roots somewhere."

"She was always very solid behind Mark."

"The point is, a preacher is not *his own person.*"

"No, he belongs to God," Robbie said.

Rosemary's lips parted, but her words died. She had never seen Robbie so resolute; twenty-one years of successful persuasion came to nothing here. She stood up and began to clear away the dishes.

"I wish you could understand," Robbie said, with an air of desperation.

And in the same tone, Rosemary said, "I had such high hopes for you."

Nine

"Yes, Judith, the bandages are off."

"Well?"

"Well, the situation is about what the doctor expected."

Rosemary can almost see Judith at the other end of the line, squaring her chin, steeling herself the way she does when she has to shoulder up to something hard.

"He's blind, isn't he? I knew it. You should've called in another specialist."

"Would you like to talk to your father, Judith?"

"First tell me what you're going to *do.*"

"I don't know. I really don't know right this minute. The doctor hasn't been gone ten minutes. Your father is waiting to talk to you now."

Rosemary gives John the receiver and reminds him to follow the cord when he hangs up. She'll be stretching her legs in the hall, she tells him. If he needs her for moral support, he hasn't shown it. Since the bandages came off, he has been virtually silent. The only mention of his blindness was an indirect one: "You'd better ring up Judith. I promised to let her know the verdict."

"Right *now,* John? But she's at her office," Rosemary reminded him.

"You have her office number," he said.

Rosemary wonders why it's so important to call at this particular moment, but she has complied. "How are you, Judith?" he asks. "Me? Oh, I'm all right." Rosemary leaves it with them.

What she tries to think about in the hall is that there has been some talk of surgery so that the verdict on John's sight is not signed, sealed, and delivered. This is what she tells herself walking to and from the elevator twice, trying to rub down the goose-pimples on her arms. She says "Good morning" to Head Nurse Krantz, who doesn't break her military stride but says "Good morning" back and offers a flicker of a smile that hides her lips. She must know that John's bandages have come off, but nothing in her manner indicates that it matters to her. This triggers a sudden surge of anger that makes Rosemary want to yell at the cool, businesslike nurse, but the urge is momentary. Rosemary isn't really mad at Nurse Krantz; she's mad at John's blindness, but she can't strike out at anyone about that. When this registers, the rise of anger diminishes like a balloon with a slow leak, and all Rosemary feels is cold.

She keeps rubbing her arms. John's words when the bandages came off made ice run in her blood. "Nothing," he said. *Nothing.* But wasn't that pretty much what she expected? The doctor had been hinting, preparing them, and if John had been able to see, they *all,* including the doctor, would've been stunned. Still, the bandages were protection from the hard truth, which, now revealed, accomplishes exactly what John said: *There's no more kidding ourselves.*

Rosemary can't read Dr. Nebbins. She can't tell whether he's hopeful or not, but he has mentioned bringing a very specialized surgeon in to talk about their options. That is the thread by which they can hang now, the thread by which they *have* to hang. Eye surgery is done all the time, and it definitely doesn't sound as grave as open-heart surgery, which is also done all the time. The more Rosemary considers surgery, the more it seems that this thread may be stronger than she first believed. Her chill bumps finally go away.

Back in the room, she asks, "Did you have a nice talk with Judith?"

"I guess so."

"What did she have to say?"

"Oh, you know Judith."

"Well, yes, but what does that mean?"

"She tried to tell me I should do this and do that. I told her I didn't want to talk about it."

"Really." A moment lapses before Rosemary says what's on her mind. "Wasn't that why you called her?"

"Why?"

"Oh, to get her opinion, her advice. She's such a *doer,* you know. She makes things happen. I thought maybe you wanted her perspective on your—" she finds a word that will do—"your situation."

"Nope," he answers simply.

Since John doesn't seem inclined to talk about his situation—his blindness—Rosemary looks for ways to make herself useful. There aren't many. She starts to straighten the items on the bedside table, forgetting for a moment that John has learned where to find each one. She turns the box of tissue back the way she found it and scoots the water pitcher over to the edge, as it was. She smooths John's covers, but as soon as she stops, he rustles them again. Time doesn't march; Time drags its feet.

"I guess we should call Melissa," Rosemary ventures.

"If you think so."

"Don't you want to?"

"It's up to you."

"You were anxious to call Judith. Why not Melissa?"

"Judith asked us to let her know, so I did. She's been checking on me every few days. She's seemed concerned."

"It's not so easy for Melissa to call," Rosemary puts in, "but that doesn't mean she's not concerned."

"That's not the point," John says, crossly. "Maybe you haven't noticed what I've noticed about Judith. I've been hearing something in her voice."

"No, I haven't noticed a thing."

"Maybe my ears are picking up shades of sound that they couldn't before."

"What is it that you're trying to say, John?" Now Rosemary is the one who sounds cross.

"Just that I think Judith would like very much to come back into the family."

Rosemary's laugh is sardonic. "Well, that's a very unusual observation. I don't recall that we excommunicated her. Possibly she pulled some legal maneuver and withdrew from our family, and I didn't know about it."

At first John twists his lips in a peevish way that clearly indicates disapproval. Then he asks sharply, "Doesn't it bother you that she hasn't been home in two years?"

The pointedness of his question cuts through the sarcasm and probes at Rosemary's maternal core. "It does bother me," she answers quite earnestly, "but I don't know a thing I can do about it. She has her own life. She doesn't have time for us." Rosemary doesn't mention that Judith wanted to fly in like Wonder Woman and take John's case in her own hands. She can't be certain that it wasn't a mistake to discourage her. Judith might've been able to wrangle a miracle.

"No one sent her away," Rosemary goes on. "I remember very well the morning she left. It'll be two years this October or maybe early November. She said she'd come to stay a couple of weeks, but it couldn't have been more than the third or fourth morning when I got up and there she was, all packed and waiting for a cab. I don't believe she intended to say good-bye. Oh, we'd had a few words, but they were mostly on *her* part. She had more reason than I did to regret what was said, but there was no apology, just a cloud of dust at her heels. No, *I* didn't send her away. If she feels excluded from the family, she has only herself to blame."

John nods slowly, but whether he is agreeing or is just too tired to talk about it any more, Rosemary isn't sure. "I don't know why I got into that," she says, a little ashamed at how she worked herself into a dither. "You knew it all. There was no point in re-hashing it."

"I wasn't blaming you for anything," says John. His voice is all at once tired and thin, and Rosemary chides herself for losing her perspective, for forgetting what John is having to deal with this morning.

"We'll wait about calling Melissa," says Rosemary.

"Yes, let's wait."

Robbie's forehead is wrinkled in that peculiar way of his, with a vertical crease that stands out between his eyebrows. Naturally he's worried by the news that greeted him at the hospital, but Rosemary wonders if there isn't something else on his mind. Mothers just have these notions, these flashes of intuition, Rosemary has called them, being something of an expert on such. No one else would suspect that the ridge in Robbie's brow was anything but worry over his father, but Rosemary has noticed that it happens whenever he gets quiet and distant, his thoughts (seemingly) nowhere about the hospital room.

Rosemary's hands are busy butterflies fluttering about the flower arrangement that has has just been delivered from the Men's Bible class. Just like men to send flowers to someone who can't see, Rosemary thinks. No doubt it was J. B. Paxton's idea, as he owns four flower shops and the arrangement came from one of them. John, however, seemed unusually grateful and has remarked a couple of times about how nice flowers make the room smell. Rosemary doesn't detect much fragrance. She thinks the flowers need to be spread out a little more, and, though she'd certainly never say so, she surmises that these are not J. B.'s freshest gladiolas.

"I've got a class coming up," says Robbie. His wrinkle is gone, along with his mood. Now he teases Rosemary about manhandling the flowers. When Robbie lets that all-American-boy-next-door grin slide across his mouth, there's no trace of a deeper layer where everything, every little thing, touches him.

"Tell me something," says John, who has scarcely spoken to Robbie. "How do you think I look?"

"Why, you look fine. You look a lot better with the bandages off, if that's what you mean."

"You think so?"

"Yes, I do."

"My eyes aren't dark circled and sunken in, are they?"

"No. You look OK, Dad, really."

When Robbie is gone, John goes through the same routine with Rosemary, who tells him again that he looks just fine. She isn't sure what he's getting at, but she doesn't intend to mention how peculiar it seems for him to talk with his eyes closed. There's something eerie about it. It really *feels* as if he's blind, but then he *is* blind.

John seems to be satisfied. He asks for a comb and takes pains with his hair. Having missed a haircut, he has trouble with those deep waves that were stylish and terribly striking when he first brushed through Darlington.

"Are you expecting visitors?" asks Rosemary.

"Nope, just trying to make the best of things," he says.

As it turns out, he has visitors. Within the hour, the doctors are springing through the door. Dr. Nebbins is a tall but not necessarily slim middle-aged man whose long face is made more pronounced by a hairline receding at the temples like inlets on a lake. At his heels is a fussy little man perhaps in his sixties, hurried and perpetually scowling, introduced by Dr. Nebbins as Dr. Geribaldi.

"How do you do," says Rosemary. "Thank you for coming by."

Dr. Geribaldi gives a firm nod, not to waste time on words, and marches to John's bedside. Rosemary gets herself to the other side, where she hovers like a mother hen, as if she might be called upon to protect John. Then Dr. Nebbins falls in beside Geribaldi and they mutter over what is presumably John's chart for a couple of minutes. John no longer has his eyes closed, but now it appears that he's straining to see, which is worse. Rosemary pats his arm and says, "They're discussing your chart, that's all." So far Geribaldi has not spoken to John.

Finally, Dr. Nebbins says, "I've brought Dr. Geribaldi in because he's operated on a number of cases like yours," and he proceeds to give a speech on the good doctor's good work at Oxford University and the Mayo Clinic. "Now I think Dr. Geribaldi would like to look at your eyes," he says.

"That won't be necessary," says John, cool as a cucumber. "I'm not interested in any operation."

If Rosemary is jolted, and she is, Dr. Nebbins is knocked for a loop. He scratches at the patch of about twenty hairs at the very top of his brow and then gives a chuckle out of the side of his mouth, as if he's suddenly decided that John is pulling his leg. "I'm not sure I understand, John," he says. Until now it's been *Mr. Gray*.

"I don't intend to have surgery, so there's no need to talk about it. Let's just say I'm not up to it."

Dr. Nebbins is still a little addled. Either he's highly unaccustomed to having a patient say no or else he just can't swallow that John has this much spunk. "We don't have to make any decisions right now," he says, "but it can't hurt to get Dr. Geribaldi's opinion. This man is a much-sought-after specialist, John."

John says, "Then you must have a whole string of patients waiting for you, Dr. Geribaldi, so I won't take any more of your time."

It's an awkward moment. Sweat pops out on Nebbins' slick temples like dew on a rose petal as he goes deep for a thimbleful of diplomacy and says, "We'll talk about this later, John." Rosemary would say something tactful to alleviate the tension, but her tongue has swollen to twice its size in her throat.

Then Dr. Geribaldi, in a voice far more kindly than Rosemary expected, says to Dr. Nebbins, "I think you should send Mr. Gray home."

"That's right!" says John. "I want to get out of here. I want to get my pants and shoes on and have my meals at a table."

"That doesn't sound unreasonable to me," says Dr. Geribaldi. "Good luck, Mr. Gray."

He scurries off like an ambitious squirrel, pursued by a damp-looking Dr. Nebbins whose parting remark is a terse, *"Later!"*

John laces his fingers behind his head and stretches out. "I guess you think I'm crazy," he says.

"Does it matter what I think?" Rosemary snips.

"Well, I *asked,* didn't I?"

Oh yes, he asks now. It wouldn't have occurred to him that before he opted to spend his life in the dark, he might've consulted with the one who would be taking care of him.

"I think you could've listened to what they had to say. That's what I think."

It's not all she thinks, either, and she's poised to say how it seems to her that he's giving up, but a candy striper interrupts, delivering the afternoon mail. Along with two cards is a letter from Melissa.

She writes: "Guess what. The doctor suspects twins. Isn't it incredible?"

"This has been a day for news," says John.

"And none of it is incredible any more," says Rosemary.

Ten

Melissa was Rosemary's *easy* child. Easy to please, easy to reason with, easy to like. But Rosemary had to be careful about saying so.

Judith was barely fourteen months old, very much a baby herself, when Melissa was brought home from the hospital, and Rosemary did tend to brag on the new, extraordinarily *calm* infant who slept through the night (while Judith was still waking up). And whenever Melissa was between naps, was she fretting, demanding to be held? Not this baby. She was lying contentedly, exercising her feet or shaking a rattle, which was convenient for Rosemary because Judith was clinging to her legs or demanding "Cookie!" or just plain whining. Naturally, when John would come home, Rosemary told how the week had gone. "Judith broke your Aunt Millie's vase and cut her finger, and I caught her tearing up the papers in your desk. Yes, I *am* tired, I'm *exhausted,* because last night Judith woke up at two-fifteen and didn't go back to sleep till four-thirty, and of course I feed Melissa at six. Oh yes, Melissa's still the *easiest* little thing you've ever seen!" Who would've thought a toddler's mind would work the way Judith's did? She promptly tottered over to Melissa and tried to bite her pinky finger off! So Rosemary had to watch herself; however tempting it was to rave about the virtues of her easy child, she could never speak in front of Judith. This did not change, either, as they grew up.

Judith had given up her bottle before Melissa was born, but at the sight of the new baby's bottle, she vehemently refused her cup. Rosemary didn't have the energy to fight it, so Judith kept her bottle for another nine months, until Melissa was drinking from a cup, too. Nor was Judith about to settle for training pants as long as her sister was getting that extra attention from diaper-changing. Finally, when Judith was three and Melissa was two, Rosemary said, "I'm sick of diapers! I'm tearing them into dust cloths!" They were pretty ragged by then. It was easier—always—to lump the girls together, to put both in a double bed when Judith outgrew her crib, to keep Judith at home until first grade, when Melissa could start in kindergarten. Judith, who was so aggressive, so overbearing, so *bold,* never wanted to try anything new at that stage of her life unless her quiet sister was at her heels.

And that was how it came to be: Melissa was always at Judith's heels, in her shadow. Whatever Judith wanted to play was all right with her. Whatever Judith wanted to eat, Melissa would have, too. Why wouldn't any child adore a golden-haired little sister who was satisfied to take whatever role she was given, the witch, the baby, the student, never demanding to be the princess, the mother, or the teacher, who never tattled, never yelled, "Not fair!" But if Judith adored her, she had a bizarre way of showing it. She bossed, scolded, belittled, until Rosemary was compelled to intervene. Judith would run to her room, screaming, "I hate her!" Then, when the noise died down, Melissa would go after her, smooth her feathers, and soon they would be playing again. Rosemary was just thankful that she had one easy child.

By the time Melissa was three, her family had moved from Macon, Georgia, to Mobile, Alabama. It was the third house for Judith, who had been born in Greenville. Being shuffled about as they were in those early years, the girls had a tendency not to play well with other children. Melissa shied into corners and Judith threw tantrums when her new playmates were not as pliable as her sister. Even in Mobile—where they started to school, where they lived for five whole years—the girls didn't develop what you would call friendships. There were hordes of children on the street, and some dropped by regularly, but drinking Kool-aid together was not, of course, the same as being friends.

Rosemary had always made a point of learning her neighbors right away—you never knew when you might need to borrow sugar—and she always started the family to church the first Sunday, for church provided a backbone that she had come to believe was essential in a day and time when nothing seemed very solid or stable. But if the girls were able to entertain themselves, all the better. She was not a *social* person herself. Not that she couldn't work harmoniously enough with others on committees; not that she didn't host pleasant gatherings for the ladies' circle. And when a new family moved into the neighborhood, Rosemary was at their kitchen door with a cake before their forks were unpacked. But kind and warm as she wanted to believe she was, Rosemary recognized that there was a level at which she snapped shut like a screen door. She did not, for example, cry in front of *anybody.* She did not let people *in,* and her girls were somewhat like her in that way. Judith and Melissa had spun their own complicated web, and intruders were just not able to get past the outer edge.

The Grays' house did not change much from suburb to suburb. Amelia Banks' house in Atlanta had its own character, and the apartment in Greenville was in a similar old neighborhood. But once John and Rosemary bought into suburbia, they could expect (in Macon, Mobile, Louisville, and later in Birmingham and Nashville) the standard three-bedroom brick in a neat row. By the time the moving van pulled away, Rosemary was out appraising the neighborhood, meeting women at the mailbox and children on their bikes, smiling, "We're the Grays from down the street (or up or across)." Thereby she learned the best places to buy groceries and children's shoes, the names of pediatricians and dentists and baby-sitters (though she rarely called sitters), and she got a feel for which neighbors she might ask for a cup of sugar (though she seldom borrowed). The neighborhood women readily gave the last word on the local school, readily took Rosemary into their hook-ups, and all, whether churchgoers or not, had opinions on the churches in the area. Rosemary had suburban living down pat.

That *sameness,* knowing what you could count on from move to move, was one side of the coin, but the other was of course the diversity, the peculiarities about each place (and the circumstances) that made it memorable. Macon was where Melissa was born. In Mobile, the girls started school. Robbie was born in Louisville. And in Louisville, there was more. John, at a prime thirty-six, began to take courses toward a college degree. Rosemary's mother, as a thirtieth birthday present, shipped Rosemary's piano to her. And Melissa got a friend. Judith would remember that, too.

Holly Hunnicutt clasped her hands at her throat and drew up her shoulders. "Puh-*leese,* Mrs. Gray! We can't have a wedding without music!"

"But I'm busy right now, dear."

"Can't Judith feed him while you play the piano?"

Judith was leaning against the door facing, twirling her dark hair around her fingers.

"Aren't you in the wedding, Judith?"

"No!"

"Please be in the wedding, Judith," Melissa begged. "You can be the groom if you want."

"But not the bride!" said Holly.

"I don't want any part of your stupid game." Judith stuck

up her nose and whirled off through the living room, out the front door.

"She never plays," said Melissa.

"She never plays *anything,*" said Holly.

Rosemary scraped the last spoonful of strained peas from the baby-food jar. "I'll be finished here in a minute," she said. "I'll play the 'Wedding March' but that's all."

"No 'I Love You Truly'?" Holly wailed.

"Not this time."

"I guess we can hum the recessional. Hurry, Mrs. Gray, the mother of the bride has already been seated."

Holly Hunnicutt was a tiny girl with whitish hair, pale skin, and faintly blue, deep-set eyes. In her bridal wear, an old white gown of Rosemary's, along with Melissa's half-slip for a veil, Holly gave the effect of an apparition that one might encounter in an enchanted forest. She looked as if you could blow her away with one puff.

But she was a spunky child, the sort that defied expectation. She didn't take piano lessons; she played the bagpipes. She took French lessons and acrobatics; no, she was not interested in Girl Scouts. Her parents were both on the faculty at the university, the mother in economics, the father in romance languages. Rosemary didn't meet them in all the three years that she lived in Louisville and provided music for Holly's weddings. However, once when she dropped Holly off at her house, there was a man in the backyard raking leaves, a bald-headed man with a white beard and unruly side whiskers. Holly commented that she had to help Papa. "Must be her grandfather," said Rosemary as she backed out of the driveway. "No," said Melissa, "it's her dad." The wedding craze, Rosemary knew, had come about because Holly was the flower girl in her grown-up sister's wedding. So, from all that Rosemary gathered, she construed that Holly was either adopted or born to her parents late in life or a stepdaughter to the man she called

Papa. But Holly didn't clarify her family situation, and, as Melissa was never invited to Holly's, Rosemary made no point of finding out anything more than she knew.

"All right, ready?" Rosemary struck the first chords: *Dum dum de dum.* Melissa, wearing a discarded suit coat of her father's, her fair hair stuffed into an old fedora, hurried to the groom's side of the picture window. As Holly floated from the kitchen door, the telephone rang. "Judith!" Rosemary called, but Judith was outside.

"Oh, *I'll* get it!" said Holly, marching into the kitchen, holding her wedding gown above her Buster Browns. A moment later, she peeped around the door, her hand on the mouthpiece of the phone, and said in a high, breathless voice, "It's an obscene call!" Then she proceeded to repeat what the caller had said, while Melissa's chin dropped to her chest.

"Give me that." Rosemary took the phone and said hello, and when the man spoke his first word, she stopped him. "What a foul and disgusting mouth you have!" she said. "You are *ill,* but listen to me." (This in her firm, patient, *mother's* voice.) "You don't have to live in a sewer. There are people who know what to do for your sickness. Psychiatrists, ministers, even the police can get treatment for you. I'm going to hang up, and when you dial again, I hope it will be to get help for yourself. Will you do that?" Silence. "I'm hanging up now."

"Wow, Mrs. Gray, I don't *believe* you!" Holly cried. "You really kept your cool!"

The phone rang again. Rosemary betrayed no emotion as she raised the receiver to her ear.

"I didn't mean anything, lady," the voice said, and the line went dead.

"That's a person we should pity," Rosemary told the girls.

"You're *brave,* Mamma," said Melissa.

"You're *wonderful!*" said Holly.

"Let's get back to the wedding."

Holly slapped her hand across her forehead and heaved a great sigh. "I do believe the mother of the bride has fainted."

Melissa and Holly hugged good-bye. Holly was tearful (she could choke up at the sight of a broken bird egg), and she promised to write every day. She did, once. Melissa sent several letters at first, but after a while her notes served only to announce something important. She met other girls in Birmingham. Though none had Holly's flair, they were, nevertheless, congenial girls who would sit with her in the school cafeteria and invite her to slumber parties, call her after school, and pass notes to her about boys. Since her friendship with Holly, Melissa was not so standoffish. Not that she would ever *seek out* friends, but she was willing to be drawn into a circle of girls who made the overture, and they did. Journeying through adolescence, Melissa was well cushioned within a clique. Always there was at least one girl who called Melissa her best friend.

Melissa graduated from the eighth grade the same week that her father graduated from college, and within a month, they were moving again.

"To Nashville, Tennessee, and this time it's permanent," said Rosemary. "Your father has promised."

"Barring unforeseen circumstances," said John, with his finger pointed. "There are not many absolute guarantees in life." But his voice had a ring to it. He had earned a degree in accounting, and he was going to work for the State of Tennessee. He was counting on stability as much as Rosemary.

They all could've predicted that Judith would balk. "It's not easy changing high schools, you know! You never consider *my* point of view!" This, of course, was directed at her mother.

"We've tried to consider the whole family," Rosemary told her.

"But it happens that only *my life* is ruined! Not *yours*—(this to Melissa) you'll be going in as a freshman where *everyone's* new, and in elementary (this to Robbie) it's no big deal. I'm a *sophomore.* Everything's already *set* by tenth grade."

"Not all *that* set, Judith," said Rosemary. "Please don't work yourself up into a tizzy. You'll break out in hives."

Judith left in a huff that Rosemary knew would pass, but John looked somewhat helpless when the door slammed. "Maybe it *is* harder when you're fifteen," he said.

"Don't worry about her. You know how she is. It doesn't have anything to do with her age."

"She has to understand that I can't turn down a good job just so she won't have to leave her friends." (John was always telling Rosemary what the children had to understand, but he rarely told *them.*)

"The thing is," said Rosemary, "I can't think of one person that she'll especially hate to leave."

"I'm going to get pictures of my friends so I can remember them," Robbie said. His long lashes fluttered. "In case I never see them again." That was Robbie for you, tender-hearted child that he was, bearing up bravely, never fussing.

"I like new beginnings," said Melissa, as merrily as if she were beginning a week at camp.

It would seem that Melissa had reason to grieve, leaving behind half a dozen girls who were devoted to her, but she was already looking ahead. It was not her nature to cling. She took in stride what life dished out. This was like her mother, except that Melissa made it seem so much easier. While Rosemary plodded on, plowed through, Melissa tended to miss the bumps by skimming along a few inches off the ground. She just did not breathe with the same intensity as the rest of her family.

Robbie charmed the new neighborhood by the end of his

first week in Nashville. Before the moving van had pulled out of his driveway, he was riding his bike with two other boys. He was so gentle with Jean Hollingsworth's puppies, so thoughtful to take old Mr. King's paper to the door when the paperboy threw it in the rosebushes, so polite with his "Yes sirs" and "No ma'ams" that his name circulated quickly through the gossip routes. "Robbie Gray? Oh, *sure* you can ask him to go to Grandma's with us." In August when Rosemary marched him into second grade, half the children in his class called out to him. The pictures he'd brought from Birmingham stayed packed away in a trunk.

Judith moped during the summer, but when school started, she followed her pattern of joining *everything.* The clubs and teams and societies in Birmingham were what she'd despaired to leave, not individuals, but the organizations at her new school welcomed her. Why wouldn't they? She was an enthusiastic participant, a tireless worker, with obvious leadership qualities. She couldn't expect to be elected president *this* year (she was president of the library club in Birmingham), but she *would* be. These people would know her! And with that, she settled into a busy year.

Melissa did not make such a splash. She was not a joiner. She was not anything outstanding. Schoolwide, she was scarcely known except for her connection with Judith, so that it came naturally to say, "I'm Melissa Gray, Judith Gray's sister." She had grown up in Judith's shadow, was used to it, didn't mind a bit. She was proud that her sister marched in the color guard, played Lady Capulet in *Romeo and Juliet,* had a brilliant letter to the editor published in the Nashville *Tennessean* when U.S. troops pulled out of Vietnam. Certainly Melissa had no wish for the limelight. She trembled whenever called on to play a hymn in her Sunday School class. And at Judith's remark that she should audition for pianist to accompany the school chorus, she could only say, "I'd be terrified."

Still, the telephone rang for her a couple of times every evening, and school functions invariably found her in the company of friends. She was quite a social butterfly within her small circle. But on occasion, with no particular place to go and no one dropping by, Melissa was content to play Chopin for hours. And Rosemary, who had instructed her in piano, who listened from another room, had the distinct notion that those were the times when Melissa was happiest.

Melissa slipped into a row near the back of the auditorium. The front half was filled with parents, some squirming, some smug, all proud, but this was not an event that tended to fire up the general student population. The debating team, of which Judith was captain, was competing at Vanderbilt University for the citywide championship. Melissa had intended to come with her mother, but that morning while practicing for a program with Robbie's class, Rosemary had broken her toe. (No, the boys were *not* supposed to roll the piano until she gave the word!) She was just back from the emergency room when Melissa came in from school. It was Melissa's first time to drive to the Vanderbilt campus, and she'd had trouble parking, so she was too late to speak to Judith. The teams were assembled on stage, and now Judith had spotted her. Melissa gave a feeble shrug, which in no way communicated why she was alone. Rosemary had not simply decided not to come; Judith should know that, but her chin jutted out fiercely, and there was nothing at all that Melissa could do to make up for her mother's absence.

There was a delay. One of the judges had not arrived, a spokesman said, "but please be patient, parents. You can't possibly be as anxious as your sons and daughters up here."

A bearded, long-haired young man in jeans and sandals sat down on the end of Melissa's row. He said something to her in a whisper, but he was six seats away. She gave him a quizzical look. He said it again, leaning her way, and when she still couldn't understand, he moved to the seat beside her.

"Mind if I sit here?" But he didn't wait for her to answer. "I was asking you what he said about a delay."

"Oh. Sorry, I couldn't hear you."

"Well?" He raised his eyebrows. "What did he say?"

"Oh—he said they'd start in a few minutes. One of the judges is late." Melissa could feel a blush coming on.

"You must be here for your boyfriend."

Her blush, she knew from her hot face, was now in full bloom. She had never been around older guys, as this one surely was, or one quite so presumptuous. Here they were in a sea of empty seats, and he was so *close.*

"I'm here for my sister."

"Good," he said. She was not sure exactly how he meant it, keeping such a steady gaze, but she smiled casually and pretended to be suddenly interested in the stage.

"That's my sister." She read the nameplate. "Judith Gray, Captain."

He finally looked, too, at Judith first and then at the others, scrutinizing them one by one, the way Melissa had felt he'd scrutinized her. She took the occasion to read the title of the textbook he carried, *Advanced Physics Applications,* and to notice that his T-shirt was silkscreened with something about clean air. She couldn't examine it too closely.

"I'm Simon Gordon," he said, quite abruptly.

"I'm Melissa Gray."

"It's nice of you to come out for your sister."

Melissa dismissed it. "Why are *you* here?"

"Curiosity. I was passing through the building and saw the sign. I wanted to see how much smarter kids are these days." He spoke like a wise uncle, and looked a bit like one, too, with his wire-rimmed glasses upon his patrician nose.

"The war had captured our attention when I was debating, the war and civil rights and the environment, which is still a priority with me but seems to have slid to a back burner as a public issue. The level of social consciousness in general has declined remarkably in a few short years. Don't you think?"

"I really couldn't say."

"You've proven my point."

Melissa had to ask, "Just how old *are* you?"

"Twenty-one."

The voice of experience! An older man who made the boys in Melissa's class seem about as mature as Robbie.

"Tell me more."

"About what?"

"Well—about the environment."

He was glad to, and the start of the debate only made him lower his voice to a whisper. He was an encyclopedia on the state of the world, the erosion of the ozone layer, the seepage of toxic wastes into water supplies. Melissa was fascinated.

As a matter of fact, she had to ask herself on the way home, *Did Judith's team win or not?*

There were no other boyfriends after Simon.

The first time he came to pick Melissa up, Rosemary had to brace herself against the door facing. *This* was the brilliant physics student from Vanderbilt? *This* was the son of a bank president in Maryland?

"Why, he's a leftover hippie," Rosemary told John, who'd missed the introduction. But he wasn't, as Rosemary was to learn over the next few weeks from Simon's freely aired commentaries. He was adamant against drugs (also caffeine, saccharine, and red dye in hot dogs). Communal living was an affront to the basic unit of society, the family, without which anarchy was inevitable. Mysticism was a sin against Almighty God.

"But he *looks* like a hippie," Rosemary declared to Melissa, who calmly replied that Simon's clothes symbolized his rejection of materialism.

"Oh, he rejects materialism, does he? Isn't money playing some part in getting him through school? Doesn't he have a car?"

"A Volkswagen, yes, but it's six years old."

Simon did not eat red meat or refined sugar. The cut flowers on the table were pretty, yes, but how much lovelier were the ones left in their natural setting! And when John told that some of the fellows at work had gone deer hunting in Canada, Simon let his head drop, like a wounded man.

He was peculiar, all right, but Rosemary had to say that she never worried about Melissa when she was with him. There were worse things for a young girl to do than to eat bean sprouts.

Melissa was a senior, and she had dated Simon for almost a year. Rosemary could not demand that she date other boys, as perhaps she should have in the beginning—and *would* have if she'd had a crystal ball. She believed, however, that once Melissa left for college, the romance would wither. She told John so.

He looked up from his glasses. "Has she said anything about college?"

"Not much."

"Where does she want to go? I hope she's not counting on Vanderbilt."

"Melissa couldn't get *into* Vanderbilt, even if we could afford it." Rosemary looked thoughtful as she tilted her head. "A state school, maybe three or four hours away, would be *just right.*"

"What does she plan to study?"

"Why, I would think music."

"Has she said?"

"No, but with her talent, it would be *unthinkable* not to."

"Maybe you should discuss it with her. If she's going to college, she needs to get her applications in right now."

"What do you mean *if?* Certainly she's going to college!"

John pulled his glasses down on his nose, Ben-Franklin style. He gave Rosemary a long, hard look, which she met without blinking. It seemed he had something on his mind, but whatever it was, he didn't get it said. He straightened his glasses and mumbled, "All right," and the newspaper went up between them.

It wasn't exactly an announcement. Melissa came in with Simon one night while her parents were watching a Perry Mason rerun, and she thoughtfully waited until Perry exposed the murderer in the courtroom. Then she said, as if she'd just thought of it, "Simon has inherited a farm."

Both John and Rosemary were at once attentive, but it was to Rosemary that Simon turned.

"My grandmother died, you know."

"Yes, we were sorry to hear it."

"This land in Virginia has been in her family for generations, but it hasn't been farmed in sixty years. My father and I are the only heirs, and as Grandmother said in her will, my father believes land should sprout condominiums." He let a smile part the dark beard, which was unusual. Smiling, he was rather pleasant-looking, Rosemary thought.

She said (trying to be polite), "No doubt you have something less *materialistic* in mind."

"I intend have a flourishing farm, just as Grandmother wanted."

While that was sinking in, Melissa said, "Simon's going on to Virginia, but I'll wait until I graduate."

"We'll be married," Simon put in quickly, "just as soon after her graduation as we can arrange it."

"It'll be a simple wedding. I wouldn't want anything fancy. We'll make sure it's no trouble to you, Mother."

"We'll probably just stand in your backyard where we can enjoy your flowers, if that's all right."

"Simon and I have no interest in all the trappings of weddings. It'll just be family."

"Just *your* family, I would think, unless my parents insist on coming. It doesn't seem sensible for them to make such a long trip for a five-minute ceremony."

In just such a tone, they mapped out the course for their future, starting with Simon's departure from Vanderbilt in the middle of a semester (and with only one other semester left before he would've earned a degree in physics), winding up with a log cabin they would build with their own hands in a wilderness that neither of them had yet glimpsed. Against such absurdity, there was no argument!

And yet Rosemary could not help herself. Those times when she and Melissa were alone, she tried reason, gentle persuasion, and pleading. Melissa was, after all, her *easy* child and surely, *surely* she could bring her around, but she didn't. Melissa's calm resistance did not waver.

The wedding drew near, and Rosemary in desperation cried, "Why did I spend all those hours at the piano with you, I ask myself! It breaks my heart to think of what you're throwing away!" It was Virginia's voice that Rosemary heard coming from her own lips, and she was not proud of it.

But Melissa said as sweetly as ever, "Be happy for me, Mother. Please, be *happy* for me!"

And Rosemary knew that it was all over. She turned back to mending the elastic in the neck of Melissa's wedding dress (how appropriate that it was called a peasant dress!). Only after she'd knotted and cut her thread did she say sharply, "Do you think Simon might possibly be married in something besides denim?"

Melissa promised to mention it to him.

The ceremony was set for two o'clock because the minister was available at that time. Except for that, Melissa and Simon might've decided at ten or ten twenty-two to have the wedding, for Simon had arrived that morning before the coffee perked.

"This is strictly out of respect for you, Rosemary," he said, indicating the blazer and dress pants that he brought on a hanger. When she saw him later dressed for the wedding, it was really too late to talk about a tie, and the hiking boots probably wouldn't show up in pictures anyway.

It could've been any ordinary day for the bridal couple, as they frolicked in the backyard like pups, as they strolled around the neighborhood in their wedding clothes. The most exciting event of the whole day was probably when Judith called from the bus station. No one expected her, but for some reason unexplained she'd taken the bus from Chicago and needed someone to meet her.

Simon thought that was awfully touching. "She must be very close to you," he said.

"Oh, I don't know," said Melissa. "We're just typical sisters in a typical family."

Melissa sincerely believed that the Grays were the average all-American family. She carried nothing from her wedding day that was sorrowful or angry or guilty. And whenever Simon marveled at how blissful and uncomplicated her childhood must've been, Melissa never denied it.

Eleven

There isn't much way to discourage visitors since John is at home. Rosemary hasn't found a tactful way to tell people not to come by, or to turn them away at the doorstep when they're standing there with a fruit basket or a cake. One of the men from John's office, a Frank Carlisle, comes by one afternoon with a gift, a bell. "So you can ring for the Missus when you need something," he says with a chuckle. Rosemary can't decide whether it's supposed to be a joke; John certainly isn't laughing. Mr. Carlisle doesn't impress Rosemary as a prankster. He has seemed genuinely concerned about John, calling more than a few times to check on his progress. Now he looks quite pleased with himself and with his gift. John mumbles a thank you. Rosemary probably goes overboard; she does that when she's embarrassed.

"He said he'll visit you again," she tells John, wondering how the man could fail to sense John's apathy.

"I don't see why."

"Neither do I. You were rude."

"I wasn't rude. He's the one who dropped in without an invitation. I don't think his bell was very funny."

"Maybe he didn't intend it to be funny. I really believe he just wants to be a friend."

"I wouldn't call him a friend, just because we work together—*did* work together."

"For four years, he said. But I don't think I ever heard you mention his name."

"I don't suppose I ever did. The state didn't pay me to

make friends. I was paid to work, and I *worked,* and I was good at my job."

"I know you were, John."

"Don't talk down to me, Rosemary."

"I'm not."

"Maybe you don't mean to, but I hear it."

"I'm sorry."

"Let's just forget it. Forget everything I said."

He gets to his feet, with some fumbling for his cane, but, nevertheless, he manages without help. Rosemary is poised to seize his arm, to assist, to do *something,* but she knows not to. John's newest mind-set is stubborn independence, which is probably better than helplessness but is no easier for Rosemary.

He misses by a good yard the doorway between the dining room and kitchen. He turns, makes a half-turn back, pokes the china cabinet with his cane.

"Wait!" Rosemary takes hold of the cane, out of necessity, knowing that John won't like it, and he doesn't.

"I'm not going to break anything."

"That was the china cabinet. You were hitting the glass."

"I wasn't hitting anything. I was tapping. That's what blind people do, isn't it? They tap with their canes."

Rosemary wants to shake him, like a defiant child. What does one do? Between the self-pity and the stubbornness, where is there a opening for people to get *through?*

"Are you going to the kitchen, John?"

"Yes."

"It's to your left."

"Did you put the milk where I told you?"

"Yes. It's the first item you'll reach when you open the refrigerator."

"You don't have to follow me around."

"I know that. I have business in the kitchen, too."

She does indeed check on her baking bread, but at the

same time she watches John's every movement. He takes a glass from the cabinet, sets it on the counter, closes the cabinet door. One, two, three. He opens the refrigerator door, locates the milk carton, sets it on the counter. One, two, three. Rosemary makes deliberate busy sounds at the stove, but she watches John, breath suspended, as if he were Robbie up to bat with the score tied. John opens the carton, finds the glass, pours. One, two, three. Closes carton, sets it on the shelf, closes the refrigerator door. One, two, three. Everything is going right; Rosemary's throat tightens, for oh how he needs this success! He eases his fingers along the counter, and when they touch the glass, they tighten around it as if that glass were a cylinder of solid gold.

Rosemary would like to cheer. She has an idea that John would like to say, "Hey, look what I did!" But instead he says that the bread smells good and she says that it'll be ready in a jiffy.

"Maybe I'll have a slice with butter and jam."

"Maybe I will, too. I'm just now taking it out of the oven."

"I'm in no hurry." John sounds a hundred percent more civil than before his accomplishment.

He starts to the table, his glass of milk in hand. Rosemary doesn't see exactly how it happens, for she is bent over the oven holding two hot loaves of bread in hand. When she hears the commotion, it's too late to do anything but clean up. Somehow John has stumbled over one of the chairs and dropped his glass. Milk is splattered; the glass is broken. In the confusion, John manages to drop his cane, too. It hits the floor with a sharp crack, like the sound of the bottom falling out of everything.

There are other little mishaps, a bump into the door facing that leaves a blue knot on John's forehead, a hand mirror knocked off the vanity in the bathroom and shattered into a hundred pieces on the tile floor, a pot of African violets tipped over onto the carpet. Nothing serious, Rosemary insists. What are a few spills? She's gone through raising three children, hasn't she? But that isn't the right thing to say. John's silence seems to answer, *The difference is, I am a man.* All in all, Rosemary is impressed by the way John gets around without his sight, but when she tells him so, he says, "Don't patronize me, Rosemary."

Then one morning as she's loading clothes into the washer, a bell rings. She has to stop and think. It's not the doorbell, not the phone, not the timer on the stove or the alarm clock—and then she hears it again and remembers.

John is sitting in his recliner, ringing the bell that Frank Carlisle brought him.

"Yes, John?"

"Could you bring the radio in? I want to hear the news."

"I notice you're trying out Mr. Carlisle's bell."

"I thought I'd find out if it was as handy as he claimed."

"What do you think?"

"It just may be. Could you get the radio now?"

So this begins a new phase, akin to the helplessness that John exhibited in the hospital. Yet there is a difference. Rosemary has things to do now that they are at home, the never-ending washing, cooking, cleaning and such. She is not simply sitting at John's side wanting to be helpful. And there is a marked difference in John's attitude. He is no longer a patient, willing to be told what is good for him. Now he is king of the mountain and Rosemary is his loyal servant, summoned by the ring of a bell.

"What is it, John?"

"Have you gone after the mail yet?"

"Not yet."

"What time is it?"

"Eleven."

"Surely the mailman has been by."

"Yes, he has."

"Why don't you see if the hospital bill came today."

He rings when he's hungry. He rings when the air-conditioning is too cool. ("It's because you're not exercising, John.") He rings for Rosemary to take his blood pressure. (One of the nurses at the hospital taught her how, for John was worried that he couldn't take his own reading. His is always just about perfect, but Rosemary doesn't dare check herself, for fear she'll blow the top out of the gauge.) John rings to say, "I just wondered where you were." And at night, he sets the bell on his bedside table and after he is supposed to be asleep (when Rosemary is finally getting something accomplished), he rings for her and asks, "Isn't it late? Shouldn't you be getting to bed?"

Rosemary knows that eventually she will have to leave John by himself from time to time, but so far she's managed to do her grocery shopping while Robbie is with his father. This is usually in the evenings, which is all right except that the produce isn't fresh at that time of day. Rosemary doesn't mention that to Robbie, of course, for the boy is doing the best he can. What she tells him is that the aisles are remarkably clear at seven PM and sometimes she even happens upon end-of-the-day doughnuts at half price.

One day Robbie comes for the whole afternoon and he says to Rosemary, "Why don't you get out and do something for yourself?"

Rosemary can't seem to think of what one does for oneself.

"Go to the beauty parlor and have a permanent."

"I gave up permanents six years ago. I think my beautician moved to Montana."

"Go shopping."

"Shopping has always been a chore, not a diversion."

"Well, visit a friend."

And Rosemary is reminded that she has never cultivated

friends, that Jean Hollingsworth is in the *neighbor* category, and there are acquaintances from church, as there used to be associations that came through school, baseball—her *children's* involvements. A twinge of sadness burrows in her stomach. For all her *busy-ness* of thirty years, she has precious little to show. But the qualm is brief; a sudden light shimmers in her eyes as she says, "Yes, I'll do that. I'll visit someone."

She takes out the phone directory and finds the address of the Eastside Nursing Home.

Buddy Grant extends his fragile hand, and when Rosemary shakes it, he clasps his other hand on hers.

"Rosemary, Rosemary. I never expected to see you again."

"You didn't tell me good-bye at the hospital."

"You weren't around. They came after me and *Whoosh!* I was gone. At my age, I don't have much say-so about things like that. But that's water under the bridge. Come, come, let's find you a chair."

This is the community room, Buddy explains, as he maneuvers his wheelchair toward one of the few empty seats in the room. All the patients seem to be out today, knitting, playing cards, or just talking—some to each other, some to themselves. A few are slumped in wheelchairs, silent, never blinking—sudden sharp reminders of another such room in a place called Ward C. Rosemary's gaze does not linger on those too long. What she remembers about Ward C (which is sketchy) isn't the stuff that makes for a light and pleasant afternoon.

The chair to which Buddy goes is at a table with two women, one of whom he introduces as Mrs. Creighton, the other as Fanny.

"Fanny Malone?" asks Rosemary, glancing at her tinted hair which gives off a bluish cast.

"How did you know, dear?" The flashy old lady claps her ringed fingers together in a gesture of glee, smiling so that her rouge-powdered cheeks squeeze into fat little balls.

"Buddy spoke of you when he was in the hospital."

"Oh, he *did,* did he?"

"Now cut that out!" says Buddy. He shakes his finger at Rosemary. "I pegged you as a troublemaker from the start."

Mrs. Creighton is unamused by their play. She yawns rather loudly, after which she grasps her walker and rises to a good five feet ten.

"Don't leave us, Iris," says Fanny.

"I'm going after my book."

"She was an English teacher," Fanny tells Rosemary in a hushed voice. "You should see her room. I'll bet she has fifty books! Reads them over and over and over, books like *Pride and Prejudice*—that's the one she's on now. Doesn't sound very interesting to me."

"Rosemary's husband had an accident and lost his eyesight," Buddy puts in.

"Oh, how sad! I'm awfully sorry, dear."

"Yes, well, thank you."

"Looks like something could be done," says Buddy. "I thought they had an operation for everything nowadays."

"My grandnephew had eye surgery," and Fanny embarks on a story, not just of the surgery but of the hunting accident, where, when, why, and how, all in dramatic narrative. Rosemary is grateful not to have to explain that there is an operation available for John but he refuses it.

Buddy nods absently to Fanny's story, as if he may have heard it more than a few times.

The animated woman finishes with a great sigh. "So you never can tell what doctors will come up with next!"

There is a lull, and Rosemary asks, "How are your feet, Buddy?"

"My feet? Why, I could dance right out of here if they'd let me."

"That's not true," Fanny puts in. "His feet still bother him."

"She thinks she knows everything," Buddy drones.

"Has your daughter come back from Hawaii?"

"Oh, yes. She brought me some strange candy made out of pineapple and coconut. I ought to let you try it. Let me go get it."

"No, don't bother, please."

Fanny Malone jumps up, spry as a pup. "*I'll* get it. I know exactly where you keep it." She waves away their protests with her tiny hands and her weighty costume jewelry.

"That woman can be a great comfort," says Buddy, "but she can overdo it, too."

"You seem to be well taken care of."

"Sure I am. Did I ever say I wasn't?"

"I suppose not." Rosemary notices that one of the young women presumably on staff is singing with some of the patients across the room. "This seems like a nice place."

"Did I ever say it wasn't?"

"Can I do anything for you?"

"Like what?"

"Oh, I don't know. I don't guess you need anything, really."

"Is that why you came to see me, Rosemary?"

His piercing eyes always make Rosemary squirm like a schoolgirl whose teacher is demanding an answer she doesn't know.

"I just wanted to see that you're all right."

"Well, you see that I am. Are you?"

"Why, yes."

"Good. Come back any time you need a little excitement."

"It's peace and quiet that I need," she says, only half joking.

"Well, you can find that here, too." Buddy raises his eyes toward the sunporch where a lone gentleman sits in his wheelchair, writing in the air with his finger.

Rosemary stays just a few minutes longer, long enough to share Buddy's candy. Fanny can't partake because it will stick to her dentures. "It's a wonderful thing to have my own teeth!" Buddy announces.

Rosemary leaves him smacking and gloating, fussed over by Fanny Malone. If he needs Rosemary's good deeds, he doesn't show it. Yet she knows as the sunshine strikes her shoulders that she will be back.

Robbie meets her at the door. "I've got something to show you."

"All right. Where's John?"

"Listening to a ball game on the radio. I went up into the attic, trying to locate a paper I did a couple of years ago, and I got to rummaging through old trunks. Look what I found."

The musty, leather-bound book is full of handwritten pages, yellowed and brittle. *"May 1, 1931,"* Rosemary reads aloud. *"Mary Spence had twins this morning* . . . Why, this is my father's writing! This is a journal that he kept!"

"Read some more. It's wonderful. It's like coming upon a treasure."

"Mary Spence had twins this morning, a boy and a girl, both weighing in at just under 6 lbs. The boy they named Jarvis. It touched me deeply." Rosemary pauses while it sinks in; these are her father's beautifully formed words. They bear no resemblence to the scrawling on prescriptions by today's physicians. This is her father speaking, with the simple eloquence for which he was known.

"You're right, Robbie. This is a treasure."

They sit at the kitchen table and read two pages together before John's bell sounds.

"Could I take it with me?" Robbie asks. "You know I'll be careful with it."

His excitement magnifies her own. This is a link between her father and her son, and with that connection, Rosemary feels *intact* in a sudden, strange way—a flimsy paper braced by bookends.

"Of course if you want to read it first—"

"No, no, you take it, Robbie. Naturally I want it back."

"I'll probably get through it in a hurry. It's the kind of thing I don't like to put down."

It's the kind of thing Rosemary will want to ponder, to muse over, to read again and again. There is a certain pleasure, too, in anticipating that journey back to a quiet town and a simple life.

Cheerfully, she goes to answer the clamoring bell.

Twelve

The morning that the Grays were to leave for Judith's graduation from Northwestern, Rosemary was called back to Darlington. Her mother was dying.

Emma Fletcher, who made the call, had lived with Virginia for going on three years, since Virginia broke her hip. Emma had put in thirty years as a schoolteacher, the classic old maid except that she was a widow. She had spent most of her adult life in Toledo, but after her husband died, she returned to her hometown for the climate. Rosemary remembered Emma's parents, Mr. and Mrs. Harvey, who ran the five-and-dime when she was growing up; but because Emma was some twenty years older than Rosemary, they were never acquainted. Virginia treated Emma much like a daughter and was forever trying to put her in Rosemary's age bracket: "You remember when you took piano from that old prune? I think Emma played at one of the recitals, too. I believe she played 'Libeistraum.'

"No, Mamma, I played 'Libeistraum.' Emma would've already been married and teaching school at that time."

"But I seem to remember that her mother and I strolled you and Emma together when you were babies."

"I believe you're thinking about Pauline Grady."

Virginia had been in good health until the day that she got her foot hung in her sheet as she was getting out of bed and wound up on the floor with a broken hip. According to the doctor, her bones were good and the break healed nicely, but Virginia would not hear of complete recovery. She had used a walker ever since, though she'd been known to stamp across the floor without it when she got mad enough. "Just put me in an old folks' home," she told Rosemary. "At least if I fall, someone will hear me yell."

"She'll have to come live with us," John had said.

"Oh, John, I don't know . . . Well, of course, that's the reasonable thing to do."

As it happened, they never came to that hurdle, due to Emma Fletcher's timely appearance in Darlington. She apparently had no money stashed away from all her years in the city; rumors were that her husband had invested unwisely in the stock market. Looking for a house to rent, Emma visited Virginia before she ever left the hospital. Virginia had, after all, spread the word that her daughter was putting her in an old folks' home. But somehow the two of them just took a liking to each other and after one conversation of about forty-five minutes, they had nailed down the terms of an agreement. Emma moved in the next day and lived in the Lowell house for the next three years. Virginia never charged her a penny for room and board; in return, Emma gave her round-the-clock attention. She was a combination nurse, cook, housekeeper, and companion, with an emphasis on *companion.* Rosemary was astounded that her mother could live in harmony with anyone, not to mention someone so set in her own ways as Emma Fletcher, but the two women managed very well. If Emma tended to behave a bit arrogantly toward Rosemary, and she did, Rosemary let it pass; she was delighted that her mother was being taken care of.

So when Emma said, "Virginia is dangerously close to death's door," Rosemary felt as if someone had whacked her across the knees with a baseball bat.

It took a little over four hours to drive to Darlington from Nashville. She went alone; naturally John and Robbie went on to Chicago for Judith's graduation.

Emma was getting off the elevator when Rosemary entered the hospital, the hospital that Doc Lowell always wanted, that went up the year after his death. Primly, Emma said, "I was just coming down to look for you," as if Rosemary might've been loitering in the waiting area, thumbing through old magazines. "I've been expecting you for an hour."

"It wasn't easy to get away. How's Mamma?"

"Hanging on."

"Is anyone with her?"

Emma bristled. "Why, certainly. Since I brought her in early this morning, I haven't left her bedside except when one of the nurses was in."

"I appreciate it," said Rosemary.

But Emma would have the last word. "You needn't worry that she's lacked attention. I've been right there." Straight-backed, she headed for the elevator, with Rosemary at her heels.

"What, exactly, happened to Mamma?"

"It's her heart."

"A heart attack?" That was, of course, how Doc had gone.

"Heart failure is what they call it." They stepped into the elevator, and Emma said, "Virginia's had heart trouble for a good while."

Rosemary opened her mouth, but nothing came out. She raised her hand to punch the number of the floor. "Three," said Emma, and Rosemary fumbled for the right button.

"She didn't want you to know. I thought you should, but she said you'd worry. She's been seeing a doctor, all right, and I did the best I could for her, the very best I knew how. I was terribly fond of Virginia."

They left the elevator, and Emma led the way to the room. She marched right in, right up to the bed, and the birdlike nurse who had been checking the I.V. tube came promptly to the door, where Rosemary lingered. "I'm Belinda Braden, or Bee-Bee, as some still say. Do you remember me? You used to come to my house when I was a little bitty girl and give piano lessons to my big sister Nell."

"Yes, how nice to see you."

"You wouldn't believe Nell now. She's as big as the side of a barn. She's married to a supervisor at one of the carpet factories up in Rome."

"Be sure and tell her hello for me."

"I will, but she doesn't come home much. They're sort of big shots up there, if you know what I mean."

"Yes, well, excuse me, Bee-Bee," and Rosemary eased nearer the bed, trying to get a glimpse of her mother. Emma was right between them, so that all Rosemary could see were the bedsheets that covered from the waist down. The way Emma had referred to Virginia, Rosemary figured she had already slipped into unconsciousness, so she was surprised when Emma said to her, "Look who's here to see you."

Then Emma finally moved so that Rosemary could take her place at her mother's bedside. "Hi, Mamma," she said.

Virginia looked up and said, "It's about time."

During the hours that Rosemary sat with her mother, Emma kept popping in to shake her head and whisper, "Doesn't she look bad?" True, she looked closer to ninety than seventy, but as Virginia had grown old in middle age, her aging since that time hadn't seemed remarkable. "She's been going down, down, down," Emma would lament, to which Rosemary would nod vaguely, thinking, *Ever since my father died.* Emma offered to relieve her time after time, but Rosemary politely refused. She took her breaks whenever the nurses were in, always leaving the chair full of her belongings, lest she return to find Emma in her place.

Virginia drifted in and out.

"When did I see you last?" she asked.

"I was here two months ago on your birthday," said Rosemary.

"You brought me a frilly blouse."

"That's right."

"It's still in the box. They ought to give you your money back."

"Don't worry about it, Mamma. Try to rest now."

"I was sick then, you know."

"I didn't know."

"I didn't want to burden you."

"It wouldn't have been a burden."

"Never let it be said that I was a burden to my daughter."

"No, of course not."

Hours later, Virginia opened her eyes and said, "If Doc had been alive, it would've been different."

Rosemary jumped. She'd thought her mother was sleeping and had let herself doze. "What is it?"

Virginia repeated what she'd said, glaring at Rosemary as if challenging her in some way.

"Well, I suppose," said Rosemary, not knowing exactly what her mother meant.

"You wouldn't have been so anxious to leave home if Doc had been around."

"That was a long time ago, Mamma."

"I never understood what I did wrong."

"It wasn't that you did anything wrong. Young girls marry and leave home, that's all. Please don't worry about things so far back in the past."

"Girls don't marry the first thing that comes along unless they're running away."

"John was—and is—a good man," she said, too loudly, and her mother scowled, as if to say what Rosemary knew: How shameful it was when a daughter couldn't hold her tongue, even with her mother dying.

Rosemary leaned closer and straightened Virginia's covers. "Let's please not argue," she said, and for a while, they were both quiet.

But Virginia had something to settle in her mind, and she would not rest. At three in the morning, she raised up and said, "There's one thing about it. You were a sweet child. Do you remember those little organdy dresses I used to make for you? You looked like a porcelain doll with your white skin, and you had such a pleasant disposition. We were a happy family in those days."

"Yes, Mamma, we were."

"If Doc could've lived a little longer—" she gave a weary sigh. "One day he was gone, the next day you were gone. Of course Doc didn't have a choice."

For thirty-two hours, Rosemary stayed with her mother. The next evening Virginia spoke for the last time. She said, "You know I have nothing but the house. It ought to bring a fair price. Don't give Emma any trouble about the will. I want you and her to split everything down the middle. She's been like a daughter to me, a *devoted* daughter, too."

Emma was at the hospital that night, insisting that Rosemary let her take a turn sitting with Virginia. Rosemary refused, but around ten o'clock when a nurse came in for a few minutes, she went to the candy machine. When she returned, munching on her peanut brittle bar, there was a gathering at Virginia's door and in the midst was Emma Fletcher, sobbing. "She's gone, Rosemary, gone. I was with her when she drew her last breath."

Rosemary slept in her old room that night, what little she slept. She sat up until the wee hours reading an old diary; then, when she turned out the lights, she couldn't rest. She couldn't stop thinking of all the things she wished she had said to her mother, and of all the things she wished her mother had said to her.

Back at home, she was always busy. Melissa and Judith were gone of course, but Robbie was an active teenager who was forever eating and outgrowing shoes, taking a big hunk out of Rosemary's time. He was not yet driving, which meant that Rosemary drove more than a hundred miles a week to deposit him and pick him up from ball practices, youth meetings at church, skating rinks, movies, and school plays; and not only Robbie, but any number of boys waved when they saw Rosemary's taxi. Robbie's ball games (which Rosemary was obliged to attend, since his father seldom managed to) and bake sales and car washes sponsored by his class (requiring adult participation of course) all took time. Keeping the house and yard took time. If John was home, he expected dinner when the 6:00 news went off; he expected the bedcovers to be turned down when the 10:00 news went off.

Rosemary was the backbone of the church, teaching Sunday School, serving on committees (she had to stop and count how many), playing the piano for the youth choir. She met with the Citizens for Better Schools once a month and was a sucker for fund-raising whenever called on to go door-to-door. "Someday you'll learn to say no," John would mumble as she darted out with a packet from some charity. She would mumble back that this was a good cause. She couldn't explain it, but she didn't *want* to say no.

The edges were blurring, even then, but not beyond what was manageable. Her carload of boys thought it was hilarious that she drove them to her beauty parlor instead of the baseball field. The sack boy thought it was hilarious that she forgot to circle around for her basket of groceries and drove all the way home before she remembered. John was not so amused. "You have too much on your mind," he said. She did, but it kept her from brooding, which was becoming a tendency, an *enticement.* Again, nothing unmanageable, but annoying that her mind was so inclined to wander into thorny places, and sometimes it was oh so hard to get out. Some dark part of her was ready at any idle moment to pull her back, back, and down, which certainly a reasonable woman could not allow. Rosemary believed she was a reasonable woman and an informed one; didn't she read *Ladies' Home Journal* and watch *Donahue?* She was not ignorant of mid-life changes and mid-life blues, which could stretch over a period of years (and they did). You felt lousy but you never gave in, and finally you got over the slump. Rosemary was convinced that all her hustle and bustle would eventually lead her to the tranquil eye of the storm.

But fortitude was not so easily summoned in the black hours before dawn, when Rosemary's eyes would suddenly pop wide open, and the ghosts swarmed in, images of loss. Sweet foolish Melissa—such a waste, such a shattering of hope! Virginia had died, and all the wrongs between them could never be made right. Judith had spent her life pulling away, cutting the ties. Lost, her mother, her daughters, all lost to her.

How often the ghosts might've gobbled her up if she hadn't had Robbie. He was the joy of her life, and she was able to hang by that thread, watching him grow up. What a marvelous son he was! What a perfect specimen of manhood he grew to be! Not in a million years could anyone have persuaded her that Robbie's gentle words—"I want to be a minister"—would be her undoing.

"You're making too much of this thing with Robbie," said John. "He's going to be a preacher, not a missionary to China."

That was when Rosemary knew that she'd lost them all, that, in fact, John had been lost to her long before the others.

She called the church office and asked if there was anyone in the hospital that she could visit, but the secretary said, "Oh, I don't think so, Mrs. Gray, not today." There were *always* church members in the hospital. Why *shouldn't* she visit? Had she said something inappropriate, visiting Josephine Ayers with the gallstones or Nan Lawrence's mother-in-law? She couldn't be sure because she didn't always listen to herself, but a vague image of Nan's mouth flying open came to mind.

"I will go anyway, thank you," she said. Certainly all the patients she had seen Tuesday wouldn't have gone home. Or was it Monday?

"But Mrs. Gray—"

Rosemary didn't wait. Sick people were waiting for *her.* It was her *duty* to visit the sick, and why should her pastor of all people object, but there he was at the desk in the hospital lobby, her own dear pastor Dr. Lyons sent to head her off! Oh, he pretended to be asking about names on his paper, but *she* knew. He was part of the conspiracy to keep her away from Nan Lawrence's mother-in-law—and now she remembered that all she'd asked the old lady was whether her gorgeous diamond ring was the one Nan was supposed to inherit when she died.

On another morning when the page in her date book was blank, she hurried to enter: *Scrub woodwork, launder kitchen curtains, clean light fixtures.* She flipped through the pages of hen-scratching that had something to do with her *purpose,* though she couldn't say exactly what. *Clean this dirty house,* she scrawled. And once she finished, she could start right back over it again. It was comforting to know that housecleaning could keep her busy for a hundred years.

But her cleaning binge was short-lived. On the second day, she dried her red, sore hands and looked around her at all that was left to do—even what she'd cleaned would get dirty again!—and her task was a mountain that she could not climb. She sank to the floor and wept, and that was what she was doing when Holly Hunnicutt called.

"Mrs. Gray? Mrs. Rosemary Gray, Melissa's mother?"

"Uh huh."

"This is Holly. Remember me? You sound *funny,* Mrs. Gray."

Another ring, and Rosemary would've screamed; that was the only reason she had answered.

"You always were persistent, Holly."

"What? Are you all right, Mrs. Gray?"

"Of course. Surprised to hear a voice from the past."

"Yes, that's me! A voice from the past." Holly's high tinkling giggle was exactly as Rosemary remembered. "What a stroke of luck! It's been over ten years since Melissa wrote that you were moving to Nashville. That's all I had to go on. I called the first John Gray in the telephone book, and when you answered, well, it's just fantastic, Mrs. Gray! And I'll bet you can't guess what *I'm* doing in Nashville."

"Probably not."

"I'm getting married, Mrs. Gray! My fiancé's a legislative aide, so we're having the wedding here. Isn't it a coincidence, that Melissa and I would both wind up in the same city again?"

"Melissa is gone. They're all gone."

"That's too bad. I wish they could come to my wedding. But I really called to ask *you.* Remember how you used to play the 'Wedding March' for Melissa and me? Oh, Mrs. Gray, it would make me so-o-o happy if you'd play for my wedding. Would you, Mrs. Gray, ple-e-ase?"

"Oh, I don't know, Holly. I'm so busy—" Now the thought of *something else to do* made her tremble.

"You *always* said you were busy!" Holly teased. "But you always gave in."

"Couldn't you play your bagpipes instead?"

"I could, but I'm the *bride!*"

"Yes, well, I guess that wouldn't work out."
Holly giggled merrily.
"When's the wedding?"
"Saturday in the park."
One of *those* weddings.
"Melissa didn't have music at hers."
"No music? I can't imagine getting married without 'I Love You Truly' and the 'Wedding March'—and you at the piano."
It was the sweetest thing anyone had ever said to her. How could she say no?
In sprawling disjointed scribble, she filled her datebook with chores through Saturday.

"Are you sure you're up to this?" asked John.
"Don't worry."
But he *did* worry. Rosemary was wound as tight as a spring in a box, and John, who'd never known quite how to handle her, was now at a genuine loss. She hiked off ahead of him toward the little gathering; and when he caught up, she was milling through the crowd, saying hello to each and every stranger. Was she playing mother of the bride?
"John, meet Holly's parents," she said, and then to the scholarly white-haired couple, "I always wondered—did you adopt Holly or was she just born to you late in life?"
"We need to find the minister, Rosemary," John urged. How he wished he could switch her off for a while.
There were some thirty guests, all clean-cut and well-dressed, which impressed Rosemary. She had expected clones of Melissa and Simon on their wedding day, eight years before. (Simon now wore his hair short, but Rosemary never thought of him that way.) They gathered at a shady spot at the edge of a brook, nice for a picnic, Rosemary thought.

"I'm the pianist," she told the young minister who had planted himself upon the knarled roots of a great oak.

"I believe it's an organ instead of a piano," he said, pointing to the truck that was just parking. Upon its flatbed sat an electronic organ, hooked to amplifiers. Holly in wedding attire, veil and all, climbed out of the passenger side of the truck. The driver had to be the groom, decked out as he was in cutaway and cummerbund.

"Oh, Mrs. Gray, I hope this is all right," Holly cried as someone pushed steps up to the back end. "Our plans for a piano fell through."

"Whatever," said Rosemary, swatting away the groom who was trying to assist her up the steps.

It was absurd, playing 'Because' on an electronic organ, and even more ludicrous that guests were actually listening. Rosemary had a stack of music books, but what good were they, with all their arpeggios for piano? You couldn't *do* that sort of thing when your keyboard was cut in half and one part was stuck on top of the other. This was an instrument for horse shows and baseball games. *Here we are folks at Yankee Stadium* and in the background, *Beeeep-beep-beep-beeeep-beep.* What a butchering of 'I Love You Truly'! It was so *hot,* too! Rosemary could scarcely breathe. Where was the boy with popcorn and cold drinks?

Everyone was watching now, and all so still. Surely it was time to get on with the wedding. She hoped for a sign from Holly, but doe-eyed Holly was gaping like the others, looking a little faint. Rosemary felt faint herself. Robbie ought to be out on the pitcher's mound by now. She was playing for him. *Take me out to the ball game, take me out to the park.* Her fingers pumped hard. She began to sing, "Buy me some peanuts and crackerjack, I don't care if I never get back!" This organ wasn't sounding too bad now!

She was starting in on the national anthem when John took her hands off the keyboard and led her away.

Her first days on Ward C, Rosemary begged to go home. "John doesn't know how to put on a new roll of toilet paper. I'm the nerve center of the household, don't you see?"

Then, when John was permitted to visit her, when he said that he was managing all right and that she should think about getting a good long rest, she took another tangent. "So he thinks he can get along without me, does he? Let him try! Let them all try! After I'm gone for a while, they may just begin to appreciate me for the first time!"

So she gave in to the good long rest. Whenever had she had time for jigsaw puzzles or ping-pong? When had someone else cooked *her* meals? It wasn't so bad, the relaxation, the quiet. Maybe she'd been looking for a place like this all along. "O. T. reminds me of Vacation Bible School," she said to one of the patients who was trying to get out of Occupational Therapy, where they made potholders and finger painted. What could anyone possibly dislike about that?

Group Therapy was more fun than the Three Stooges. These people were apt to say *anything!* One frustrated writer wanted to read his novel aloud at every session, except that he had no novel. He read from a blank legal pad, just as eloquently as if he'd had real words before him. Sometimes he'd stop and say, "Excuse me, that was a typographical error." Rosemary thought his story about espionage in the Middle East was pretty catchy. Her own contribution to the group sessions was limited to dry one-liners. She liked Group, all right, but not as a forum to bare her soul. No sir. They needn't ask her how this or that made her *feel;* whatever she answered would send the more lucid patients rolling in the aisles. Her *feelings* were the one part of her that were her very own. No one had a right to them.

And that was why the individual session with her psychiatrist was her worst hour of the day. Dr. Laura Harding, a grandmother herself, was forever rattling locked doors, probing into tender dark corners, nudging at barriers. "Tell me about that, Rosemary. Does it upset you to talk about it? Why do you think it's so painful?" And she was so very patient. Rosemary couldn't exhaust her with wisecracks. "You're making good progress," she'd say, and Rosemary would wonder if she'd slipped and told the doctor something important.

Days and nights meshed. Weeks ran together, so that Rosemary had no sense of the passing summer. Three weeks, four, seven, nine. She was finishing her sixth basket in O. T.

Now that she'd settled down from her fury over John, he was coming to visit her twice a week.

As he was about to leave, he said in a trembly voice, "Take care of yourself, Rosemary."

And sweetly she said, "No, I'm letting these people take care of me now."

Melissa flew in from Virginia. Rosemary wanted to play Old Maid cards. Judith flew in from Chicago. Rosemary took her to the TV room and they watched an hour of news, for Rosemary was sure that one of the newsmen had been reporting on her.

Robbie visited often, but never for more than a few minutes. It broke his heart to see the dead look in his mother's eyes, to touch the stranger in his mother's skin.

"Just tell me what I can do to help you, Mother. Please let me help you if I can."

"Could you do anything about the Olympics? Who decided to hold the Olympics in our hall? The noise keeps me awake all night!"

A time came when Robbie looked down at his white knuckles and said to his mother, "I'm not going into the ministry after all. I've changed my mind."

It was Rosemary's twelfth week on Ward C. That was the day that she began to recover.

Thirteen

Rosemary is shelling peas when Robbie returns his grandfather's journal. He has read it through twice in a week and a half.

"How was it?" Rosemary asks, clasping the book to her bosom.

"My grandfather was a remarkable man," says Robbie, which doesn't answer her question but is good enough.

Rosemary turns through a few pages—like a child who just *will* shake the box—but momentarily she hands the journal to Robbie. "Lay it up there with my recipe books, will you? So it won't get dirty." She must wait until evening to start her reading; otherwise, her pea-shelling would never get done, nor would any other chore.

"How long do you think you'll take?" Robbie wants to know.

"Why, months, I hope! I'm in no hurry. I think I'll keep this dangling like a carrot before me. It'll be my treat at the end of each day." She's been considering this all the time that Robbie has had the journal. John, who has become a great fan of the radio, listens to a nightly program reminiscent of the old Lux Radio Theater. Rosemary occasionally listens, too, but she has slotted the hour for her time with her father's journal.

Robbie nods in a noncommittal way, prompting Rosemary to ask, "Is there some reason why I should hurry through?"

"Not unless you can't stop when you get into it, which is how it was with me."

But there is something left unsaid. A mother knows these things. So that evening when she settles in the armchair in her bedroom, Rosemary opens the book in her lap, wondering what it has to say to her and also what it had to say to Robbie.

Robbie makes himself scarce for a while. He calls to ask, "How are you? How is Dad? How far are you in the journal?" But the summer session is in full swing and papers are due, and Robbie alludes to a difficult case at the center, which, if Rosemary can read between the lines, is keeping him from getting much sleep. "Now if you need me—" he says at the end of his three-minute conversation. That's Robbie for you. Rosemary insists that they're managing just fine.

And for the most part they are. These days, John is able to stay alone for short intervals while Rosemary runs errands and takes care of business. She shops at her convenience, which is normally late morning, and delights in buying produce that was just that minute brought out, bread right off the delivery man's truck. The butcher is on hand to wrap her a package of two pork chops, and the checkout lady knows her by name. The little things one takes for granted!

Sometimes when the sun begins to dip behind the rooftops across the street, John likes to walk in the yard. Rosemary walks beside him but assists only with her voice. It's all right, when he gets into the alyssum border, for her to tell him he's stepping on the flowers, and it's all right to say, "Come this way" or "More to your right," but let her try to guide him around a rosebush and he balks like a mule.

"Don't *lead* me, Rosemary. Just tell me which way to go."

And so she gives directions. She also gives a running

account of what is blooming where and what she needs to do to it next Yard Day.

"These junipers are looking dry. I need to cut them back, too."

"Does the grass look dry?"

"It's beginning to."

"It feels dry, walking on it."

"Watering doesn't do the job like rain."

Rosemary bends down to jerk up a dandelion and continues pulling up a handful of weeds. John stops a few feet ahead of her. "Rosemary?"

"Right here. Just getting rid of some weeds." She catches up with him. He can always tell when she drops behind.

"My scarlet sage is looking droopy," she says, farther on.

"Now where's that?"

"Against the house, under the girls' bedroom window."

"Scarlet, you say?"

"Yes, it's a bright pretty red when it's healthy."

John veers in that direction. "Now where?"

"A little more to your left and, oh, three or four steps."

At the bed of scarlet sage, John kneels down and first makes a wide sweep with his hand, touching the tops of the tubelike flowers. Then he runs his fingers lightly up and down one plant. "And this is bright red?"

"That's right."

"I don't think I ever noticed these flowers. Isn't that peculiar?"

But that doesn't seem as peculiar to Rosemary as seeing John on his knees before a bed of scarlet sage, John, who never gave a hoot for flowers, who downright resented Rosemary's one extravagance, her yard, who never saw or looked for beauty there. She almost tells him so, too, but then he stands up, making a sound in his throat that's something between a groan and a sigh, and it seems to Rosemary that he already knows.

Curled up in her armchair, Rosemary reads:

"February 6, 1933. We are up to our eyebrows in measles. I made six housecalls this morning in a drizzling rain, all to the cause of red measles. At Kirby Jones's house I saw Kirby's two boys who were so sick they couldn't even fuss and then I went across the hall and saw Kirby. Poor man, if you put him beside a cadaver, the only difference would be that Kirby has spots. I worry about Virginia because we are seeing so many contagious patients in the office, and she doesn't remember ever having the red measles herself. But she's a trooper and declares that she must be immune to every germ in the book by now. She was in the office by seven-thirty and when I got back from my housecalls a little after nine, she'd already treated an infected toe and a couple of cases of pinkeye, which is also in the schools. The principal has asked me to make them a speech on hygiene again this year when we get through this measles epidemic. I think I'll ask Virginia to go in my place. She'd be fine. I wonder if she'd do it."

Rosemary is summoned by John's bell.

"My program's off," he says when she gets there.

"All right."

"Where were you?"

"In the bedroom, reading. You knew where I was."

"Reading that journal that Robbie found?"

"Yes, the same as every night for the last couple of weeks."

"It's kind of entertaining, I guess."

"Well, yes. Was there something you needed, John?"

"We didn't take my blood pressure today."

It takes just a minute to determine that his blood pressure is right on target, but it's a wasted minute as far as Rosemary is concerned, prompting the edge in her voice. "I'll finish the entry I was reading and then I'll put the journal away for tonight."

"If you wanted to read some of it to me," says John, "it might be interesting."

"Oh, I doubt that it would mean much to you," Rosemary fumbles, ashamed at her selfishness but annoyed, too, that he should ask this of her. "It's not just your everyday leisure reading, John, and of course you didn't know my father."

"That didn't seem to make any difference to Robbie."

Robbie recognized the journal for the treasure it is, Rosemary wants to say. But it occurs to her that the *book* is not what she's reluctant to share; it's the whole experience of reading it alone, silently, letting her father's words jump from the page straight into her heart.

"I'll get it," she says.

John is lying back in his recliner, smiling contentedly, when Rosemary begins to read: *Today Obie Denton died hanging a barn door.*

July brings earlier nights, barely noticeable at first, but sometime well into the month the crickets began to call while Rosemary and John are meandering through the yard, and Rosemary is reminded that the days have been getting shorter all along.

It's still hot as blazes but in Rosemary's mind, summer is fading. The sun has a direct bearing on her moods, she has recognized for a long time. From the onset of summer through autumn, she has a distinct impression of loss, as the sunlight hours gradually diminish. But after that shortest day in mid-December, no matter how harsh the winter may prove to be, Rosemary's mood becomes one of expectancy as longer days push her toward spring.

But these are just silly notions that she has never told anyone, and when she looks at John, who no longer sees any sunlight ever, she makes up her mind not to let any such foolishness cloud her sensibility. Now when they are outside in the evening, Rosemary may remark, "Isn't it so much cooler since the sun goes down earlier."

Then after darkness settles she reads to John from Doc

Lowell's journal. It would please him to listen any time of day, but Rosemary tells him, "We'll get through it too soon unless we pace ourselves." She doesn't tell him that sometimes she steals away with the book when she's supposed to be sewing on her frock for Robbie's graduation; later she shares with John the passage she's read in solitude. So far she's kept only one excerpt from him, and that is a lengthy, profusely sentimental outpouring written the night of her birth. There's nothing in it that she would mind for John to *know,* but she's sure he couldn't appreciate the depth of emotion that comes through to her, and she couldn't bear to read those precious sentiments aloud, knowing he didn't.

One afternoon Rosemary has to take the lawn mower in for repairs. She always asks John if he wouldn't like to come along whenever she goes out, and she asks him this time. They go through the same little song and dance.

"It's too hot to sit in the car."

"You could go inside with me."

"Oh, I don't think I'm ready to stumble around in public yet."

"You wouldn't stumble around, John."

"Well, I'm not ready anyway."

"Someday you're going to have to do it."

"Someday I will."

Coming home, Rosemary rounds the corner at her street and sees John standing in front of the house yelling. She doesn't take time to pull into the driveway; she stops on the street and jumps out, calling, "John! What is it, John?"

He turns around and around. "It's a fire! The house is on fire!"

Now Bonnie Truxler's mother hobbles over from next door, followed by Bonnie, wrapping her wet hair with a towel.

"A fire?" shouts Bonnie. "Did you call the fire department?" John shakes his head helplessly, and Bonnie runs back to call.

"What's the commotion?" her hard-of-hearing mother wants to know.

Rosemary is with him now, grasping his hands, telling him it's all right.

"Is it burning? Is the house burning down?"

"Why, I don't see any fire at all, John."

There isn't one. The smoke detector is having a fit because Rosemary did indeed leave the oven on with a ham cooking in it, and some stray crumbs in the bottom began to smoke, and that is the extent of the trouble. The firemen are good-natured about the false alarm; they take it a whole lot better than Bonnie and her mother, as Bonnie had to come right out of the shower and her mother ripped her hem out, climbing through Bonnie's rosebushes.

John cannot stop shaking. "I feel like such a fool," he says.

"Nonsense," Rosemary tells him. "You did the right thing getting out and calling for help. It very well could've been a fire."

"But it wasn't, and I looked like a fool."

"You mustn't worry about it, John."

"Bonnie acted awfully put out. Who else was out there watching me make a fool of myself?"

"No one much until the fire engine came." He doesn't need to know that neighbors came out of the woodwork. You'd have thought it was a garage sale. "Really, John, you mustn't let this worry you. You were able to get out of the house when you thought you were in danger, and that's what's important. What Bonnie and her mother think doesn't amount to a hill of beans."

John's bell is well used for the next couple of days. During that time, Rosemary doesn't even go out to move her car into the garage, and she lets Yard Day pass unmentioned, for John is terrified to stay in the room by himself. Finally, it seems to sink in that Rosemary isn't going to leave him alone again and that she's going to jump whenever he needs her, so he gives the bell a rest.

But Rosemary is certain that the incident is very much on his mind and that, in fact, it triggers what happens at his next doctor's appointment.

Dr. Nebbins calls Rosemary into his office after he's examined John and says, "We need to talk about scheduling, Mrs. Gray. You must be very happy that your husband is going through with the surgery."

John sits there looking pleased with himself.

When Rosemary gets her bearings, she says, Yes, she's happy, and then Dr. Nebbins does the rest of the talking. Not all that he explains registers, but he's been through the same speech with John already. What impresses Rosemary most is his comment, "There are no guarantees," which isn't unreasonable to say—about *anything* really—but somehow she had considered the surgery an absolute answer that John refused, and now it occurs to her that he may go through a great deal of trauma and still have nothing.

"Are you sure about this, John?" she asks, the first thing after Dr. Nebbins dismisses them.

"Yes. What do *you* think?"

He's a great one for asking what she thinks after he's already decided.

"It seems the right thing to do," she says.

All the children think so, too. It's the first time that Rosemary can remember—maybe the first time ever—that they are all agreed on anything. This surgery, Rosemary begins to feel, is ballooning into something more than a medical matter, especially when Judith drops the brick that she's coming home. No doubt she's coming to see that the doctors toe the mark, but still, *she is coming home* after two years.

"I think she's been looking for an excuse," John says.

"So you're giving her one."

"That's not why I'm going through with this."

"Why *are* you?"

"Don't you know?"

Rosemary doesn't say what she thinks, that John got scared of living in the dark. "I think I know," she says.

"Well, then." John switches on the radio and Rosemary dismisses it, too. It's Judith's homecoming now that's on her mind.

Fourteen

In a way, Rosemary marked the beginning of her adult life at Judith's birth. Adulthood began with motherhood, which was not, of course, how things were *supposed* to work. From one angle, Rosemary could say that she had been quite grown-up to make a living for herself and her mother, that her attitude toward marriage (as a solemn lifetime commitment) exhibited maturity, but having a baby was something else altogether. Becoming a mother added a whole new dimension that changed a woman forever. Actually, Rosemary was still thinking of herself as a girl—or, stretching it, a young woman—when there came to life this extension of herself that somehow rounded out her corners, brought to completion her own development.

This tiny person depended on her for *everything,* which was scary at first, but Rosemary found early on that maternal instinct was not a myth. She seemed to just know what to do. It was mostly a matter of using common sense; however, John was just about the most sensible person that Rosemary had ever known, and he had practically no feeling for what worked with Judith and what didn't. "She won't break, John. Just relax," Rosemary would say as he tried to hold the whimpering baby, but John remained as wooden as the Indian outside "Downey's Best Peach Cobbler in Georgia." Soon the whimpers would escalate into yells, and Rosemary would take Judith, talk to her and pat her. Naturally, the crying stopped. It didn't seem like any great feat to soothe a fussy baby, but John certainly didn't have the knack.

Neither did Rosemary's mother, who came to stay a week and teach Rosemary what she ought to know. Catching the earliest bus home she could get on the seventh day, she lamented to every passenger who would listen that her daughter didn't give her credit for knowing anything about babies (with all her experience as a nurse, too!) and that her grandchild was already spoiled rotten.

It was true that Judith had her preferences, that she was an unusually alert and active baby, but Rosemary didn't consider those *bad* traits. She was sure that Judith was exceptionally bright, and that was why she liked being in the middle of things instead of stuck off in another room in her crib. John was not so patient with Judith's whims. "Get her bottle!" he'd say every time she made a peep. Rosemary, of course, could tell by the nature of her cry whether she was hungry, wet, hurting, or bored. "How can a baby be bored?" John challenged, but what could he know about Judith's disposition, being away from her five days out of the week?

Judith was demanding, to be sure, but it was hard to say during that first year which practices (like rocking and singing Judith to sleep) came about as the result of the baby's demands or because Rosemary thought that was what mothers were supposed to do. The bottom line was, they had a way of doing things—mother and child—and Judith was not inclined to change.

But changes *had* to occur, for there was a new baby to consider—never mind that Judith was just fourteen months old herself. Rosemary thought her heart would break right in two when she was rolled away from John and Judith at the hospital door, with Judith reaching for her, screaming "Mam-ma!" It was worse than getting to the hospital by herself and having no family nearby during the delivery. John didn't get back for this big event, either, for the lady who was supposed to keep Judith wouldn't let him leave her in the shape she was in. "It wasn't a tantrum," the woman later declared to Rosemary. "It was a fit of hysteria!" Since they'd only lived in Macon some three months and John had even fewer acquaintances than Rosemary, he was stuck with keeping Judith himself until Virginia arrived from Darlington.

After a week in the hospital, Rosemary came home to Virginia's announcement, "Without you around, the baby warmed to me and we got along fine." *The baby* was Judith at that point, but suddenly the new *calm* infant who snuggled into anyone's arms became the baby, and Judith, who was hardly old enough to qualify for *big girl,* was just Judith.

They gave her attention, certainly. As a matter of fact, Rosemary made a point of giving her *extra* attention, but Judith wanted *all.* Rosemary tried involving her in Melissa's care—even a peaceful infant has to be diapered, fed, and bathed—but Judith didn't care about washing little toes; no, she slapped the washcloth at Melissa's face. When time came for bottles—Judith had to have one, too—Rosemary couldn't let Melissa's bottle out of her sight, for Judith would lick the nipple. Generally, she was about as interested in taking care of the new baby as she was in eating her spinach.

There were *reasons* for Judith's behavior, reasons that Rosemary tried to take into consideration, but as the child discovered clever new ways to make herself a pest, Rosemary's fuse grew shorter. She was seeing that babies didn't *have* to be a lot of trouble—Melissa wasn't—and wondering if John was perhaps right in his contention that she'd spoiled Judith. They both recognized that Judith was born with a stubborn streak, but John's theory was: "You can't give in! She'll soon be giving *you* orders if you don't take a firm hand now!" Rosemary had believed that patience and understanding would eventually bridle Judith's stubbornness, but matters were getting worse instead of better.

Oh, how she loved the dark-haired, spirited little girl! How she longed for Judith to be *good,* so that others would see in her the endearing traits that only Rosemary identified. It was hard enough to be tolerant of a difficult child, harder still when an *easy* child made comparison inevitable, and downright impossible when friends and strangers alike (and sometimes father) pointed out the difference between the two children.

One day Rosemary's fuse burned out. Judith had put in overtime that week, and while Rosemary was filling John's ear with complaints, the willful child sank her teeth into her baby sister's little finger. Melissa had never screamed so! The sudden yell served to frighten Judith, as well as her parents, and she grabbed Rosemary's skirts.

"Naughty girl!" said Rosemary, pushing her aside, hurrying to check the damage and to comfort Melissa. "There, there, it's all right," she crooned, kissing the tiny finger where little teeth had left red dents.

"Judith needs a spanking," said John. "Here, I'll see to Melissa." (That wasn't hard to do because Melissa was already quiet.)

Rosemary spanked Judith's hands, and she howled for fifteen minutes. Rosemary would not hold her or try to calm her in any way. At last, Judith lay down in front of the sofa, drew herself into a little ball, and began to trace the patterns in the rug.

"This is just the first of a whole string of hard lessons she'll have to learn in life," said John, trying to be philosophical, but, never having seen Judith quite so subdued, he tended to sound a little uncertain.

From the doorway Rosemary glanced at Judith, balled up on the floor, and what she felt was just the barest twinge of tenderness. What she *saw* was the bratty child that others most often saw, and it made her want to shake Judith and cry, *I have been entirely devoted to you, and this is the thanks I get!*

The thing that scared her was that Judith was just a year and a half old. Just a *baby,* and yet what power she wielded! If she could turn the family inside out *now,* the possibilities for the next two decades were hair-raising. How grateful Rosemary was for one child with Melissa's temperament. *But can I handle Judith?* she wondered, *or will she send me to an early grave?* It was the first time that she had entertained such doubts about the child who was now pulling the nap off the rug; it was by no means the last.

Those incidents, occurring so early in Judith's life, were naturally not part of her memory bank, but a tone was set even then. Just as Judith had no concept of life without Melissa, she had no concept of what it was like to be petted and pampered by her mother. In her earliest memories, Melissa was petted and pampered, while she was being scolded. Her mother's voice registered a sharp "Stop that, Judith!" and a weary "Not now, Judith," with the smiles and soft musical words reserved for Melissa. Melissa was sweet; Judith was naughty. That was how she remembered every childhood scenario. Whether or not in reality the black and white hats had been so perfectly defined, the camera of Judith's mind snapped them that way and that was how the images were preserved.

The trouble with having a sister like Melissa was that she *was* good. She did indeed possess all those pleasing traits that people praised, which meant that Judith couldn't find much to dislike about her. What she *did* dislike about her wasn't even Melissa's fault; it was that everything came so easily for her, friends, true love (as in the case of Simon), approval—most of all, their mother's approval. Melissa didn't even *try* to please; she more or less did what came naturally, but it somehow wasn't in her nature to do anything wrong. Melissa pleased their mother without trying; Judith never seemed to please her, no matter how hard she tried.

One afternoon a neighbor dropped in, and Judith heard her mother say, "Oh, we don't do much celebrating of birthdays around here," with a laugh that seemed a little too gushy for Rosemary. "The children's birthdays, yes, of course, but John and I never make much of ours. Since he's on the road, I doubt that he'll remember what Thursday is. Oh, he might. He might call that night or bring me a little something Friday. But it's not important really. What's a birthday by the time you're twenty-seven?"

Judith was seven, and birthdays meant presents. The idea that her mother's special day might pass unnoticed struck a note of sorrow in her, and she decided that she would not let that happen.

"We have to get Mother a gift," she told Melissa.

"All right. What?"

"That depends on where we get it." It was a perplexing matter because there were no stores in their neighborhood. Judith thought hard and concluded that she would have to ride her bike across the highway and buy a gift at the supermarket.

"But we're not allowed to cross the highway," said Melissa.

"That's a silly rule. There's a traffic light, and other kids ride their bikes to the supermarket all the time."

"But Mom has told us not to. I don't think we should."

"I'll do it. I'll take my bike out tomorrow afternoon, and Mother won't know how far I go." That wasn't exactly the truth. While Melissa worried about disobeying, Judith worried that her mother *would* know she had crossed the highway. She would have to know, for there wasn't any other place that Judith could buy the gift, but surely her mother

would see that her reason for disobeying had been a good one.

Then Judith tackled the matter of what kind of gift she could find at a supermarket. All that came to mind were the heart-shaped boxes of candy that must've been left over from Valentine's Day but would certainly be nicer than a bag of apples. Once, as Judith was pushing the cart past the candy display, her mother had remarked, "John gave me a box of candy like that when we were young." The candy was probably the best gift that Judith was going to find.

She looked up the number of the A & P on the General Lee Highway and called the store. Yes, there were still plenty of those heart-shaped boxes and the smallest one would cost five dollars and twenty-three cents, including tax. Next came the business of getting into piggy banks, which, luckily, weren't the kind that had to be broken. Judith counted a dollar and ninety cents from Melissa's bank and three dollars and nine cents from her own. She added the two amounts on paper, and then she counted all the money together. Both times she came up with four dollars and ninety-nine cents.

"How much do we need?" asked Melissa.

"Twenty-four cents, I think," but Judith didn't trust her subtraction, so she wrote down the problem and asked her mother to check it.

"Are you having this kind of arithmetic already?" Rosemary asked.

"No, I just thought I'd get ahead."

"You'd do better to spend your time on your assignments," said Rosemary, but she confirmed that the answer to the problem was twenty-four.

Judith reported to Melissa, "What we need is another quarter."

"Where will we get it?"

"I've been thinking about that."

"Well, what?"

"Well, isn't that tooth of yours ready to come out?"

It seemed an easy enough way to get money, not that Judith still believed in the tooth fairy, but every tooth *was* worth a quarter. Judith had already lost four, and no others were loose at that time, but Melissa hadn't lost any, and she'd been wiggling a lower front tooth for a month.

"We have to get it out now," said Judith, "or at least by tonight."

"So the tooth fairy can leave my quarter."

"Uh huh."

Melissa wiggled the tooth again. "I don't think it's ready."

"Sure it is."

"Maybe I should ask Mom."

"You can't do that! She'd want to know why you're in a hurry to get it out. *I* can do it. I pulled all my own."

"Yours just fell out. Mine doesn't want to fall out."

"I know where Dad keeps his pliers."

Judith's scheme might've worked if her mother's flower bed hadn't been muddy. When Rosemary came inside to change into old shoes and heard moans and groans, naturally she sought out the source. She arrived at the door of the girls' bedroom just in time to see Judith, straddled on Melissa's stomach, give a jerk with the pliers and shout, "I've got it!"

Rosemary's little shriek alerted Judith that they had been found out, but she jumped to her feet and hurried to announce cheerfully, "Melissa's tooth came out!"

Rosemary rushed in, hurling questions without waiting for answers, questions that didn't especially *need* answers, like "Where did you get those pliers?" when she had to know where Judith got the pliers, and "What in the world have you done?" when Judith had just told her and was in fact holding up the little tooth between her thumb and forefinger. And then the same question, really, but to Melissa, with blood spilling down her chin as she dashed toward the bathroom: "What has she *done* to you?" As if it wasn't plain to see.

"It's just a tooth," Judith interjected. "I've lost four!"

"But how could you go into your sister's mouth with pliers? How could you *think* of pulling her little tooth that was barely loose? What in the world did you have on your mind, Judith? Don't you have any feeling at all?"

"It was all right with Melissa."

"Don't you know that's because she trusts you? How could you do such a cruel thing—to take her first baby tooth!—knowing how she trusts you?"

Such was the gist of the scolding that continued until Melissa was back, sucking on a washcloth at first, and then showing off a perfectly fine tooth hole.

Even then, the plan might not have been ruined if Melissa hadn't tried to take up for her sister.

"Don't fuss at Judith, Mamma. It didn't hurt much."

Rosemary hugged her. "That's a brave girl."

"I *wanted* her to pull it. I wanted to get a quarter. We needed another quarter for your birthday gift."

And she went on to tell, as Judith fell like a brick on the bed, what they had planned to do. The only good that Judith could see in the whole mess was that they did get to buy the candy the next afternoon. Their mother drove them to the supermarket.

"I'll never forget that you gave your front tooth for my birthday present," Rosemary told Melissa.

And to Judith she said, "I appreciate the thought behind the candy, but don't you ever *ever* ride your bike across that highway until I say so!"

When she was twelve years old, Judith made up her mind to be a lawyer and she never wavered in that course. Rosemary was satisfied that she'd make a good lawyer, as skilled as she was at presenting her side and as diligently as she worked to get her way. "If I ever went to court, I'd want you pleading my case," Rosemary told her once when Judith was perhaps fifteen. Judith later did not remember the circumstances that prompted the comment or the sigh that came along with the words; she remembered the remark as the nicest compliment ever paid to her by her mother.

Rosemary knew that Judith was smart—everyone knew—but Judith doubted that her mother appreciated *how* smart or what that meant. Dummies didn't get into Northwestern University on a scholarship. That was something a mother could brag about! But what did Rosemary have to say to Mrs. Payne, whose daughter Beth was going to a community college some forty miles from home? Not *Judith has a scholarship to one of the finest universities in the nation.* Not even *Judith has a splendid opportunity to go to Northwestern in Chicago, but oh how far away it seems!* No, Rosemary said, "Judith is going to college in Chicago," as if it were just *any* school. And when Mrs. Payne mentioned how far away from home that was, Rosemary replied merrily, "That suits Judith just fine. Doesn't it, Judith?"

There at the escalator in the department store, Judith replied so vehemently that the people who had already gone up looked back down. "You are so right! I can't *wait* to live my own life in Chicago!"

Mrs. Payne's eyebrows shot up. Rosemary gave a startled little smile but otherwise appeared to let the remark slide like an inconsequential raindrop. She told Mrs. Payne how good it was to see her, sent good wishes to Beth, and nudged Judith onto the escalator.

In that incident, something seemed to jell in Judith's perspective of college. Northwestern was a prestigious university with a fine law school, and Judith was proving something to herself, as well as *hoping* to prove something to her family, to please or impress them—her mother in particular—but all those notions were fluid until Judith's bold declaration suddenly gave them one distinct shape, the shape of *flight.* Attending Northwestern meant a severing of the apron strings. Anywhere in the whole state, the apron strings would still confine; one had to go *away* to be a separate person, and that was what Judith was doing. Rosemary's rigid demands would no longer hold her back. No longer would she measure herself by her mother's expectations.

Rosemary and John drove Judith to Chicago. Judith sensed that their reason had more to do with the expense of flying than with the need to see her settled comfortably in her new surroundings, but she couldn't prove it. The trip was pleasant. Judith wondered how different her life might've turned out if she'd been an only child.

When time came for her parents to leave, Judith got an awkward one-armed hug from John, who said, "If you need anything, anything at all, you call collect anytime." It was the best he had *in him* and it made a lump rise in Judith's throat.

Rosemary hugged and kissed her and said, "This is awfully far away from home, Judith." But very quickly then and on a merry note, she said, "But you'll be fine, I'm *sure* you'll be just fine!"

And with a stiff upper lip, Judith agreed that she most certainly would be.

Judith went home for the Christmas holidays and then for summer in time for Melissa's wedding, and the next year she spent a week at Christmas again. But by that June she had a summer job in Chicago, and after that, her visits back to Nashville were brief. A couple of days at Christmas, a few at the end of June or the end of August, never long enough to get comfortable in her old bed. By the time Judith graduated from law school, Chicago was home; home was Chicago.

There was still some obligation to visit her family, but her visits tied her up in knots for weeks after, so that it was much easier *not* to go back. No one seemed to care too much that she missed a Christmas here and there. They still communicated by phone, which seemed most sensible for the conversation couldn't get terribly heated in three minutes, and at three minutes Judith could hear her father in the background telling Rosemary to hurry up.

But if they had *needed* her, that would've been different, as was the time that her father called to tell how her mother had—in his words—"gone to pieces." Judith was on the first plane she could get out of Chicago. She wasn't allowed to see her mother on Ward C, but she stayed with her father for a week, cooked and kept house and told him that everything would be all right.

Judith never really understood what happened to her mother. When she was finally able to visit on the ward after Rosemary had been confined for a month or more, she tried to elicit some answers from the staff people, but they were all closemouthed. Naturally she understood the principle of confidentiality, but this was her *mother* and it was her mother's sanity at stake; that was why she probably appeared a little pushy so that finally she was told she'd have to leave if she continued to upset her mother. *Upset her mother,* of all things! Rosemary's vacant eyes were fixed on the television as she waited for some imaginary report about her to come on. "One of the women who brings our meals is an investigative reporter," she said quite matter-of-factly. "She's been much too interested in my pot holders."

A woman with white glasses shaped like cat eyes leaned

toward Judith as they sat in the common room and whispered, "You must be the daughter."

"I'm one of the daughters, yes," Judith answered, pulling back a little.

"You have a lovely mother. You should appreciate her."

"Why, I do," said Judith.

The woman daintily adjusted her showy spectacles and said knowingly, "It's those who're supposed to be the smartest that can't see the nose on their face."

For some reason, her enigmatic saying prompted Judith to snap, "I don't see that this is any of your business."

"Suit yourself, Missy," and the busybody disappeared.

Judith didn't know why, but more times than she could count the cat-eyed woman had come to her in dreams, and time and time again she would wake in a cold sweat, frightened by the notion that she had sent away the one person who could have made her understand her mother.

When Rosemary was well—they all said—Judith came back again. It was late fall, and Rosemary wore a jacket to work outdoors. Judith joined her in the backyard where she was digging up canna and tulip bulbs, and tried very hard to make easy conversation. Soon, however, Rosemary had stood up and was leaning on the shovel, firing questions in an all-too-familiar way.

Did Judith ever do anything but work? What about a social life, friends, men in her life? Didn't she realize that the older she got, the harder it was to find a husband? Had she ruled out marriage altogether? Hadn't it occurred to her that careers dwindled and old age could be very lonely?

It was easy to forget that her mother had been ill. She seemed very much her old self.

"I'm simply concerned that you're alone, Judith."

"Mother, I *do* have friends. I go out as much as I care to. I'm not alone."

"Oh, but that's not the same thing as family."

"Family?" Old bitterness rushed in, and suddenly Judith was saying, "A family doesn't always seem to fulfill a person's needs."

Rosemary did not—perhaps did not care to—pursue that line. "You may begin to think of marriage when you're forty and find that the pickings are scarce."

"I have a wonderful job, Mother. I haven't had a chance to tell you, but I've left the Public Defender's office and have joined a firm with four of Chicago's leading defense attorneys."

"I've never understood what reward there could be in defending people who are guilty."

"Every person deserves the best defense available."

"So you've told me."

"I have a good life, Mother."

"I just worry that you're alone."

"Strange that you should push marriage for me, when *your* marriage has been such a disappointment." Judith saw a cloud in her mother's eyes, but it was like arguing to the jury: Her momentum was up, and she couldn't stop. "It *has* been a disappointment, hasn't it, Mother? But you don't have to answer. I grew up in this house, remember? Maybe that's why I'm not too anxious for a husband and children. I don't want a family like the one I grew up in."

Silently, Rosemary sank to her knees and shoved her hands into the soil.

Judith could not be sure whether her mother related their words to her father or whether he overheard. She suspected he must've been at the kitchen door, and certainly he would've had no trouble hearing her courtroom voice. She could not imagine that her mother would've repeated the conversation.

That night her father came to her room. She was reading by a dim lamp; no doubt her mother was asleep. "Judith, I think you should plan to go home pretty soon," he said, looking at his feet which were planted just inside the door. "I was hoping you could stay a good long while, but it just doesn't work, does it?" He raised his eyes to her briefly but began to survey the room, the bulletin board where old invitations and blue ribbons were tacked, the dresser where a mirrored tray held perfume that was ten years old.

"Give Rosie some time. She's—well, she's so *fragile* right now."

It was strange hearing her father using a word like *fragile.* Judith wondered if she knew her parents at all.

"You're probably right. I'll call the airlines in the morning."

"You have a good life away from us, Judith. I'm glad for you. I hope you understand that I can't risk losing your mother again."

"I understand," she said. In an odd way, she did, but that didn't make it any easier.

Fifteen

Melissa decides to come home, too. John remarks that she can't let her sister outdo her, to which Rosemary huffs, for that is not at all Melissa's way. She has no inclination to compete with Judith, never has had. "If she cared about that sort of thing," Rosemary insists, "she would've gone to college instead of off to the wilderness."

"I keep telling you," says John, "it's not a wilderness. It's fertile farmland."

"Well, anyway. She's not coming home for the sake of appearance because it doesn't matter to Melissa how a thing *looks* or whether Judith is doing it or whether we'll be impressed. She wouldn't be coming home if she didn't just plain *want* to. Face it, John, she loves you."

John makes no audible reply but the upturn of his mouth at one corner shows that the idea pleases him. He never has been one to talk about love, which is all right with Rosemary for she isn't the mushy type, either, but where her family is concerned, she has certainly won her merit badge in devotion. Over and over and over she has been required to prove her love, and that is what strikes her as unfair, for John is accepted as he is, his inadequacies ignored. Undiluted loyalty from his children is his reward—for what? Rosemary doesn't deny that he has been *good* to them. He was a good provider. He patted heads a lot—on weekends—but he was never, never *involved* with them. That's what it boils down to. He wasn't there. *Did that work to his advantage?* Rosemary wonders. There *she* was, *always,* fixer of bikes, dispenser of Mercurochrome and tender loving care, cook, maid, tutor and chauffeur, and also the one to blame if the picnic was rained out or if chicken pox popped out on the morning of the school play. Even when John was physically present, he wasn't *really* there. Family life went on around him, while he straightened the papers in his already orderly rolltop desk or raised a newspaper barrier in front of him.

"I'm *glad* the girls are coming home, you understand."

John frowns. Not having been privy to Rosemary's thoughts, he doesn't make a connection at first, but he waits, and she makes it for him.

"It would please me, too, if they were coming home because *I* was going into the hospital."

"They did visit you in the hospital, Rosemary, remember?"

"I don't remember much about any of that," she answers tersely.

"Well, they were there, all the children at various times."

"All right, they were. What do you want for lunch?" It seems to Rosemary that the more she elaborates, the more *jealous* she sounds, which is silly, for she is not jealous. She just can't help wishing that her children were as tolerant of their mother as they are of their father, that's the thing. It doesn't seem like a lot to ask, but she couldn't possibly ask. She decided a long time ago that anything a mother has to ask of her children is too much.

John's eye surgery is first scheduled for the week after Robbie's graduation. This is John's request, on the basis that Robbie should have the spotlight on his graduation day. But if Judith and Melissa are coming home anyway, John reasons, they ought to see their brother get his diploma, so he asks Dr. Nebbins to move the surgery up. Now the plans are for John to enter the hospital the day after Robbie graduates. Rosemary stands by while John works it out with the doctor and the girls, rather dazed by the way he is taking care of things.

There are preparations that she should be making, too, Rosemary knows, but on these sultry August days she can't seem to tackle anything new. She is finishing the handwork on her dress, but without enthusiasm. Who will know or care what she wears to the graduation ceremony? Nor can she muster the energy to set about cleaning the girls' room, a chore left undone—like a bunch of other chores—since John's accident. Robbie's room will be available, of course, and Rosemary has continued to keep it clean, but one of the girls will sleep in their old room. *Will it be Judith or Melissa?* she wonders. Not that it matters. She just bets Judith will choose the room that was never hers. Rosemary had no choice about where to sleep whenever she went back to her mother's in Darlington, and she well remembers all the ghosts that inhabited her old room.

More often now, she's drawn to her father's journal. She lays aside her hemming to slip in a couple of pages before John's outrageous bell calls her. She leans against the sewing machine and reads:

"September 14, 1944. Sonny Blake arrived yesterday, a war hero with a chest full of medals but without his legs. I don't understand war or the larger issues that the world powers ponder, but when my own little corner of the world is invaded, it tears me to the quick not to be able to do something. 'You wouldn't have let them do it, Doc, would you?' he said to me. 'You would've found another way.' What a heavy load to lay on a small-town doctor!"

Rosemary's private reading has taken her far ahead of what she reads to John. Now as she follows Doc's earlier recordings and his later ones, both at once, Rosemary is aware of a subtle contrast. That attitudes change over a decade is not an acceptable reason—in theory, yes, but not as it applies to Doc because Rosemary *knew* him and he was unchanging. Still, the farther she reads, the more contemplative becomes the journal which began as a chronicle of Darlington's births, deaths, and ailments. In the evenings, Rosemary reads to John about getting a pea out of Katie Emerson's nose. Later, in the shadowy lamplight which never seems to disturb John's sleeping, she reads:

"December 10, 1944. Rosemary started in about a Christmas tree the day after Thanksgiving. I put her off as long as I could. Last week I got word to Alvin Skinner and he found me one, which we put up Sunday. Rosemary wouldn't trim it without me. Oh, what joy shined in her eyes when we stood back to look at the decorated tree. I'm sure I must've felt the same joy and wonder too once upon a time, but that seems like a lifetime ago."

"February 2, 1945. Groundhog day and my birthday. The old groundhog couldn't have seen his shadow in the drizzle we've had today, so that must mean that winter is on its way out, and none too soon. Virginia had a big supper for me, all my favorites and a birthday cake. Now I know why she's been holding back the sugar, saving it for this. Somehow this fiftieth birthday hits me hard, but bless Virginia's heart, she went all out to make it a cheerful occasion. She tried her best to put the Winningham woman off when she called about her mother's intestinal pains, but as I said to Virginia on my way out the door, 'This is what I'm all about.' "

"I don't guess we'll get through it before I go into the hospital," says John.

"No way." *He won't get through it but I will.* There is an urgency now to finish, which seems funny to Rosemary, for she *knows* the ending, or she should. She was, after all, a witness to the respect and affection that a whole town doled out to her father. She played a role in the blissful family in which he took such pride. She was *there,* and how could anyone who knew him mistake the devotion that her father had for his patients, his dedication to healing? How Doc Lowell's story ends is not the thing she needs to know. It's *What does it mean?* In her father's wisdom, surely there is a gem for her. And for Robbie. She hasn't forgotten her original impression that Robbie found something for himself in his grandfather's words. That presumption is reinforced each time he calls and asks, "How far are you in the journal?"

John's bell is as shrill as a child's scream.

"What is it, John?" she asks, coming from the bedroom where the open journal lies facedown on her bed beside the crumpled dress without buttons.

"Aren't you going to mow the yard? Today's Friday, isn't it? Didn't you miss the last two Fridays?"

"Yes, yes, and no. I did miss two Fridays when the part had to be ordered for the lawn mower, but last week I had it back."

"You usually get out in the yard while it's cool."

"I'm finishing my dress, John."

"I just wondered."

Rosemary marks her place in the journal and changes into her yard clothes. It seems like a good idea to put up the journal for a while. She has less than twenty pages left to read. Besides, if she doesn't finish her dress soon, she may cut it into shreds. Besides that, she has not swept one cobweb out from under the beds in the girls' room, and they'll be home next week. And besides that, she had entirely forgotten it was Yard Day.

Rain, much needed and long awaited, begins just before midnight Sunday. Rosemary is at the door to the backyard when the drops hit, big drops, so that at first she seems to hear each individual one as it splats, but faster they fall until finally the sound is a roar, embellished with intermittent thunderclaps.

It was not the noise that woke her. It was more likely the silence, for when she went to the back door the night was curiously soundless. But the air was charged with the promise of a storm, and within minutes, a gusty wind was blowing over a pot of geraniums. Against the sky, bright with lightning cutting across it, was the silhouette of the willow tree bending and swaying. Rosemary did not want to come in, for the restlessness matched something restless within herself, but of course she did.

Quickly she locks the door. In Darlington, before the days of air conditioning, all the windows would be open and her mother would hustle through the house, shutting out the storm, sometimes getting drenched if the wind gusted from a certain direction. There was something wonderfully dangerous about thunderstorms in those days. Rosemary feels no threat from this disturbance, with all the storm windows and doors closed up, but she watches from the kitchen sink, marveling at the grand display of light, movement, and sound.

Some moments later, when the storm is at its peak, she tiptoes into the bedroom. She fumbles in the dark for her father's journal and comes to sit at the kitchen table with the last pages before her.

"March 14, 1947. Bailey Cook from North Point was in town yesterday for the Sutton girl's wedding, which Virginia, Rosemary, and I attended. A wingding if ever Darlington saw one. Evidently Bailey's wife is related to the groom. Bailey's just recently taken a young ex-Navy doctor into practice with him. He says it's working out fine, that the fellow knows medicine and understands rank. At times I think I'd like to come upon someone like that. Who will carry on when I can't? Not that I'm expecting anything like that for a long time, but I guess the reason it's on my mind is because Bailey told me I ought to let him give me a good checkup. He said I looked wrung out. So was he, he said, before his new man gave him a thorough examination, put him on a strict exercise regimen, and took away all his vices. My only vice is hard work, I told Bailey. He said maybe that was where I needed to cut back, but I don't know how and don't know if I could stand not being everything that

everybody wants me to be. The greatest burden in my life is my greatest joy, being Doc to a whole town. But sometimes, the way they all depend on me, it's more than I can live up to; I don't work miracles. I just occasionally preside over one. But it's not as much what people ask me to do as what they expect me to be. So that's why I'm wrung out, but all the same, I might just run up to North Point and let Bailey take a look-see—if I ever get the time."

"May 14, 1947. I delivered a stillborn at three AM and had to tell Alvin Skinner at eleven that his x-rays show a lung tumor. Alvin won't talk about going to Atlanta where there's a chance that a specialist could do something for him. He's never spent one night away from the old homeplace. How useless I feel! There was Alvin, speaking quietly about the hereafter, and I was wanting to rant and rave, so angry was I that I couldn't make him well. Maybe the good Christians have the right idea about the soul that is immortal and the place of eternal rest. I'd like to believe that when death makes a mockery of my feeble efforts with Alvin, a soul in him will soar to something beyond his rotting flesh. Oh how I'd like to believe that death wouldn't get the last lick!"

"May 22, 1947. Rosemary will be thirteen this week. Virginia was going to let her have a few little girls over for a slumber party (the kind where they don't slumber, I hear) but Rosemary just wanted a family to-do, so we may take her to the circus that is setting up out on Highway 10. Rosemary doesn't seem to have many friends. Virginia worries about it, but how, I ask her, could anyone fail to like our Rosemary? Funny that Virginia would worry about that when she's such a homebody herself. I say that in the most loving way, for how could I have ever managed without Virginia, without her strength, without her faith in me? If Rosemary grows up to be anything like her mother, her husband will be a lucky man."

Like that, Doc Lowell stops writing, leaving the last pages blank.

Rosemary closes the book, tucks it between *101 Desserts* and *The Economy of Cooking* on a high shelf, and switches off the light. The rain has settled into a steady drizzle. The broken pot of geraniums seems the only evidence of the storm.

Rosemary has read to the end of her father's journal. Surely there is gold between the covers if only she can extract it, but this is all she can work out, rambling through the dark house: that her father would've been disappointed in her, for a copy of her mother is the thing she has spent thirty years trying not to be.

Breakfast is at nine o'clock, which doesn't much please John, as he's been up since seven. Then, just as they sit down, the telephone rings. That doesn't much please John either, though it's Rosemary who answers.

The chirpy voice that could belong to an eight-year-old girl turns out to be Fanny Malone's.

"What's the matter, Fanny?" Rosemary asks quickly, for she can't imagine any other reason for her to call.

"Buddy's had to go back to the hospital," comes the mournful answer.

"Is he all right?" Rosemary asks.

It's a senseless question but Fanny's reply is no more intelligent. "Why, yes, he's just having another operation."

Buddy's feet, it seems, are the trouble. "You know he hasn't walked since that other operation," says Fanny. "And oh the pain he has! His daughter and son-in-law came and took him away yesterday afternoon."

"Away?"

"To the hospital!"

"I see."

"I wouldn't have bothered you, but none of us here can go to see him, you know, and he's very fond of you, Rosemary, though he'd rake me over the coals if he knew I said it! Just a minute, dear. Will you just hold your horses, Lyman! I'll quit when I'm good and ready! So sorry, Rosemary. Now what was I saying?"

Rosemary is thinking how she's neglected the little man, how she never so much as wrote a note saying, *I'd like to visit you again but I can't leave John by himself.* Her intentions are noble; why is it that she's always letting down the people who count on her?

"I'll go to see him," she promises. No doubt he'll still be in the hospital when John goes in on Thursday, but she has no intention of waiting until then.

It's just as well that she doesn't go until the next morning when Robbie has come home. By then she has the girls' room in order, which must mean she's ready for them. By then Buddy has some of his spunk back.

"They kept me in that ice-cold recovery room till sometime last night," he fusses, but in a weaker voice than usual. "They said I was talking crazy."

To Rosemary's wry smile, he lifts his finger and says, "That's not very nice, what you're thinking."

"I'm glad you're doing so well, Buddy. Here, I made you some banana bread. One of the nurses said it was all right."

"I don't like bananas—I've seen too many mashed bananas at the home—but I appreciate the thought just the same." He fumbles with the adjustments to the bed, making it do everything but what he wants, until finally he lets Rosemary help. "Just raise the head a little bit. That's it. You come in handy sometimes."

He looks tired and pale. The nurse told Rosemary she could stay "just a few minutes," so she gets right into telling Buddy all she has to say—about John's surgery and the day the smoke detector gave him such a fright so that she no longer leaves him alone, about Robbie's graduation the day after tomorrow and how he's been working and studying so that he couldn't stay with his father for her to go out. She wants Buddy to understand why she only came once to the nursing home He dismisses it with his feeble hand

Judith is coming home after two years, she tells him. Melissa will be home, too, without Simon and the children but they were here Christmas. Melissa's expecting twins. "And another thing," she says, looking at her hands. "I've been reading my father's journal."

Buddy purses his lips and nods.

"Robbie found it in the attic. It starts in 1931."

"Thirty-one! Why, you couldn't have been more than a pup."

"Not even a pup. I came along in thirty-four."

"Give or take a few. Go on about the diary."

"Journal, though I couldn't tell you the difference." Rosemary smooths her skirt, brushes off a speck of lint. She isn't sure she should've brought it up. "My father was a small-town doctor. Everyone adored him, and I thought he was just about perfect. He died when I was thirteen."

"Let me guess, Rosemary. You learned from his journal that he was actually a very naughty man. What terrible thing did he do?"

"It's nothing like that. He didn't do *anything* bad."

"Well?"

"Well, I'm being silly. I need to go, Buddy. I promised the nurse I wouldn't be long."

She stands up, but he motions for her to come closer, and when she bends toward him, he grasps her arm with his thin purplish hand.

"Agnes thought her daddy was pretty swell, too, till she found out he had a skeleton in his closet."

"I tell you, there was no skeleton—"

But he doesn't listen. "Back in his young days Buddy Grant was pretty wild. Sometimes little men try too hard to prove themselves. This little man had a brush with the law. Spent some time in the state penitentiary."

"You're not making this up, are you, Buddy."

"*No,* Rosemary. Pay attention."

She sits down on the edge of the bed. Buddy still has a remarkably solid grip on her arm.

"I repented before Almighty God and I paid my debt to society, but I couldn't get over the notion that I owed Agnes, too. Like I said, she thought her daddy hung the moon. It seemed only right to set her straight. So fifty years after the deed was done—and Agnes forty years old, mind you, old enough to know there's no Santie Claus—I told her what was what. You could just hear that hero-image of her daddy splintering. That was when she more or less wrote me off. Couldn't take having a father that was just a plain little man."

"But you're not a plain little man."

"I'm not what she thought I was. For the record, she's not what I thought *she* was, either, which was the forgiving sort."

"I'm sorry, Buddy."

"I didn't tell you so you'd worry about it. I don't worry about it. I'll tell you something else, too. It's better in some ways than having to be a hero."

Rosemary knows exactly what he's trying to do. At first she *doesn't* know how much she can believe, but no spark of play lights Buddy's eyes. "I'd better leave now," she says, but he doesn't let go of her arm.

"You've always struck me as sensible, Rosemary—at the core."

"I hope so."

"A spry young thing like you oughtn't to hang around old folks' homes or old men in hospitals or be digging in old books. You should have better things to do than listen to old bones rattle."

"Maybe there are secrets in the rattling of old bones."

He scowls. Rosemary has the impression that he's offended by her jaunty reply. But he says, "Then you probably still believe in Santie Claus, too." He lets his hand drop to his side. "Go on home to your husband, Rosemary. That's what you've *got,* a husband who probably loves you a whole lot, so go home and take care of him."

Sixteen

When John was six years old, when his father left for the last time, his Aunt Millie's dry appraisal was, "Eustace wasn't cut out to be a family man. There's a knack to taking care of a family that Eustace plain don't have." All in all, John had seen more of the town mayor than he'd ever seen of his father, for the mayor at least drove by in his motorcar twice a day; nevertheless, he'd formed a solid impression, and if his father *wasn't* a family man, then in John's young mind, a family man was a good thing to be.

Aunt Millie was a big-boned woman, not especially tidy in her appearance and rough-looking by nature, but her heart was as soft as the oatmeal she fed John for breakfast till he was grown—too soft, in the case of her brother Eustace, whom she'd also raised. Out of the best intentions Millie had overlooked harmful tendencies in Eustace that might've been yanked up by the roots like Johnson grass had a firm parent been on hand. Ten years his senior, Millie was the kind who seemed to turn from girlish into matronly in a snap, without a brush with adolescence and youth. By contrast, Eustace was the kind who never grew up.

"That's just how he is, a born rascal," Millie explained to the baffled teacher at the little one-room schoolhouse where Eustace finally completed five grades. Forever the prankster, he brought in garter snakes to scare the girls and the desperate young woman who was trying to teach, and created havoc in the classroom by the notes he wrote, notes to which he signed someone else's name. He sent to one chubby girl the message, *You are a fat pig and stink like one. Jane E.* The parents got in on that, Eustace understood, but as the quarrel took place away from school, he missed the fun. Most of his other notes brought situations to a head within the classroom, which Eustace enjoyed immensely, even though he often wound up with a whipping.

Then he started teaching the other boys to gamble during recess, using dice that he'd somehow obtained in real, play-for-blood crap games on the sleazy side of town. This was ultimately why he dropped out of school. The schoolboys who'd first lost their pocket knives to Eustace had wound up taking money from home to stay in the game. When the parents figured out what had been going on for at least a year, they stormed in on the poor teacher, who went to Millie for the dozenth time. This was far more serious than garter snakes, she declared, knowing all the time that Millie was as much a victim as the rest of them. True to form, Millie bailed her brother out of his latest scrape, paying back week by week more than twenty-five dollars to irate parents. This time, however, the teacher had succeeded in frightening Millie, warning her that if any of the parents called in the sheriff, Eustace might well wind up in a school for wayward boys under lock and key. Fearing this—for she couldn't count on Eustace to behave at school—Millie simply told him in the careless way that was hers, "If I was you, I'd stay away from school for a while." He never went back after that.

Millie didn't hesitate to say—years later, telling John—that letting her brother quit school at thirteen was a mistake. (She freely acknowledged a whole bunch of mistakes with her brother, none of which lost her a wink of sleep, once they were water under the bridge.) Trouble compounded trouble as bad company, bad habits, and a bad reputation took their toll. One night a fire was set to the sheriff's house. As the fire bell clanged, Eustace started stuffing clothes in a cardboard suitcase.

"Why?" Millie demanded. "You didn't do it. You've been right here."

"But I know who did," he said. The screen door slammed, and Millie did not see or hear from him for five years.

"Your daddy just had it in him to wander," Millie would tell John. "Never could stick to anything." When Eustace returned, being all of nineteen years old, he'd seen twenty-two states (so he said). He'd been a cowpoke in New Mexico and a clam digger in Maine and everything in between (so he said) but nothing ever worked out, through no fault of his own (so he said). He was home to stay. But three weeks later, he was off to Detroit to make his fortune on the assembly line. That lasted a few months, and he came dragging back without a penny.

Never again did he mention *staying.* He knew he wouldn't. So did Millie. Even when he brought back the skinny, sad-eyed girl who would eventually become John's mother, Millie knew he wouldn't stay.

Her name was Deidre. She was twenty years old and had come from some remote hollow in Kentucky—without her parents' blessings it seemed, for when Eustace left her the first time and Millie suggested that she might ought to go back to Kentucky, she sobbed, "I can't ever go back." For all her naive ways, she knew a great deal about some things, one being fine needlework. Millie, who supported herself as a seamstress, was able to incorporate Deidre's talent into her business, and together they eked out a meager living. Deidre was beginning to make something of herself. Then Eustace came back.

It was the same story, over and over again. John was born, and his father stayed around until he was a year old, which must've been a record. Sometimes Eustace left to find work. Sometimes he left after an argument, and Deidre would go to Millie, weeping, reproaching herself for imagined wrongdoings. She adored her husband and would do anything for him if he'd just come home. Such a fragile thing she seemed. Millie wondered, *How many times can he break her heart?*

She was indeed fragile, weighing about a hundred pounds on her healthiest day, which was before John's time. One of his father's complaints was that she was *sickly.* That stuck with John, though the image of his frail mother faded. Consumption was the cause of her death, but as Millie put it, "She stopped living when she lost Eustace."

Eustace had left two months earlier, upon finding out that another baby was on the way. "That does it, Dee," he told her. "Two's just plain over-eggin' the puddin'." Before he went, he kissed John's tousled hair, kissed his tearful wife on the cheek, and said, "Tell Millie 'bye for me. This time I won't be back."

It was hard growing up during the Depression, hard growing up without parents. John didn't doubt that he was loved by his Aunt Millie, but in comparison to the real mothers he knew, her shortcomings shined like soot on the nose. She seemed no more cut out to raise children than her brother had been, but John could forgive her since she was just a stand-in for a parent. He never lost sight of the kindness she was performing in taking him in, and he tried his best not to be any trouble.

The hardest part about growing up was knowing that he'd been abandoned by a no-good father and harboring hate to which he couldn't give voice. Oh, Aunt Millie would say how shiftless her brother was, but she'd say it in a loving way, as some people would speak of naughty little boys. John never dared to tell her right out how he genuinely hated the man. But he did what he could do to erase the blemish of his father, and that was to legally drop his own middle name, which was Eustace. "Don't that seem a little harsh?" his Aunt Millie wanted to know, but John's regret was that he didn't go on and change his last name, too, for his gesture hadn't accomplished what he'd hoped. Hate and bitterness and shame for being Eustace Gray's offspring were still like worms eating away at his insides.

John had quit high school to work (which was a necessity), but he wasn't sorry when his country called him to fight the Japanese. The anger that churned within him found an outlet, but when the peace treaties were signed, John's anger went right on boiling.

Then he met Mark Hogan. Mark was a young preacher in Birmingham, Alabama, and John, who finally had his high school diploma, was there training to be a salesman for a line of men's clothing. The two were eyeing a new Ford sedan (which neither could afford) when they got to talking and John said, "I don't go in much for religion. I had my fill when I was a youngster." The young preacher looked as if he wanted to hear more, so John told him.

"There was this tent set up just out of town and rumors were that the people had snakes. Well, any boy would want to see that, and I did. Oh, it was lively, with lots of singing and dancing through the aisles, and some stooped-over woman all of a sudden jumped straight up in the air and shouted that she was healed. When they brought the snakes out, that held my attention all right. But when the preacher went to yanking people out of their seats and dragging them up to the front, it started not to be so enjoyable. Then that preacher stood at the end of my aisle and pointed his finger at me, and that bony finger was about eight inches long. Well, I don't mind telling you, I darted out the other end and hightailed it home, and that was enough religion to last me a lifetime."

Mark Hogan laughed and said, "I don't go in much for snakes."

"What kind of religion do you go in for?" John asked him.

"Same as the apostle Paul," he said. "Love, joy, peace, longsuffering, gentleness, goodness, faith, meekness, and temperance."

John figured he was quoting Scripture, but for some reason he didn't come off like other Scripture-spouters who shouted warnings to sinners. "Doesn't sound like something to get stirred up about," John told him, meaning it in the most courteous way.

But Mark Hogan didn't let it go at that. He brought out from his coat pocket a worn little Bible and with a flip of the flimsy pages began to read about new creatures, about old things passing away. He said, "Getting a new heart isn't something to yawn about, either."

After that, John had to hear Mark preach, and then he got to reading the Scriptures out of a Bible that Mark gave him, in which Mark had taken the liberty of underlining that verse: "Therefore if any man be in Christ, he is a new creature: old things are passed away; behold, all things are become new." Day after day John read his Bible, and night after night his friend Mark Hogan talked it, and in the end John got a new heart. He knew it was so, for the old anger and bitterness toward his father went away, and he was just sorry that the man had been what he was, sorry for what they all had missed.

When Rosemary Lowell popped up in his path, John wasn't necessarily thinking about marriage, but that didn't take long. He was twenty-seven years old and had spent the last ten years pulling himself up by his boot straps—which was no easy chore—with not much money to spend and not much occasion to meet young ladies. The spinster-types baked wonderfully fluffy biscuits but once the meal was over, a fellow couldn't keep from watching the clock. The pretty girls somehow turned out to be more worldly than John bargained for. So he didn't go out much, but he was definitely noticing young women more and more. He was definitely open to meeting someone who would make him want to slick back his hair and straighten his shoulders, but someone who'd let him sort of take the lead. He wanted to impress her and at the same time be impressed by her feminine ways, and that was how it was with Rosemary.

Very soon John was thinking of her in terms of marriage, hinting at it, and getting the feeling that she was hinting back. It was too bad his Aunt Millie never got to meet Rosemary. He made a special trip just to tell her about the wonderful girl he'd found, to which his aunt replied, "You'd better grab her while you can." But not a week later Aunt Millie fell off the roof while trying to get a cat down, and she died without ever knowing the remarkable girl who was going to make up for all the bad and hard times and lonely years that had been the bricks and mortar of John's life up until then.

Though John had truly stopped hating his father, it was nevertheless his intention to be the man that his father had not been—solid, reliable, a family man. Naturally he had to be away from home some of the time. His job was selling, and to sell, a man had to keep the road hot. Rosemary knew this, of course; she knew before she married him what his job required. But it seemed that at some hazy point she began to hold it against him.

How sorry he was to miss the birth of his first child! He'd certainly planned on getting the news in the father's waiting room and hurrying to Rosemary's side; he'd counted on it as much as Rosemary had. He wanted to tell her that, and of course to sympathize with how alone she must've felt—though it wasn't his fault—but when he finally got to the hospital, he didn't know what to say. She was so distant and, besides that, getting along so well without him that it just seemed silly to rush in with the foolish little speeches he'd rehearsed.

Then when Melissa was born, plans went awry again, and once again John simply couldn't figure out what Rosemary expected of him. At first he thought she blamed him for having to stay with Judith, though he had no choice whatsoever and Rosemary should've realized that. He apologized anyway. "I'm sorry I couldn't get back," he said. "I'm sorry I missed this one, too."

But Rosemary said it was all right, that she'd managed just fine, the way she'd managed the first time, and it certainly seemed from her cool reply that she hadn't needed him.

So when Robbie was born, John made sure he did everything he was supposed to do. He brought her to the hospital, paced for hours in the father's waiting room, and went in to see Rosemary the minute they gave him the OK.

"Hi," he said, giving her a quick kiss. "How do you feel?"

"Oh, I feel all right."

"You still sound a little groggy."

"That's because I am."

"Well, you look fine."

"I'm sure *that's* not so," she said, brushing at her hair with her fingers.

But she did look wonderful, and John said, "You do. You really do."

"Let's not talk about my looks, John. Have you seen the baby?"

"Yes."

"Tell me about him."

"What's to tell?" John asked in all seriousness.

"Who he looks like and all that." Rosemary was sounding a little aggravated, though John had not the faintest idea why.

"He looks like any newborn baby, red and wrinkled. I

dare anybody to say he looks like me." John grinned at his joke, but Rosemary didn't.

"You don't seem very proud of him."

"Sure I am. I *am* proud. I just don't know what you want me to say, Rosemary."

She turned her head trying to hide a tear that was easing down her cheek. After an awkward moment, she got her bearings and said, "I don't know what to say, either. Maybe if this was our first, but I don't know, John. Why don't you just go on home and check on the girls."

Sometimes he couldn't tell what Rosemary wanted; the rest of the time it seemed he couldn't make what she wanted happen. Moving was, for some reason John didn't grasp, a difficult thing for Rosemary. Maybe she had a solid case when they were transferred three times in four years while the girls were babies, but most of the time John believed she simply sank her roots in too far down. He liked new faces and new beginnings, himself, but he felt obligated to say to his boss that relocating so often was hard on the family. It was for that speech, he suspected, that he found himself without a job when the company merged with a bigger one. They were living in Mobile, and John went to extreme lengths to avoid another move. He sold home cleaning products. He sold encyclopedias. Then he got into selling a line of third-rate shoes which bought them another two years—for a total of five—in Mobile.

At that point an opportunity that John believed was golden presented itself. This time the Grays were off to Louisville, Kentucky, the headquarters of a new pharmaceutical company that John had been hired to represent. There were two years of high sales. Robbie was born, and Rosemary was reasonably settled with her hook-ups and chairmanships. Then the Food and Drug Administration began calling in some of the pharmaceutical products, which John could not possibly have foreseen, but oh how foolish it made him look in his mirror, and in the mirror of Rosemary's eyes.

Some unexpected good, nevertheless, had come out of John's association with the pharmaceutical company, aside from the good sales that had enabled him to put back a little money in savings. The company had also paid for him to take a Saturday course in marketing at the university. This was supposed to make him a better salesman, but what it accomplished was to whet John's interest in going to college. As he heard himself offer sensible answers in class, it occurred to him that getting a college education wasn't as farfetched as it always had sounded. As he met other men his age who were working toward degrees in business, he began to see possibilities that would put an end to living on the road and uprooting his family every couple of years.

So when the Grays touched down in Birmingham, John promptly enrolled at the University of Alabama. Rosemary believed he was going through a mid-life crisis, which may well have been the case, but she was a good sport about what seemed to her a whim. She even took on piano students to supplement John's not-too-impressive income. He was selling home cleaning products in a small territory, having made contact with someone he'd known in Birmingham during his sales training days. He'd come full circle, it seemed, with not much to show for himself, but he didn't let that thought drag him down. He just worked harder to make his grades and to sell those detergents and polishes.

Finally, his valuable college degree earned, John moved his family for what had to be the last time. His job with the State of Tennessee simply had to work out—that was the sum and substance of it—for Rosemary was all set to send her roots way down to China.

She whistled as she ripped open boxes and rolled out new

shelf paper. John couldn't remember ever seeing her quite so animated. Robbie happened to ask her where-all she'd lived, and before all their round eyes she began to flit about, singing a little ditty: *"Darlington At-LAN-ta, GREEN-ville and MA-con, MO-bile, Louisville, Birmingham and NASH-ville."* The kids started laughing and joined in on the tune (it was a tune that went with a nursery rhyme, barely familiar to John); then somehow they were holding hands, dancing around in a circle, Rosemary and the children, even Judith.

Clumsily, John shifted back, out of their way, like the leftover when teams were chosen. He assumed a distracted pose, or tried to; then a box of glasses on the counter caught his attention and he suddenly became very busy setting them in the shelves.

"No, John, they have to be washed first," called Rosemary, and the capricious little dance came to an abrupt halt. "Besides, those are my best—can't you tell? They go in the china cabinet. But I'll do it. I'd *rather.*"

"All right, I'll work in another room."

"John, you don't know where the things came from, so you can't know where they go. Please, just let us do it. We've packed and unpacked so many times before, we know what to do. You don't have the foggiest notion."

Too many things, it seemed, were things about which John had not the foggiest notion. About the plumbing under the kitchen sink. About the lawn mower's quirks. About what the girls were allowed to do and not allowed to do. Now John was willing and available to be whatever his family needed, but what did they need from him? Not much more, it appeared, than they had needed when they danced around the kitchen in their own tight circle.

And before the children had come along, there was the other circle that Rosemary had formed with Bertie MacArthur and Amelia Banks, both of whom knew before John did that he was going to be a father. Rosemary was the kind of person that people came to depend upon. They'd never moved from any place that people didn't moan, "What are we going to do without Rosemary?" Those same ones weren't always clear on John's name, however, that hard name of his. It wasn't just now dawning on John that Rosemary was one to naturally take over, but it was just dawning on him that she wasn't going to stop taking over at this point in their lives.

Who was to blame? John guessed he was. He'd been on the road too long. He'd let too many things slip out of his control. It had been simpler for Rosemary to take charge in matters of the children's education and discipline and religious training, but something in him had diminished as he gave away those chores. All the time his family was knitting their little circle that left him out. Whatever John initiated, Rosemary took over and squeezed him out. The zeal he'd shown in bringing her into the church had dwindled as hers grew. The two of them had more or less seesawed through their marriage.

Three years into a desk job for the state, John was offered the chance to go on the road. The pay was essentially the same. He would travel across the state, auditing state-owned institutions, from Monday through Friday.

When he told Rosemary, she kept right on rolling dough. It didn't surprise her, she said in all kindness. He never had exactly been the family man type. But it was all right. She and the children would manage.

Seventeen

Judith steps out of a striped cab. "Everybody's gotta have a gimmick," the cabbie drawls to Rosemary, who raises her eyebrows at the unseemly paint job. Then to Judith, "Where do you want your bags, Miss?"

"The front doorstep," Rosemary pipes in before Judith can answer. "Not through that messy garage." Judith nods, and the driver obeys.

She pays him, tips him well, no doubt, for he says, "Hey, *thanks,* Miss." Rosemary and Judith are left at the doorstep. Now the perfunctory hug, clumsy because of the luggage at their feet. Rosemary tries to open the door, but it hasn't been unlocked all day.

And when she's made the hike through the garage and the kitchen and has come around to let Judith in, while Judith still bakes on the hot doorstep, John calls out, "Melissa's on the phone."

Melissa is at the bus station. Her local ticket agent was mixed up on the schedule, and here she is, an hour and a half early, cheery as a bluebird, waiting for her mother to pick her up.

And so this is Judith's homecoming. Rosemary barely gets the door open before hurrying to answer Melissa's call. Then, while Judith and her father are exchanging those first greetings, made all the more awkward by his blindness, Rosemary is hauling the suitcase and travel bag back toward the bedrooms, prompting Judith to call, "Mother, just leave those, *please.* You shouldn't keep Melissa waiting." Rosemary has not said a proper hello before she says good-bye, swinging her purse strap across her shoulder, heading after Melissa, whose arrival in town coincidentally seems to overshadow Judith's. *This is not the way it's supposed to be,* Rosemary tells herself, seeing that Judith is still clutching her handbag, sitting primly beside John, like an uneasy patient in the waiting room.

By contrast, Melissa is the image of a capricious waif, standing on the sidewalk in front of the bus station, waving as she catches sight of her mother. She picks up her antiquated blue suitcase (which Rosemary took to the hospital when Robbie was born), flips her loose, straight, sunbleached hair back from her face, and hurries the best she can toward the spot where Rosemary is parking. How she waddles already! Her jeans accentuate her weight-gain, and her loose shirt, which ought to be a maternity blouse but isn't, accentuates her indifference toward fashion.

Rosemary parks and hastens to meet her, calling, "Let *me* carry that suitcase, Melissa, put it right down!" They meet in a warm, loving embrace, and Melissa laughs at her mother's gentle scolding: "You'll *hurt* yourself, lifting that heavy bag, you silly girl. Why didn't you wait for me to come inside? It's too *hot* out here. You could've had a sunstroke!"

Rush-hour traffic is at its peak now, which keeps Rosemary on edge, but she doesn't necessarily mind the time she has Melissa to herself. There has never been enough of that; there never *is,* with the middle child.

"And how are my grandchildren?" she wants to know.

"Couldn't be better. I have new pictures."

"Good! And Simon's well, I suppose."

"Yes, busy getting started with the bees."

"What bees?"

"Didn't I tell you? I've been in such a whirl over *twins* that I probably forgot. Anyway, Simon's going to raise bees."

Rosemary's disapproval is not disguised, though she says, "I suppose Simon wouldn't do it if he thought there was any risk to the children."

"Oh, it's all right, Mother. It's much more scientific than I ever knew. Say, when did they tear down the skating rink? *Dawn's Tanning Parlor* —I can't believe it!"

"That happened at least two years back."

Melissa sighs dramatically. "The wheels of progress. In the country, time doesn't fly so."

She seems terribly earnest for Melissa, but Rosemary can't help adding, "It may not *seem* that way."

Melissa laughs. "That's right, time *seems* not to fly but it's no different, is it? You know something, Mother, you sounded just like Judith then!"

"Oh." The word comes out bland.

"I'm *thrilled* about seeing her. She's there already, you said."

"Just barely."

"Oh, won't it be exciting, Mother, all of us together again? I'll miss Simon and the boys, of course, but being back here without them and with Judith this time, why, it'll be just like the old days!"

So startled is Rosemary, she sails right through a yellow light.

"I didn't remember that you were such an aggressive driver, Mom."

It seems to Rosemary that there are a great many other things she doesn't remember. But she will, no doubt, before her visit is over.

Rosemary is surprised again when Judith chooses to settle in her old room.

She says, "I told Melissa to take the double bed. She might not be comfortable in one of our twin beds. Not that it matters to *me*."

"That's very thoughtful of you, Judith." Rosemary tries to be gracious; why does she seem condescending?

And the tone has not escaped Judith. She lifts her chin and Rosemary no doubt could see her nostrils flare if she were closer. Judith fiddles with her rings as she loiters about the kitchen. Rosemary drops a spoon and with one swift, graceful gesture, Judith picks it up. It seems she wants to be useful. Is she waiting for an engraved invitation to help in the kitchen or what? How silly it is that a mother should have to walk on eggshells with her daughter, but if Judith leaves *this* time in a dither, she well may be *gone.*

Melissa comes in and begins to take plates from the cabinets. "Five places, Mom?"

"Just four. Robbie was here this morning but he had to go back to work."

"Will we even *see* him before the ceremony?" asks Judith in that put-out way of hers.

"He promised to get home as early as he could in the morning." Rosemary ventures, "You could put the silverware around if you'd like, Judith."

"I'll be happy to but I thought Melissa was taking care of that."

"I'm doing it, Mom," says Melissa.

"I'm probably in the way," says Judith.

"Not at all, dear."

The "dear" seems to have an effect. Judith looks behind the door and takes an apron off the hook. "Now," she says, slipping it over her pale pink blouse and matching pants, "I guess I can get out the ice."

It's really not time yet, but Rosemary says, "Good idea."

Dinner is not fancy but the table is loaded. Melissa remarks in a complimentary way that you couldn't squeeze another dish on, and Rosemary decides the table *is* too crowded. What can you do, though, when you don't have a dining room? You make do with your small kitchen table, that's what. Judith perhaps *means* to be complimentary when she says it looks as if they could feed the starving Africans, but Rosemary isn't sure whether to say thank you to that, so what she says is, "I suppose I'm wasteful."

Judith tries to say no, but Melissa chimes in rather loudly, "Oh, Judith, that's so *sad.*"

"Well, I'm *sorry.*"

"The children especially, with their little bloated bellies."

"Yes, Melissa, but must we talk about bloated bellies just as we sit down to eat?"

For once, Rosemary finds herself agreeing with Judith. Suddenly nothing seems very appetizing.

Melissa's appetite is fine, however. "It's wonderful to be eating for three," she says. "No one gives you a funny look when you pile your plate high." But that's not necessarily true, Rosemary notes from Judith's raised eyebrows.

Further into the meal, Melissa remarks, "You do exceptionally well with your eating, Dad."

"I try," he says, uncomfortably. He barely touches his food after that, either because he's conscious of being watched or because of the direction the conversation takes.

"I think it's wonderful the way you've adjusted," says Melissa. "It shows real strength of character."

"It's just too bad you couldn't have had the surgery earlier," says Judith. (John doesn't reply that he could have.)

"Then all you've had to learn to do and all the *anguish* you've gone through wouldn't have been necessary."

"Assuming the surgery is a success," says Melissa.

"There's no reason to think it won't be." Judith scowls at her sister, but the reprimand is lost, for Melissa is spearing the last of her baby limas onto her fork.

"I wish I could be that sure of everything, Judith, but who can say?" John folds his hands in his lap. "We'll do what we can do, and if it doesn't work, maybe that's the way things are supposed to be."

"If it doesn't work, we'll do something else," Judith says, too insistent. "There are other hospitals and other doctors."

"Who's for cherry pie?" Rosemary pipes in.

Melissa is, but Judith shakes her head and John seems not to hear. "There are some things beyond our control," he says.

"John, wouldn't you like a nice slice of cherry pie?"

He mumbles no and continues saying to Judith, "I wouldn't want my family to be bitter."

"I don't like losing and I don't lose very often."

"This isn't exactly a case of winning or losing, Judith," says Melissa.

"It certainly is!"

"Coffee, anybody?" Rosemary's chair makes a loud scraping noise.

"I think Melissa's right," says John. "There's no contest here. What will be will be. From here on, it's in the hands of my Maker."

"I'm putting on coffee anyway, in case any of you change your mind."

"I'll help you, Mother," says Melissa, and *her* chair makes a loud scraping noise.

But not as loud as the noise in Rosemary's head.

"The hands you'd better be confident in are the surgeon's. Are you sure you *trust* this doctor? Because it's not too late to get someone else."

"This fellow's fine. I believe he knows his business."

"Then why aren't you more hopeful?"

"I *am* hopeful."

"Then what's all this about *what will be will be?* That's a defeatist attitude."

"That," says Rosemary, "is a kind of courage you may not understand, Judith." No one speaks. Judith turns up a defiant gaze toward her mother, but cherry filling dripping from the pie server takes Rosemary's attention. "And doc-

tors are just people, aren't they?" she goes on, brightly, cutting a slice for herself. "People with human frailties like the rest of us. There's only so much you can ask of a human being, even one who sometimes presides over miracles."

She licks the pie server and drops it into the sink. She washes her sticky hands. When at last she takes her pie to the table, the talk is starting up again, like a sluggish engine on a cold morning, on the topic of beehives.

Afterward, she wishes she hadn't said so much or hadn't made such a *point* of saying it, and she wishes she hadn't directed it to Judith. But Judith appears to be unpacking instead of packing, and Rosemary takes that as a good sign. Melissa is still telling her father everything he's always wanted to know about bees. John seems fascinated. Rosemary takes the opportunity to admire her impatiens, blooming clouds of red, yellow, and white, and the new geraniums she's potted, and all the shrubs that have perked up so since the rain. Once outside, she finds a dozen little things to do.

The light fades into a grayish-pink haze. It is that quiet, cool time of evening that Doc Lowell used to call *twilight.* Rosemary can hear him. *"I'll be home at twilight."* She can see him at the gate, his tired shoulders drooping so that the coat of his wilted suit hikes up in the back. There was a rosebush just inside the gate. Sometimes Doc would break off a bud and stick it in his lapel. What would he think of all these flowers? Rosemary wonders. Her mother never paid much attention to the yard. There were no flowers to speak of, just one rosebush.

Sometimes Rosemary would be chasing lightning bugs when he got home, and he'd catch one for her. She could put them in a Mason jar and watch their fairy-lights flicker for a while, but then she had to free them. "It serves no purpose to let them die," Doc would say. Now Rosemary scoops one up and covers it loosely with her other hand, so that the pale yellowish glow comes from the spaces between her fingers. She's grown up now and no one can tell her not to let it die, but she opens her hands and it flies away.

She *is* grown up, fifty years old, a wife and mother, a grandmother, and her father would be an old man if he were alive, old and feeble like Buddy, but she could never smash a lightning bug or let it die in a jar. Her father's words have become the ground on which she has plodded through half a century, and that is why his journal now disturbs her so. It has shaken her foothold. There is the business about her mother, for one thing. *How could I have ever managed without Virginia, without her strength, without her faith in me?* Doc wrote. But it was the other way around. Doc was the solid oak, Virginia the clinging vine—or so it appeared in Rosemary's young eyes. When Doc died, her mother was entirely helpless. But now Rosemary is confused. At thirteen she took over and her mother *did* depend upon her, and for the three remaining decades that Virginia lived after that, the mother-daughter thing was never quite right. Could it have been different, Rosemary wonders, if her image of her mother hadn't been so set in stone?

There's the business about medicine, too. One cannot have read sixteen years' worth of commentary by a doctor and not recognize the shadows at the edges of the limelight. A doctor *is* subject to human frailty—like a salesman or an auditor—but that isn't what Rosemary *wants* to believe. Her father was *Doc* and he was *important* and she counted for something because of who he was. Why did he have to record his failures and shortcomings? *I delivered a stillborn. I don't work miracles. Oh, how I'd like to believe that death wouldn't get the last lick!* Rosemary aches to think that he died without coming to terms with that.

She's used her father as a measuring stick, and now she wonders about all the people who didn't measure up. John for one never quite has. *She* never has, for that matter. Ironically, she's often thought that her father was the only person in her life who would've been entirely pleased with her, and now that notion is ripped apart, too. Oh, the secrets in old bones!

But what she needs to know is not revealed. Who *is* Doc Lowell? Not until she is satisfied with the answer can she know for certain who Rosemary Lowell Gray is.

And that is what she's wondering when Judith calls her in to attend to Melissa.

Melissa's stomachache has Judith and John worried, fearing something is haywire with the pregnancy, but Melissa blames it on the long bus ride with nothing but snacks to eat. Rosemary puts her to bed and promises her that she'll be all right in the morning. That always worked when she was a child. She smooths her hair back from her forehead and says, "Sweet dreams," and Melissa's color is better already.

"It's great to be home," she says. "Just like old times. Simon gets a kick out of all the stories I tell about our family."

"Let me guess. About the time Judith painted a tattoo on your arm with permanent magic marker and then tried to scrub it off with bleach?"

"Oh that! I'd forgotten."

"Or the time you were waiting for her inside the church but the choir met at the parsonage instead, and Judith never missed you?"

"And they locked me up. No, I didn't forget *that.*"

But she's smiling. Rosemary says, "Maybe things seem funnier looking back."

"*Everything's* funny, looking back."

"Melissa's fine," Rosemary tells John and Judith. "Considering the meal she devoured, I'm not a bit surprised at her stomachache."

John listens to his radio program and then to the television news at ten, during which he dozes off in his recliner. By the time Rosemary has changed into her nightclothes, John has roused up enough to get to bed, so they say goodnight to Judith.

But Rosemary doesn't sleep, and sometime much later, she goes to check on Melissa, who rests peacefully. Across the hall, Judith's light is on. Her door is ajar, and Rosemary sees her, propped against her pillows, reading out of Doc Lowell's journal.

"Excuse me, Judith." Rosemary pushes back the door, her voice low but not at all timid. "Where did you get that?"

A startled Judith finds her defense attorney's voice and answers boldly, "It was on the chest of drawers in Melissa's room—*Robbie's* room, I should say. Is anything wrong, Mother? Because this was very much out in the open. Otherwise I wouldn't have taken it."

"Oh, *well.* Robbie must've been looking through it again this morning." Rosemary tries to make up for overreacting with a shrug and a little smile, but Judith remains silent and unmoving, waiting for her vindication. And so, with some difficulty, Rosemary says, "I didn't mean to snap, Judith. There's no reason why you shouldn't be reading it."

Judith's glare softens and for a moment she seems to grope, too, unaccustomed as she is to accepting apologies from her mother. "You're sure it's all right then."

"Yes, it's all right." Rosemary glances at the open book. "You've read that *much?*"

"I'm just skimming. But it's fascinating. It's like knowing my grandfather for the first time."

How peculiar, thinks Rosemary. The journal *reveals* a man to one, *obscures* the man to another.

Judith wants to know where and how it was found, and how it has come to be hidden for so long, to which Rosemary has no good answer. The journal has great appeal, to be sure. As Judith turns through it, scanning, she suddenly laughs. "Listen to this," and Rosemary crawls upon the bed beside her while she reads:

"October 11, 1940. Rosemary brought home her first report card Wednesday. I had promised her an ice cream sundae at Halleby's if she made straight A's, and she had all A's except for a B+ in Deportment. That makes no sense to me, for I know Rosemary to be exemplary in her deportment. But there is the B+ so what was I to do? Right or wrong, I took her to Halleby's. I had in mind to make some sort of compromise, say, to leave off the cherry, but knowing how Rosemary loves cherries, I couldn't do it. Now if her grades go down I will have a take a firm hand, but Rosemary does love those pretty little maraschino cherries!"

Rosemary grins, but she is aware of something hot and wet behind her eyes. Judith says, "Isn't that *priceless?*" and Rosemary nods, afraid that if she speaks, her voice will betray her.

Judith reads another, an earlier excerpt, having turned back a few pages. This time Doc is trying to understand why Rosemary didn't win the "Little Darling of Darlington" beauty contest.

"What a happy child you must've been," says Judith, "being loved like that."

It strikes Rosemary as an odd thing to say, or perhaps the strangeness lies in the wistful nature of Judith's tone.

"Very happy," says Rosemary, *and never so happy since,* she thinks. "My childhood was serene and secure—up until I was thirteen."

"You still had Grandmother."

"Yes." And Rosemary remembers that her mother, too, was devoted to her in her childhood, but those gloomy years after Doc's death are the ones she can't shake. "Your grandmother loved me in her own way—and I loved her," she says by way of afterthought. "We should've been a family, just the two of us, but we weren't. I blamed her for not being strong enough for me to lean on. She blamed me for—everything, for growing up, I guess, because I never could please her after I grew up."

Judith's eyes turn to the open book and she says, "Grandmother should've kept a journal."

Rosemary raises her eyebrows.

"It's an intriguing form of communication, like letters in a way, but letters are usually answered and the reply may play a part in what the *next* letter says. Reading a journal, you get inside a person's head, and things that seemed unreasonable may begin to make sense. The impressions you were left with may change, like your impression that you never pleased Grandmother."

"On the other hand, the secrets that you learn from the rattling of old bones may only disillusion you."

"Then it depends on what you have to lose." She pauses, flipping a couple of pages. "You didn't happen to keep a journal when we were growing up, did you?"

"Me? There was hardly time, Judith."

"I know. But it might've been a good thing, don't you think?"

Like a bright light dawning, it occurs to Rosemary that Judith has not been talking about *her* any of the time. She regards her daughter carefully, the bold, independent daughter, never quite so vulnerable as in this moment.

"What would I have said?" asks Rosemary. "Days passed, years passed and pulled us along. Most things I didn't plan. They just happened, and I managed the best I could. I tried to make a good childhood for you, Judith. If I didn't, I'm sorry. If your memories are unhappy, I'm sorry, but I don't know how I could've done any better."

"Don't apologize," says Judith, defensive now.

"Then what? What do you want from me, Judith?"

"What did you want from Grandmother?"

Rosemary is jolted. She pops up, as if the jolt were in her seat. "It's not the same at all. Her love was smothering, and when I *had* to grow up, she heaped guilt on me that weighs me down still. But Judith, I let you become independent. It wasn't easy to pull back, but I did, and if I did too soon it was so I wouldn't do to you what my mother did to me."

Judith's eyes are wide and glassy at first, but she blinks and blinks again, and then she says, "But it *is* the same thing, Mother. I've never pleased you, and the guilt is overpowering. Isn't it funny?" She laughs a false, hollow laugh, her palms flat on her temples. "Isn't it really funny when you think about it?"

Resolutely, Rosemary seizes her daughter's hands, squeezing as if she might squeeze sense into her. "I have *always* been proud of you, Judith."

"Oh, don't say—"

"*Listen* to me." She is the mother now and sure of herself. "If I'd kept a journal, I would've said how proud I was. 'Judith made the honor roll. Judith made the debating team. Judith pulled Melissa's tooth to get money for my birthday present and I ran her up one side and down the other, but who else would've come up with something like that? Judith has a wonderful job in Chicago. The world she moves in is one I don't understand, but she continues to make me proud, over and over again.' There now."

She squeezes Judith's hands again, but this time more for her own benefit. "The only times you haven't pleased me are probably the times you've reminded me of myself."

Judith, her cheeks flushed, starts to say something, but Rosemary shushes her. "It's late. We'll both topple out of our seats during those boring speeches tomorrow if we don't get some sleep."

Like the obedient child that she never really was, Judith slips under the covers. Rosemary smooths them around her, taking the journal—not for further searching but to put up. She switches off the lamp and says, "Sweet dreams."

Robbie's college graduation, which Rosemary has anticipated for, oh, twenty years, begins at two o'clock as a solemn event. "There he is. I can see him beginning to march," Rosemary whispers to John, whose effort to be present was no small measure. The ceremony is held on the football field. Random clouds blow by during the processional, but the sun peeks out between them. If one can believe the weather forecaster, there is "a chance of late afternoon showers." Rosemary's family laughed at her; she brought five umbrellas.

After much pomp and circumstance, as the dozenth speaker—the one finally giving the keynote address—is introduced, a great roll of thunder shakes the earth and a crack of lightning zigzags in a darkening sky. A couple far down in the front get up, and another over to the left, and then a whole herd of teenagers trample across the feet of Rosemary and her family.

"What's happening?" asks John.

"People are leaving. I think it's starting to rain."

They are shooting up all through the crowd now as the drops begin. On the podium, the black robes and mortarboards squirm. Someone rushes up with an umbrella for the speaker. Rosemary doesn't hear how he ends his two-minute address; nor can she make out what the next dignitary who comes to the microphone says. But evidently the ceremony is over, for the graduates now stand up and the music starts. You can tell who the parents are. They sit on the edges of their seats, reluctant not to get their money's worth out of Junior's graduation, but poised to flee the minute the recessional stops.

Rosemary has, of course, passed out four of her umbrellas. Her family is not especially uncomfortable, except for all the commotion around them.

"Robbie's found us. There he comes." No need to whisper now. He runs up to the clear row in front of them and grabs his umbrella.

No need to join in all the pushing and shoving, either, the five of them agree. When the rain lets up, as this kind of shower generally does in a matter of minutes, Robbie can go after the car.

"What about your diploma?" Judith wants to know.

"They're going to mail it," says Robbie.

"But it's official, is it?" Melissa asks. "You're a bonafide graduate."

Robbie flips his tassle to the other side. "Now I'm a bonafide graduate."

"Well, it was a nice ceremony," says Rosemary.

"Not bad at all," says John. "I'll bet it came out under forty-five minutes, which must be a record."

"But we didn't get pictures!" Rosemary remembers.

"This is worse than the day we had the family portrait made," says Melissa, grinning. "Remember that?"

"Don't we all!" Judith answers in mock exasperation, but then she smiles, too.

The parking lot is a tangle of cars. The last of the drenched crowd are making their way through the gates. But the Grays remain relatively dry and unruffled at their seats. Rosemary is astonished by the behavior of her family. Calm acceptance has not been a virtue of the Grays through the years. Minor difficulties have thrown them into major tizzies. More often than Rosemary likes to remember, they have disintegrated—collectively and sometimes individually—over what in the long run amounted to little more than simple inconveniences.

But here they are now with this auspicious occasion ruined, not to mention that there will be no pictures of all of them dressed up around Robbie in his scholarly attire, and it doesn't seem to matter. No one is scowling, complaining, or trying to fix blame—not even Rosemary. She doesn't even feel an urge to, and that is the most baffling of it all.

Eighteen

The family portrait was Rosemary's project, which was not to say that herding her family toward the studio on a Saturday afternoon was her idea of fun. It was just one of those things that had to be done, like making entries in baby books. Someday the children would be glad to know that they all said "Da-da" first. Someday the family portrait of the Grays would be a treasured heirloom, like the one that had hung in the Lowells' living room, the blissful Lowells—Rosemary (in long white baby dress) on Virginia's lap, Doc at their side, looking proud and dignified. Something for posterity.

If Rosemary didn't take the responsibility, no one would, but oh who would they all blame in years to come? Even John, who didn't exactly accuse, ever. But she could see him as a doddering old man, telling a granddaughter in a crackling voice, "No, we don't have a family portrait. Your grandma never got around to that."

But John was a good thirty years from being doddering and that far from being sentimental. He was a hurried man who despised hurrying, who had come through eight years of Saturday classes to regard that one day of the week as his own prize for working the other five. His college degree had brought him to that comfortable plane known as the forty-hour week, and he made the most of it. He might take the car to the service station; he might deliver Robbie to a baseball practice or pick up a can of bug spray at the hardware store; but there was a general understanding that Saturday was his day *off.*

Add to that his strong dislike for being photographed (which was basically why Rosemary hadn't seen to a family portrait years before). It was his natural tendency to duck the camera so that candid shots showed him as a blur, and only when there was no civil way out of it did he consent to *pose.* In those straight-on shots, John somehow came out looking like a character in a stomach antacid commercial. Little wonder that his response to the portrait announcement was the same annoyed grunt he'd given Rosemary when she flushed Judith's diaper down the commode.

The girls, who made lovely pictures, had better things to do, or were sure they could find better things. Robbie didn't exactly complain, but he quickly made the observation that getting his picture made would mean getting cleaned up. "I guess I'll have to wear Sunday clothes on Saturday, won't I?"

To which John added, "Yes, and I'll get to put on a tie each day for thirteen in a row."

But Rosemary had anticipated all the muttering. That was why she waited until the week before the appointment to break the news, even though she'd scheduled it two and a half months earlier. She allowed her family ample time for commiserating, and then she said, "Well, it's settled. Saturday at one o'clock." And when she said in that particular tone of voice that something was settled, it was.

The red-letter day dawned bright as a jewel. Waking up on that sparkling May morning, Rosemary nudged John. "Didn't I pick a good day to go for a family portrait?"

John rubbed his eyes and squinted against the sunlight. "There is no such thing as a good day to have a family portrait made," he said.

She hadn't expected him to admit it, so her delight was not diminished, delight that the weathermen had obviously been wrong about the rain. Surely, on a morning like this, worry over wet clothes, muddy shoes, and stringy hair could be tossed aside.

Robbie was already out on his bike. Rosmary tried to raise her window, intending to call him, but it didn't want to budge. "He'd just better not get scraped up," she said, "especially not on his face." John's sideways glance made her add, "You know what I mean."

"This comedy is scheduled for one o'clock, you say."

"One o'clock." He wasn't going to ruffle her today. No one was.

"Is that before or after lunch?"

Rosemary stopped pulling on the window. How could lunch have skipped her mind? She'd been so sure that she had considered all the angles. The photographer had first said three-thirty, and she'd told him no, that everybody would be worn out by then. An early-morning appointment, on the other hand, would've meant the kind of hustle and bustle that surrounded getting ready for Sunday School. One o'clock seemed a good compromise, but lunch had not occurred to her.

"We could wait until we got back."

"Starve us? After we're being such good sports about this?"

"Well, I suppose you'd like to have lunch at ten-thirty then. You know how long it takes this bunch to work our way through one bathroom. Naturally, having lunch after we're dressed for the portrait is out of the question."

A smile played on John's lips. He tended to find humor in the strangest places. But Rosemary would not be ruffled.

"So we'll have brunch, that's what. We'll skip breakfast, and in a couple of hours, I'll fix brunch."

John was now nurturing a full-fledged grin. "That's just fine with me."

"Then it's settled." She turned back to the window and gave a hard tug. It flew up.

Robbie heard the noise and called, "Hey, Mom, when's breakfast? I've been up since seven."

Glances were exchanged all around the table, and not very subtle glances at that. Rosemary pretended not to notice. It didn't take a genius mother to figure out that John had told the children not to hassle her. Good enough.

But later Robbie must have forgotten, or, more likely, he asked out of simple curiosity, "Why couldn't we have our pictures made on Sunday when we're all dressed up anyway?"

"The studio isn't open on Sunday," Rosemary answered sweetly.

The subject door was opened. Melissa said, "It's supposed to be eighty degrees today. It would be a great day to start on a tan."

"Only you just blister," said Judith, her wry smile a reminder that with her own naturally golden-brown skin, *she* didn't fool with sun-baking.

"I promise you, there will be other sunny Saturdays," said Rosemary.

Robbie popped up from the table and wiped his mouth on his sleeve. "I'm going out while I can."

"Don't go far, Robbie."

"Yes, ma'am."

"I mean it. If I couldn't locate you when time came to get ready, you know it would be a disaster."

"I know, Mom." He didn't look back.

She cut her eyes toward John. "I can tell he's scared to death."

Before time to begin prodding the others, Rosemary treated herself to a bubble bath and wound a few rollers into her hair. She wanted soft waves that would fall around her ears, a natural, youthful look, not squeezed-up beauty-shop curls. Someday her children would say, "Didn't Mother look young for thirty-eight?"

She was about to polish her nails when Judith came in with a seam to mend. The sleeve was coming away from the shoulder. Any other seam might not show, but this one would, and this was her dress for the photograph.

"When did this happen?" asked Rosemary as she set up the sewing machine.

"I just saw it when I was pressing the dress."

"You didn't know about it?"

"Actually, I *did* rip it when I wore it last, but I'd forgotten." Judith squared her jaw, and in her eyes Rosemary identified the *Don't tread on me* look. Oh, Judith knew well how to ward off a scolding. With that defiant jaw and steely glare she was saying, *You know I am to blame and I know it but I won't admit it and you won't get an apology without a clash which I'm sure you don't want at this particular time.* Yes, it worked; it had worked more often than Rosemary cared to remember. Judith knew how much she despised clashes and to what lengths she would go to avoid them. It was not the way to handle a child, but there was no changing the rules at this point. Judith was going on eighteen. Rosemary did what she could, which was to give a long exasperated sigh, her way of saying, *We both know you're at fault, but I am the longsuffering mother so you're getting by with your mistake this time.*

Their little game played out, Judith let down her guard and said, more kindly, "Can't you just whip it up with a needle and thread? It doesn't look too bad to me."

"That's because you don't know very much about it. Hand-stitching wouldn't last at this seam. If you want to help, find Robbie and your dad."

"How about Melissa?" Something smug seeped into her voice.

"I thought Melissa was here."

"She's at Annette's."

"I'd like to know what she's doing at Annette's house."

"It's not *my* fault," Judith said with mock innocence.

"Would you please go after her?"

"I'll be happy to."

The sleeve had a mind of its own. It would not go in right. Rosemary jerked the material away from the machine and began to pull out stitches. She was trying the seam yet another time when Melissa passed the door and called, "I'm back, Mom."

"Melissa?"

"I have to take a shower. It's my turn in the bathroom."

Rosemary was intent on the annoying sleeve.

Judith came back to wait, peering over Rosemary's shoulder at first and finally settling at the dresser to polish her nails.

"Your nails probably won't show," said Rosemary, thinking of her own, which would have to go unpolished.

"Have you seen Melissa?" Judith asked, once again smug.

"She came in a few minutes ago."

"I just wondered if you'd seen her."

"What's going on, Judith?"

"It's not for me to say."

"Has Melissa done something wrong?"

"You know Melissa *never* does anything wrong, Mother."

Rosemary snipped the thread and handed the dress up to Judith. "There had better *not* be anything wrong, not today, not an hour and twenty minutes before we're supposed to be at the studio." She swept past Judith and called, "John, are you and Robbie ready?"

"Robbie's dressed and I'm waiting for my turn in the bathroom," he called back.

Things were moving right along. The gnawing in Rosemary's stomach couldn't be anything but simple indigestion.

There was a matter of which to do first, put on her dress (which had to go over her head, which meant she'd have to take out her rollers) or put on her makeup and risk smudging her white collar when the dress came down over her face. Decisions, decisions! She took the rollers from her hair—a little too soon, but no matter—and slipped on her dress. That was when she noticed the billowy clouds moving in front of the sun. It came naturally to stick out her lower lip in a pout, thinking, *It's not fair!* Why couldn't things ever happen the way they were supposed to?

She stood at the window, watching the menacing clouds gather, wondering how it had been with her parents when they had their family portrait made. She was just a year old then. Had she spit up on her dress or, worse yet, on her mother's? Had she started yelling when the photographer began to place them in the proper pose? Likely as not, her father would've had to quiet some hysterical woman on the phone before he could leave the house, making them late, so that his brow was shiny with perspiration when they arrived for the picture. And yet, when that moment in time was captured by the camera, the Lowells appeared calm and complacent. That was what Rosemary had wanted for the Gray portrait, an aura of calm complacency. A rainstorm did not set the stage for calm complacency.

But Doc would've just laughed away any calamities that tried to spoil their picture—Rosemary was sure of that—and her mother would have, too, at that time in her life. Oh, life was funny, full of surprises, joyous! Rosemary remembered times around the piano when they couldn't sing for laughing at Doc's mistakes, mostly contrived. She'd known him to *cry,* he laughed so hard, like the time he told about the thermometer that Nurse Dexter lost in Mrs. Mulgarry's wrinkles. Virginia doubled up and finally fell to the sofa, and Rosemary laughed till she hiccuped. Doc just had a way of making people feel happy.

Rosemary went back to the mirror. She felt a headache coming on, and no doubt those dark clouds would dump on them between the parking lot and studio, but she would not be ruffled. She couldn't see her family laughing their way to the studio, but she might inspire *calm* in them if she could keep her head.

She hadn't heard John, and when she saw him in the mirror, she jumped, catching her mascara brush in the edge of her hair.

"I just came to get my coat and vest," he said apologetically.

"It's nothing a little soap and water won't take off," said Rosemary, managing a level tone. Luck was with her; the bathroom was empty, and she was able to wash the mascara out of her hair, the only damage being that the curl went out, too.

John was still in their room, starched and spruced up—and waiting for her. She could tell.

"What's on your mind, John?"

"This portrait," he answered quickly.

"In a couple of hours, it'll all be over. Don't worry. I'm sure your picture will be fine."

"No, it's not that. Here's what it is, Rosemary. You've got to see that the Grays aren't the Lowells."

"That's crazy, John. *I* know who we are."

"I can't strike the pose of a patriarch."

"You're just nervous."

"That's not all. I found Robbie out in the garage working on his bicycle chain, all dressed in his good clothes."

Rosemary groaned.

"It's not worth going into a tizzy over. None of it is."

"What else?"

"Judith is made up like a movie star. She looks old enough to be your sister. And did you know Melissa was sunbathing at Annette's house? She has a red nose and two white circles around her eyes."

That was when Rosemary dropped the mascara on her white collar.

It was John who picked up the portrait some weeks later and placed the gift to posterity above the mantel. Rosemary had seen the proofs and selected the least comical. She didn't rush to see the finished product.

But that night, she was drawn into the family gathering at the mantel, where John and the children were actually giving earnest appraisal to the portrait. Rosemary had expected howls. She'd felt like howling herself when she saw the proofs, but for some reason she'd cried instead.

"Not too bad," said Judith, "considering that I was soaked by the time we got to the studio." Judith *would* judge the portrait on the basis of her own image, and she was smiling approval. Rosemary had no illusions that they could pass as sisters, but Judith easily looked twenty-five. Aloof, sophisticated, a little arrogant—and Judith loved it.

"What do you think, Mom?" asked Melissa. "My sunburn didn't show up too much, did it? I look sort of rosy."

"We did the best we could." Makeup had covered the white circles reasonably well, but Melissa's nose looked like a plum. "What does it matter? There's Robbie with grease on his tie, and me—after all the trouble with my mascara, I only got it on one eye."

"I promise you, no one can tell," said John.

"My hair is as limp as a mop, and Judith's hair is in her eyes—"

"It's supposed to be that way," Judith put in.

"The grease doesn't show too much," said Robbie.

"It doesn't matter. It's over, and I'm tired of thinking about it."

"I can't understand why you're so disappointed," said John. "You wanted our family and that's what this is. It's *us.*"

"The Grays!" Judith swept her hand toward the mantel in a regal gesture. "First place for the most authentic family!"

"That's right, *authentic,*" said John. "We're not Sears catalog cutouts. *This* is who we are." He had tried to relax, really tried, Rosemary knew. No fault of his if his pained smile gave the impression that his belt was too tight.

"Dad, you don't look like you have a headache this time," said Melissa.

"Mom does," said Robbie.

"I did. I had a terrible headache." Rosemary began to turn out the lamps in the living room. "Oh, well, it won't be something you'll fight over when your father and I are dead. I guess that's good."

"We might," said Judith.

"I'd take it," said Melissa. "I mean, I wouldn't pack it away and let the moths eat it. I'd do *something* with it."

"I'd *like* to have it," said Robbie, "but don't talk about dying."

"I expect it will be a while," Rosemary told him.

"You might put it in your will, though," he said.

Rosemary had a sudden urge to laugh, but she didn't. She said in her best mother's voice, "I'm touched."

She was the last to leave the living room. With the lights out, the Gray portrait looked almost like it was supposed to.

Nineteen

Rosemary has been thinking since early morning about what to say to Robbie. She recognizes that there will be other good opportunities, some better than today, but the bee in her bonnet won't let her wait.

They all change into dry clothes, though certainly they are in better shape on returning from the ceremony than the majority of the crowd. John takes a nap. Judith and Melissa dry their hair. Rosemary stirs up a batch of cookie dough and rolls it out. She knows Robbie will come prowling in the kitchen.

He does. He pinches the cookie dough and cuts himself a double slice of leftover cherry pie, which is all right with Rosemary. He's twenty-one and a college graduate. He can worry about his own teeth from now on.

"I want you to take the journal," she tells him. "Since you didn't know your grandfather, I think you should have that connection to him."

A big wide-open grin comes to his face, but then he seems to reconsider. "I wouldn't want to take something that means so much to you," he says in all sincerity.

"I *knew* him. That's my connection. I have what I have, which may be more real than what he chose to put down on paper. But for you, his reflections will mean something. I hope they will anyway."

"Of course they will. They *do*."

"I had the feeling that you found something in the journal

for yourself. Perhaps an observation that affected you somehow?"

"If you mean a particular line, no."

"Really?" Rosemary stops with the cookie sheet in midair, the oven door open.

"As a perspective on sixteen years of his life, the journal is wonderful. It *did* affect me, the whole of it, but not in the way you might've hoped. I feel no inclination to become a doctor, Mother."

She starts to tell him what she's been thinking, but he keeps talking. "I was impressed all right, seeing Grandfather entirely immersed in doing what he did. He had a gift and he was driven to give, and from cover to cover he was always giving."

"And always searching," says Rosemary, just realizing it. The journal gave her no peace because Doc was still trying to find peace when he wrote his last lines. And something else occurs to her, that she is a lot like him.

"For all that he did, which was every bit good, he never felt it was enough. It set me to thinking. The job I'm supposed to be taking next month is challenging and worthy and all that, but I can't believe it would ever be *enough.*" He clinks his fork against his plate again, and the ridge suddenly rises on his brow. "I shouldn't have started about this. I didn't intend to bring it up until after the surgery."

"Bring what up?" asks Melissa, leaning into the kitchen. Judith comes up behind her, and John's bell sounds in the bedroom.

"What were you about to tell us, Robbie?" asks Rosemary.

He tries to dismiss it. "I can wait."

But he has waited, on her account, and Rosemary needs to be free of that. And he needs to do what he needs to do.

"What about Dad?" asks Judith. "That was his bell."

"Yes, do wait till I get your father," says Rosemary. "He wouldn't want to miss this."

There were other things she might've said to him, Rosemary is thinking as she is drawn unaccountably into the living room, but speeches are not in her nature, and frankly, she was a little choked up when Robbie got around to telling what was on his mind.

Maybe she'll say it in a journal. She smiles, thinking what the first line might be if she penned it today. She thinks of the poster Melissa used to have with that slogan, *Today is the first day of the rest of your life.* Sometimes it takes a catchy phrase to drive a point home. You can look back and you can look forward, but you can't hold to something back there that no longer is, and you can't wait for something that never quite happens, for all you have is *now.* Life is always beginning.

The Grays are beginning in a big way, she thinks, raising her eyes to the family portrait. Robbie is about to embark in the direction he has chosen, believing *he* is chosen for it. There is Melissa, nurturing the promise of not one new life but two. For John it's the beginning, too; the outcome of the surgery notwithstanding, he's starting fresh, a man of courage. Judith, firstborn, is beginning at thirty, a daughter stamped approved.

Rosemary of course is beginning because *they* are, and they are what she's all about. Good or bad, they're all tied up to each other, *with* each other, *in* each other; *apron strings* some say, but today the ties seem more like a lifeline. *This is who we are.*

The sun has come out since the rain and the grass, the trees, the flowers all have a new sparkle. Even the air sparkles. Rosemary is caught unexpectedly without a chore to do. Melissa has gone to buy groceries (with Judith's money, much to Rosemary's embarrassment), for the girls insist on making dinner. Judith has taken Robbie to pick up his car at the site of the graduation. John is on the telephone with Frank Carlisle (the bell giver) who evidently has just heard about the surgery. Rosemary sits down at her piano. She can scarcely remember the last time she played, but her fingers find their way around a simple minuet and then wander into a Chopin prelude. Miss Markham was a great promoter of memorization, and not just in regard to recital pieces. "Once music is written on your mind," she said, "your fingers never lose it." Forty years, and Rosemary's fingers remember. Remarkably, measure by measure, it comes back.

What's written on the heart is not easily lost either, thinks Rosemary. She is getting past the splintered hero-image of Doc Lowell. The perfect and the imperfect are blurring, the edges softening. She is beginning to reconcile the larger-than-life figure in her memory with the simple man who wrote the journal. She knows who he was. He was a good doctor. He loved her. He was her father.

So thoroughly absorbed in her music is she, she doesn't notice that John has settled in the wingback chair. She plays from one of her books now, another Chopin, 'Etude, Opus 10, Number 3.' Fluid, reflective pieces suit her mood. But at the end, John says, "What *was* that one you used to do for me?"

Startled, she says, "I didn't know I had an audience."

"Remember the one? The woman on the Grand Ole Opry played it all the time."

"Oh, *John,* it's been a hundred years since I tried 'Down Yonder.' "

" 'Down Yonder'! That's it. You can still do it, can't you?"

She toys with a couple of different keys until one feels right. "I can try," she says reluctantly, but once she's off and running on the rousing old tune, she has fun with it. John applauds her, which may be the first time since her last recital in 1947 that she's been applauded. "Go on, do something else," he says, "something you like." But she plays something *he* will like, a Sousa march, and this time he waits for another without saying anything.

She follows with a string of lively pieces, vaguely remembering John in a seersucker suit, saying, "If I can't tap my toes to it, I doze off." That must've been in Darlington when they were getting to know each other and every little word or gesture was a revelation. It had to be then; not since that time has she played the piano like this, for John's enjoyment. After all, she didn't *have* her piano until they were in Louisville, and then John was always on the go, and she was always busy. There are any number of reasons why John had to be blind before they ever spent an hour like this, but most of the reasons seem now to be tied in with wasted motion.

"I've exhausted my repertoire," she says.

"Surely not."

"Don't you want to walk in the yard?"

"It's wet, isn't it?"

"I doubt that it's wet, the way the sun's shining. It's turned into an absolutely splendid afternoon. You know how it is after a hard rain when the sun comes out and everything looks washed and bright."

"I'll notice that sort of thing if I get another chance," says John, not at all sadly, but Rosemary feels a stab of sorrow.

He hasn't seemed jittery before, but now as he taps a rhythm with two fingers on the arm of his chair, it occurs to Rosemary that the surgery is—and perhaps *has been*—heavy on his mind. So she tells him, "In any case, what*ever* happens, we can always walk in the yard in the evenings and I'll play 'Down Yonder' till you beg for Bach, so there, you mustn't worry." And in a braver voice she says, "I'll be here."

She more or less expects John to be relieved, reassured, but he nods and says matter-of-factly, "That's why I'm going through with it."

Somewhat puzzled she says, "I've been here all along, you know."

He seems to understand what she's getting at. "Well, I had to come around to it."

"I realize of course that the surgery is an ordeal."

"Not just an *ordeal,* Rosemary." He leans forward, using his hands as he explains, speaking as if he finds it incredible that she doesn't *know* this. "As long as the operation was *out there* for me, the darkness wasn't final, you see." And she does see, that if the surgery doesn't work, the darkness *is* final.

She nods, and it takes a moment for her to realize that John is waiting for her to answer. "Yes, I understand," she says, "but why are you willing to take the chance now?"

"Now," he says, "I know you can take it either way."

"Me?"

"There wasn't any question about *me.* I *had* to take it."

"There shouldn't have been any question about me, either," she says indignantly, "not after I've invested thirty years in you."

He leans back against the wing of the chair, closing his eyes, faintly smiling. "I guess you're right. You always are. Play me another tune, Rosie."

It strikes her that the last time he called her Rosie was their wedding day, as he was showing her Amelia Banks's house for the first time. How wise and strong she believed her new husband to be! And yet how hard she has tried through the years to be the strong one, as if maybe she didn't trust her instincts. She must've stopped being Rosie that very day.

How long ago that seems. Now, as she starts to play again, thirty years of marriage are suddenly condensed into one vivid impression. She and John are both strong and they are both weak, and neither is a hundred percent without the other. It must've been the same with Doc and Virginia Lowell, and maybe that's how it's supposed to be.

Rosemary plays on, not measuring time except by the fading gold light. John follows the rhythm, tapping on the arm of the chair, tapping out a beat, even after Rosemary's fingers are still, tapping to music that must come from his head, for the room has become as quiet as a prayer.